I0587999

The Jet Jewel

© C.M. Bakker, 2021.

First edition

ISBN: 978-1-8383181-0-9

https://cmbakkerwrites.wordpress.com

Cover art: Erik Bakker

All rights reserved. No part of this publication may be reproduced, stored or transmitted in any form or by any means, electronic, mechanical, photocopying, recording, scanning, or otherwise without written permission from the publisher. It is illegal to copy this book, post it to a website, or distribute it by any other means without permission.

C.M. Bakker

The Jet Jewel

To Genevieve, who was at the beginning
To Rachel, who ploughed through it, making it fertile
And to Erik, who was still there at the end

1

With her hand on the door handle of her aunt's terraced house, Hannah hesitated. She had been so sure Aunt Jess would be on her side. But would she? The ball in Hannah's stomach bounced up and down and sideways. Maybe she should come back later. But she would have to tell her at some point. And Hannah was like a daughter to Aunt Jess, surely she would understand.

Gah! Hannah gripped the door handle tighter, hot as it was from an unusually relentless British summer sun. *See, this is why they wouldn't hire you as a policewoman! Make a decision already!* Right. No sense in delaying the execution. She took a deep breath, turned the key, and pushed the door open. The hallway was little more than a square yard where you could stand and decide whether you wanted to go into the sitting room, back outside, or up the stairs. In this case, it was another chance to reconsider. Behind door number one: all the familiar cosiness Hannah had grown up with. Door number two was getting more attractive by the minute. It was also still wide open, showing the vivid blue Aunt Jess had applied to the outside of it as layer number… at least nine that Hannah could remember. If there was one thing she and Aunt Jess had in common, it was a love of vivid colours. Still, with these temperatures a vanilla-coloured top and cream wide skirt had seemed the best option. Not least because look-at-me clothes did not fit her mood today. Don't-look-at-me clothes, or even don't-see-me clothes, those would be perfect.

Hannah winced. Thinking about colours and clothes would not solve her problem. She was stalling and she knew it. She was trying to fool herself. On purpose! How deep had she sunk? One last deep breath before she closed the front door, picked up the post from the mat, and entered the drawing room.

"It's me!"

Flowery sofa, blue cushions, orange rug, family photos everywhere. Yep, still felt like home. Aunt Jess came in from the garden through the double doors, a broad-rimmed, bright red hat on top of her greying curls. As was to be expected, Aunt Jess was the only one in Nottingham who didn't seem to mind the ongoing humid heat.

"Oh, Hannah, dear! I didn't hear you come in. Up to my ears in rustling dead leaves, you know. Everything seems to be dying this summer, no matter how much I water." She pulled off her violet gardening gloves and took the post from Hannah. "I thought you'd be at work today. Come to help me out in the garden? Hello, darling." She kissed Hannah's cheek and sailed off into the kitchen.

"There's nowhere I'd rather be than here," Hannah called after her. It would be true… in any other circumstance. As always, Hannah stopped at her favourite photo, the oldest of the lot. A beaming three-year-old Hannah held her newborn cousin Sean. In the top left corner the camera had captured a curled lock of Aunt Jess's blonde hair, the same colour as Hannah's and her mother's, Aunt Jess always said. The three of them, together. In the picture and in life. A happy family. Life may have changed, but the picture remained, filling Hannah with a nostalgic sense of hope whenever she looked at it.

She turned away from the photo and pulled out a chair from the shiny white dining table. The sunlight bouncing off the yellow parasol just outside reflected in the surface of the table, filling the room with a warm glow. No place like home… to break someone's heart.

Hannah perched on the edge of her chair when Aunt Jess

emerged from the kitchen with two tall glasses of iced tea, chattering about some girl whose story she'd found online and to whom she'd written a letter. Hannah never understood why her aunt didn't just email these people, but strangely, most of them were delighted to receive an actual letter and wrote back to her the same way. The stamp collection she'd built up this way was almost as large as the pile of family photos. Today, Aunt Jess waved a moss green envelope bearing a Chinese stamp under Hannah's nose.

Hannah pulled away. A gulp of iced tea cooled her down a bit, but wasn't great for the bouncing ball in her stomach. Right. Better get it out quickly.

"Aunt Jess…"

"Yes, dear?"

The letter opener tearing through the envelope ripped her courage to shreds. Clutching her drink with both hands, she tried to find the words, but the only sound was the soft clinking of ice cubes in her glass. Hannah stared at those instead of her aunt. By now Aunt Jess would know something was wrong. Her gaze would be leaving the sheet of paper in her lap to settle on Hannah's reddening cheeks. Knowing that did not make it easier to talk.

"What's wrong?" Aunt Jess's voice sounded worried, not angry. Yet.

"Last night…"

"Yes?"

"…Ben proposed."

Aunt Jess clasped her hands over her heart and beamed. "Oh Hannah, that's—!"

"I said no."

And there it was, after a moment's puzzled hesitation, the look of disapproval. Hannah's already sweaty palms heated up even more. Marriage. What was Ben thinking? Did he know her at all? But Aunt Jess adored him. Of course she did. He was just as old-fashioned as she was, in some ways. Same ideas about the man being the provider, although he was always very gallant and not overbearing.

Hannah's eye was drawn to where she knew was a picture of Ben and her together. He had his arm around her shoulders. More protective than loving. But maybe that's what you get with all those muscles. She'd always liked that picture, but now she thought she looked pale next to his dark skin. Ben leered into the camera. *Don't look at me like that!*

Aunt Jess slid her glass onto the table. "Oh, Hannah..."

Another moment of silence. Hannah hoped she would get away with no more than that, a hope destroyed as soon as Aunt Jess found the words.

"How could you do that to the poor boy? You said you loved him! Why would you not want to marry him?"

"I just don't!" Hannah didn't think she could get any hotter, but the thought of being stuck with Ben, or anyone or anything for that matter, put her hackles up. "He never said anything about marrying me before, and I never thought about it. Come on, I'm twenty-four. There are so many things I still want to do and they don't all include him."

Aunt Jess leaned over the table. "You two have been together for years. Where did you think it was going to end up?"

"We were just having fun! We never even... I mean... He was always joking about who his next girlfriend was going to be. I had no idea he was getting serious about it. Us, I mean." Hannah slumped back in the chair. She kept her eye on the fast-melting ice cubes and bit her lips closed. Had she really been so naive? Or had it just been convenient not to consider any consequences? Ben had told her as much last night, after she turned him down. 'You never think ahead', he'd said. Was he right? That little voice in the back of her head that hadn't shut up since last night was fighting for attention again. Something about her reluctance to talk to Aunt Jess being proof that she actually agreed with him. But that was *not* what she wanted to hear. Little voices have a lot to learn before they grow up to be big voices.

Aunt Jess sat up straight, her blue eyes fixed on a potted plant and her hands clasped in her lap. It must be quite a shock for her. She'd always thought Ben was perfect. Attentive, thoughtful. He'd even tried, probably against his better judgement, to pull some strings in his department and get Hannah a job with the police. He *was* nice, sure! But… you know…

Aunt Jess sighed. "I just didn't expect something like this from *you*."

Now that was just mean. "Don't compare me to Sean! That's not fair, he's a… a…" Aunt Jess's pained look was all she needed. "I'm not like him. I don't take the easy way out. I know when people aren't giving me the best deal, and this was not the best deal for me."

"You think marriage is a deal? Some kind of impersonal transaction? Did you stop to think how Ben feels?"

"Of course I did!" The heat inside her began to surpass the heat outside. "But that doesn't mean that I should just comply! I'm not going to marry him because I don't want to hurt his feelings."

Aunt Jess took a sip of iced tea. "Naturally. But you should have seen this coming. Everyone else did."

"Then everyone else can marry him! You've never needed a man! Why should I be dependent on one?"

Aunt Jess looked like she'd been slapped in the face. "Just because you've never seen me depend on a man, doesn't mean I've never needed one. Look at what you've been doing the past two years. You haven't held on to one job for more than a few months. Ben wants to take care of you. Why don't you let him?"

"I don't need him to. I've never once been fired. Those jobs weren't… the right deal." Take care of her. What other superfluous things would he bring to the table? A set future? Children? She shuddered.

"Hannah, you're taking these things too lightly. You think everything has to be easy, because it always has been for you, but you need to grow up. At some point you will need to make decisions in life that are more difficult than whether or not you should join the police. It's a blessing having someone around to help you make those decisions, not a burden."

"Unless they're the wrong decisions, like Sean makes all the time." Ah, yes, the perfect way to divert attention: hit them where it hurts. Hannah opened her mouth to apologise for her hot-headed reply, but the ice in Aunt Jess's voice was enough to cool her down thoroughly.

"Are you sure you're not making the wrong decision right now?"

That hurt. Even more than a comparison to Sean. The only other time Aunt Jess had ever questioned her judgement was when Hannah decided she wanted to join the police. Aunt Jess had been right then, but she should not have chosen this moment to remind Hannah of that. That was low. "Yes. I thought you'd at least credit me with that much sense."

Hannah stood up, flounced into the garden and stepped over the little wooden fence that separated the garden from the side street. Aunt Jess called her back, but she didn't listen. Without even a goodbye, she started back to her apartment, fighting the red in her peripheral vision.

The one thing she had expected Aunt Jess to do, support her in this decision, had been denied. Anger, she'd counted on. Disappointment, yes, and sadness. But how could Aunt Jess question her judgement on whether or not she wanted to marry someone? That's the rest of your life! Talk about thinking ahead!

Halfway down the road she stopped, brushing back a blonde curl that resisted being tied into a ponytail. Wiping her forehead with the back of her hand, she pulled her sunglasses from the tiny blue handbag she carried, and put them on. *The wrong decision!* She bit back a frustrated growl and stomped on.

And then Aunt Jess had compared Hannah to Sean! In their extended family of three, the percentage of black sheep was quite high. Ben had never told either Hannah or Aunt Jess what exactly he had arrested Sean for, but they both knew they had

Ben to thank for the fact that he was never charged. Not that it had made any difference.

Hannah had tried to talk to her cousin, too. They did have a special bond after all. In fact, the only secret Hannah kept from Aunt Jess involved Sean. But he had waved away her concerns, making her feel like an accomplice to whatever he was into.

But a refusal of marriage was not a criminal act!

Around the corner another river of asphalt flowed down the hill. In front of a cafe a dumpy man sat melting into his chair under an orange parasol, sipping diet cola and sweating profusely. Most pedestrians tried to stay in the shade on the other side of the street, but in this part of town even the sunny side was quite busy, so Hannah had to slow her pace. Her train of thought was still thundering along, though.

She could have handled things better. She could have been more mature about it and shown that she wasn't as unprepared to handle grown-up life as her aunt seemed to think. If only it wasn't so mindbendingly hot! This was Britain, why wasn't it raining?

And why was this idiot of a man blocking her path? She almost bumped into him. *I'm thinking here. Go away!* The idiot didn't move. Jaw clenched, she yanked off her sunglasses and looked up at him to tell him exactly where she thought he should go. But then her eyes met his and she recognised the grinning face of her cousin.

"Got out of the wrong bed this morning, Nana?" he sneered. Being about a foot taller than Hannah, he literally looked down on her.

"Stop it, Sean, I'm not in the mood."

"No, really?"

Hannah ignored him and walked past. The only thing she could expect was more sarcasm.

But he didn't give up. He turned and joined her. "Where are you going?"

"Home."

"Okaaay, so where have you been? It's only eleven, and when you take a day off, that's usually the time you get up."

"That's not true! I…"

His eyes twinkled. He was only trying to aggravate her. And succeeding, as usual.

That frustrated growl finally came out. "Why are you following me?"

"What's wrong with you anyway? Anything I can do?" His face had gone serious. He must have realised this was not the time to provoke her.

She swiped her forehead again. "Ben proposed, and I turned him down. And now your mum is angry."

Sean made an effort not to laugh, but failed miserably. "Oh, I see! Well, she shouldn't be. I told her you wouldn't want him as your slave forever."

She skidded to a halt. "My slave? What's that supposed to mean?"

"Oh, come on! He's always following you around. Like a little dog, making sure you have everything you wanted. D'you think he would've ever gone skydiving if it weren't for you? Has he ever opposed you or given you a reason to fight with him? Noooo. He's just been there night and day, laying offerings by that great big pedestal he has you on."

"Don't be ridiculous. We were just having fun, that's all." She wrinkled her nose. "At least I thought so."

Sean shook his head. "And I thought you were supposed to be the smart one."

"So what are you, the pretty one?" How dare he be so cheerful.

He put on a quasi-serious face. "No, Hannah, I'm the bad egg. *I* would say I'm the rebel, but I guess it depends on from which angle you look at it."

Here we go again. He babbled on, an upbeat version of the story she'd heard so many times before. With Hannah being so perfect, someone had to provide some balance, blah blah. In the frustrated version of this speech he had once accused her of wanting to join the police just to spite him.

"Don't you have somewhere to be?" she interrupted his monologue, glancing at him. He should have been a model, or an actor. That would probably have been more lucrative than this borderline or sometimes blatantly illegal stuff. He wasn't exactly handsome, but his face was interesting nonetheless. Her best friend Julie, a French girl, once said that he looked very British, with his thin frame and bony features, topped with shaggy light brown hair.

"Nope!" Sean said, still grinning. But then his grin turned mischievous. "Actually yes, I think I'll go and turn Mum against you. She might disinherit you and I can finally claim my rightful place in the family."

"Very funny."

"Did he cry?"

"What?!"

"Did he cry when you said no? He's such a softie, I bet he cried."

She sighed. "Unbelievable, Sean. He's with the police, he's not a softie."

"That's not a no. He did cry, didn't he!"

"Stop it! I'm not discussing this with you if you only want to make fun of us." She glared at him, but all he did was smirk. Her palms itched. "No, he didn't cry! Just go home, will you. Be juvenile with your friends or something."

"Fine, I'll leave you to wallow. Eat some ice cream, you'll feel better!"

"Thanks, grandma, I will."

"Hey, I'm only trying to help."

"No, you're not."

"No. I'm not." His smile became friendly. "Hey, I'm sorry. You'll get over it." Then he put on a pair of flashy, mirrored sunglasses and was back to being Sean. "Well, I'm off to Mum, see what I can do about that inheritance. Byeee!"

She stared at his back for a moment, then put her sunglasses on and continued on her way home. Typical Sean, never serious about anything. Hannah used to be the same, but here was another piece of evidence that she *had* matured.

Still, even Sean said she'd been unfair to Ben. How many more people would have to say it before she acknowledged it? Because they were right, of course. With a sigh she came to a halt, taking off her sunglasses again and squinting in the harsh sunlight. Why had she let it go on this long? Why had she not realised that she hadn't been in love with Ben for such a long time?

She never meant to hurt him. Or Aunt Jess, for that matter. She should go back. Saying sorry to Aunt Jess would not be as complicated. She'd had some practice. After all this, she didn't even care that Sean would be there to see her grovel.

Feeling lighter already, Hannah hurried back along the street for the third time that morning. But when she reached Aunt Jess's house, her heart jumped. The blue door was ajar.

2

Sunglasses in hand, Hannah pushed the door open and crossed the hallway to the living room door. "Aunt Jess, I'm sorry, I—"

Halfway open, the door stuck and she bumped into it. A curse on the other side. The door gave way, but all Hannah could see was her cousin's back as he moved out from behind it. Her skin tingled. Something was wrong. Why had Sean left the door open? Flashes of blue and orange behind him. The cushions, the rug. Same as always, but less bright somehow. A fraction of a second later the realisation hit. In Sean's hand. A gun.

Footsteps. Running. A dark man with black Beethoven hair, wearing some kind of heavy cape-like overcoat, disappeared into the garden. Sean swore again, and chased him over the little fence.

Hannah tried to move, but shock had her rooted to the spot. Who was that man? What was Sean doing with a gun? Should she follow? Her hand moved towards the phone in her bag, but hovered as the rest of the room came into view. Her breath faltered. Dropping her sunglasses and her bag, she covered her mouth with her fingers and sank to her knees. On the orange rug lay a woman, a large red stain covering her chest. It wasn't Aunt Jess. It couldn't be! On hands and knees Hannah moved towards her.

This wasn't Aunt Jess. This woman may have her hair, and her nose, and her lips, but this was not her wonderful aunt, the woman who'd raised her, who always had a laugh in her eyes, even when she was angry. Frantically checking for a pulse, Hannah fought the growing sense of futility until it suffocated her. She leaned back, gasping for air, wiping clouding eyes with her palms. Why? Who would do this?

Staring at the dead woman in front of her, Hannah took the hand that had fallen over her aunt's stomach and caressed it, clutching the fingers to her chest. *Oh, Aunt Jess…* How did this happen so fast? Hannah had only just left. She swallowed. And now she had to leave again. Sean had gone after the killer. He could be in danger too. With a last kiss on her aunt's hand, she placed it back on her stomach. When she closed the eyes staring at the ceiling, she let her fingers brush the cheek. *Bye, Aunt Jess.*

Forcing back her tears, she ran into the side street. For a moment she hesitated, searching for a hint of where Sean and the attacker had gone. The rows of houses were baking in the sun. A dog had found a tiny patch of shadow to fall down in. Nothing seemed out of the ordinary.

The sound of a car braking ripped through the air, followed by angry shouting. Hannah sprinted in the direction of the noise. Left here, then right. Halfway down the road one of Aunt Jess's neighbours was talking to an angry woman in a little red car.

"Just like that! Yes, I saw them! And in this heat!"

"Mr. Singh!" Hannah shouted, "Which way did they go?"

Mr. Singh pointed up the hill. "Up there, Hannah. Was that Sean with a gun?"

"Call the police!" She raced to the corner, just in time to catch a glimpse of flying coat tails across the square. *Come on, Sean!* He still hadn't caught up, chasing the man up the stairs leading to Mill's Park.

Hannah shot after them, feet pummelling the steps. At the top of the stairs… nothing. Panting, she kicked the ground. Too slow! She scoured the field surrounding the windmill. She wasn't that far behind. Where could they have gone? Her eyes darted around. The windmill, locked. The field, deserted. They couldn't have doubled back. Where else was there?

On her left was the old, overgrown wall where the miller's cottage had once stood. That was too high to climb without a ladder. *Oh! The door!* She had never seen the weathered wooden door open before, but now it was ajar. Squinting against the sun she bridged the few yards to the opening and with her hand on the rusty latch, flung herself through it.

Her foot caught on something soft, and the next moment she was on the ground in the dark.

The ground was soft and smelled of pine needles. But there was more underneath her than forest floor.

Sean pushed her aside and grumbled, "Get off me!"

She jumped to her feet and helped him up. "What happened? Where is he? Where are *we*? Why is it so cold? And dark..." She looked around, but the killer was gone, leaving them alone in an inky bubble streaked with the even darker shadows of thin, straight tree trunks. In the dark she couldn't even make out if he had left footprints.

Left without the need for immediate action, Hannah directed all her adrenaline-fuelled anxiety at her cousin.

"What did you do?"

"*Me?*" Sean pointed at his chest. "*You* made the gate disappear! Now how are we going to go back?"

Hannah's gaze flicked back to the V-shaped tree behind them. Black spots dancing in front of her eyes darkened her vision further. No gate. Trapped. Trapped where?

She flexed her hands into fists, whipping around trying to find an exit, but no gate, or door, or strange light stood out. Trembling, she stepped over the trunk of the tree. *Please work. Please.* But the other side of the tree looked exactly the same. She went around it, only to see Sean mirror her dread.

He was scared. She had to be strong, for him. Nobody else would. Not now. Hannah sagged against one of the trees, not finding any of the strength she craved. The silent darkness of this strange forest filled the hole Aunt Jess had left inside her. Was it even real? Or was this the place everyone goes to when they've lost the one they love most in life?

Sean rubbed the back of his head and grunted, but said nothing. Hannah tried to read his face, but in the scant moonlight that seeped through the branches, she couldn't find anything more than she already knew. Something she felt just as bitterly.

"Oh Sean!" Whimpering, she leaned her head against his shoulder and he put his arms around her. There was no need to say anything, the loss weighed as heavily on him as it did on her.

The fact that they had no idea where they were or how the world around them could suddenly have switched from an oppressively hot summer morning to a chilly night, was of little importance next to finding themselves without the one person who had always been there. Around them, sometimes between them, but always close, Aunt Jess had been a mother to both of them, guiding them, supporting them and loving them. She had always been the one they would go to for help. But now Aunt Jess was gone. Who would help Hannah with that?

She pressed her forehead into Sean's t-shirt and tried not to cry. But when she turned her head, her cheek against his chest, and she opened her eyes, the fabric in front of her darkened where Sean's tears fell. A sob shocked her body and she buried herself in his arms. Aunt Jess, her Aunt Jess, was the sweetest person in the world. And Hannah had left her in an argument. She should have stayed! She should have at least said sorry!

How long they stood there, not wanting to go back to reality, but simply holding on to that little bit of safety and familiarity, she could not tell. When she finally let go of Sean, she shivered, and he rubbed her arms to help her get warm.

"Ehm…" she said while drying her cheeks, "I suppose we should find out where we are, so we can go back."

He stared at the ground, then took a deep breath and nodded.

"Yeh, we can't stay here forever. Wherever we are."

Hannah took in her surroundings, but nothing familiar stood out. All she could see in about a ten yard circle around her were silvery patches of pine duvet. No doors, or gates, or even those weird upright whirlpools they have in science fiction films. As far as she knew, none of the parks and woods around Nottingham were so dense that only the tops of the trees still bore needles. Certainly nowhere around Mill's Park.

She reached for her bag, but it wasn't there. Must have dropped to the floor when she saw…

"D'you have your phone?"

Sean reached into his pocket, and handed her the device. No reception. Naturally. No internet either. Great. Flashlight would have to do. A glint at her feet caught Hannah's eye. The light from the phone reflected on the matt surface of the gun. Using the hem of her skirt, she lifted the weapon by the barrel. Her stomach turned. Instinct told her to throw the awful thing as far away as she could, but she'd have to keep it until she could turn it over to the police. But where was the nearest station? Where was the nearest anything? To the left, darkness. To the right, creepiness. Straight ahead, trees. Behind her—*Oh, decide already!* She took a few steps in a random direction, walking more steadily when Sean followed her.

"This is so bizarre…"

Sean shrugged. Hannah bit her cheek. No, bizarre didn't cover it. But there were too many questions swimming around in Hannah's brain to think of the proper word. This was Sean, he shouldn't need the proper word from her. *Talk to me!*

"So what happened to you?"

He rubbed his head again. "I followed him through the gate, and when I saw I had run into this non-existent wood in this non-existent darkness, I stopped, and he hit me from behind."

"Let me see." He bent over, and she raised her hands to check him. They were shaking. Biting her lips, she examined him as well as she could in the dark, eventually establishing there was nothing worse than a bump on his head. He straightened, and for a moment neither of them knew what to say. Sean coughed and folded his arms over his chest.

Hoping her voice would sound steady, Hannah asked, "Who was that? Do you know him?"

"No!" For Sean, that was a fierce reaction, making Hannah almost glad she couldn't see the expression in his eyes. "I don't hang out with murderers!"

"I didn't say that. I meant, did you recognise him? You could have seen him somewhere. She must have known him, right? Otherwise, why…" Her lower lip quivered and she took in a sharp breath. Lowering her voice and trying not to sound too bitter, she forced herself in a different direction. "Why didn't you shoot?"

He hesitated a moment and looked away. "I don't know how."

"What? What about all those selfies with your mates, posing with guns?"

"It was a fake, all right? I've never shot a gun. I was afraid I'd hit someone else instead!"

The weapon weighed heavily in Hannah's hand. "Well, this is not a fake. We saw what it did…" She swallowed, pushing away the memory by shining the flashlight around again, searching for any way out of this nightmare. "I think there's a sign there."

Her voice mingled with his.

"There's a light there."

He was right. A tiny light shone in the distance. The far distance. On the other side, not five yards to the left of where they stood, a path cut through the trees. It was too dark to tell if the white post a little further down was actually a sign, but for once Hannah had already made up her mind.

She took a step towards the post. "Maybe the path will take us to the light. And anyway, the sign might tell us where we are."

He looked at the light again and opened his mouth, but then turned. "Okay, let's do that."

The path was hardly more than an animal trail. Perhaps it had once been well-used, but now most of it was covered by long grass and weeds, leaving only a narrow strip of sand to walk on. A very old and weathered white wooden arrow told them that Nottingham should be a quarter of a mile to the left of where they stood.

"That's ridiculous," said Sean, "There's nothing like this forest anywhere near Nottingham. I say we go back to the light and see if we can at least borrow some warm clothes."

"I don't know. Maybe it's a different Nottingham...?"

He looked down on her, hands on his hips. "Well, sure, there's Nottingham-on-Avon, High Nottingham, Nottingham-by-the-Sea... Seriously, Hannah!"

When she shot him a poisonous look, he continued, "The light probably means there's a house there, we could ask the people..."

"It could just be a lamp or something! The sign says that Nottingham—or at least some kind of village or something—is a quarter of a mile away. We'll have more chance of finding someone who can help us there."

"The light is closer."

"It's cold! I don't want to do the extra walking if it is only a lamp."

He threw his right hand in the air as if flinging something over his shoulder. "Fine! We'll do it your way, as usual." He grumbled some more, but followed her in the direction of 'Nottingham'. After about ten minutes they came to the edge of the forest, where the path sloped downward. Soon a bank rose on one side, while thick bushes grew on the other, blocking even more of the path.

Sean held back so Hannah could lead. She would have preferred to walk together, but the hedgerow made that impossible. Sean was unusually quiet. Although that made sense considering what had happened, it only made Hannah's thoughts circle back to the same horrific image over and over again. After a few minutes she couldn't take the quiet anymore.

"My feet are frozen. I've got sand in my sandals."

He didn't answer. Of course not. Ridiculously mundane thing to complain about. But what else could she say? Something positive? Nothing came to mind. Something generic like 'we'll be fine' seemed hugely inadequate. Would it even be true? All the other things she could think to say involved questions. Questions he would no more have the answers to than she did.

Not wanting to disturb him any more, Hannah walked on in silence, trying not to drown in her own thoughts. How much further would they have to go? They rounded a bend and a village came into view up ahead. Lights shone behind the windows of several houses and what seemed to be a pub at the end of the road.

Never before had Hannah been so happy to see a pub. She upped her tempo and turned to Sean with a smile. "You see? I told you there would—"

She stopped. He was gone.

3

Roderick put his glass on the woodworm-ridden table in front of him, playing with its stem for a moment. It would run out in a year or so. Not that it mattered, really. Nothing mattered, really. He picked up the bottle and filled his glass again. It was more habit than enjoyment nowadays. But when it's the only thing you do…

He stared into his wine, the flames of the fire behind it leaping around in the red liquid, dancing like the people at the parties they used to have up at the castle. Now he had only their memories to keep him company. And the wine. For another year or so.

His gaze drifted from the wine and settled on the fire. He frowned, as if he saw it for the first time. Why had he bothered to light a fire tonight? He came here almost every night, but he never lit a fire. What was different today?

He glanced around, casting his eye over the long dining hall tables and benches, lined up and dusty, as always. Nothing new there. The workers hadn't used them in years. The comfortable chairs in the alcove by the tall windows, flowery patterns fading, the little tables in between; they were all there, exactly as they always were. No-one to fill them or move them. No-one but Roderick.

A sigh escaped from his pool of self-pity. He was reaching for his glass when there was a knock on the door. His mouth half open in anticipation of the wine, Roderick froze. That was certainly different. No-one had knocked in years. Staring at the door, he had half convinced himself he'd imagined it, when another knock sounded, louder this time.

He got up and opened the door, eyeing the visitor beneath half-closed lids. Tall, but quite thin, with pale skin and straggly hair, the young knocker would not easily be mistaken for a gentleman. And why this state of undress? Wearing nothing but torn breeches and some kind of undershirt, this man was not merely a stranger, he was strange. And not very impressive.

While Roderick observed his odd dress, he noticed that the strange stranger returned the look.

"Hi. Can I come in?"

Then, remembering some of his past charm and hospitality, Roderick smiled. "Certainly."

Stepping aside, he waved the newcomer to the corner of the long table where he had put his bottle of wine. A visitor, even a peculiar one, was very welcome after all this time.

Sitting down on the bench closest to the fire, the young man looked around. "What is this place?" he asked, "Some kind of factory?"

Roderick scratched his chin. It must be difficult to distinguish the building's purpose after all these years, especially with only the light of a small fire in the capacious dining hall where he had come to drink. The majority of the complex was actually situated on the other side of the mill yard, but there weren't any chairs there. Nor glasses.

He ducked behind the counter that stretched along one side of the hall and came up holding another wine glass. "It used to be," he said as he poured the visitor a drink, "a textile mill. Lace, to be precise. But that was back when my hair was the colour of yours. It has been closed down for years. I come here every so often to reminisce and to drink to good times past."

He handed the stranger the glass, but the boy put it on the table with a soft 'thanks' and tapped the stem with his fingertips.

Roderick sat down opposite, scrutinising his visitor. "Excuse me for asking, but why are you not dressed? Or at least wearing a coat?"

The boy frowned. But whether that was due to anger or confusion was hard to tell. "Well… Where I was before… it was hot."

"It was hot. At the end of October?"

His eyes widened under another frown. "October? It's the middle of July!"

He was undoubtedly a very odd fellow. It took Roderick a while to pick one of the various questions this man's arrival prompted, during which the newcomer kept fidgeting with his wine, and glancing around glassy-eyed. He was making Roderick nervous just looking at him.

"Can I help you in any way?"

"Nah. Well… maybe. I, er… came here looking for a warm place, but I left my cousin going the other way, towards where the sign said would be Nottingham."

Roderick waved his hand to set the boy's mind at ease. "Oh, but then he will—"

"She."

"She…" Roderick hesitated before he finished his sentence. "Will be fine, the village isn't far. Why did you not go with her? You would have had more chance to find someone in the village. Besides, a woman on her own in the dark…"

He snorted. "Yeah." Then continued, "We sort of… disagreed, so we split up."

"She will be fine," Roderick repeated. What could possibly have possessed this young man to leave a family member, and a weaker one at that, alone in the woods? Even if the last robbery had been some time ago. One never knew what might happen. He frowned at his visitor. At least the boy finally picked up his wine and took a sip. Apparently it wasn't quite to his taste. He could be a little more appreciative. "Don't you like it? It's a good year."

"More of a cider man." He gave a little apologetic smile and then tried another sip. He still made a face, but it seemed to defrost him somewhat.

Roderick studied the boy as he fidgeted and shivered. After all these years. Years of solitude, and the first visitor was… him. An undressed, uncultured, dare he say unfit specimen. If this was the alternative to solitude, which was to be preferred?

Yet, perhaps this was too quick a judgement. His current apparel might belie his habitual behaviour. Roderick took a sip of his own wine, while his visitor pulled on his nose. *Perhaps not.*

* * *

Sean took another sip of wine, though it made his tongue stick to the roof of his mouth. The alcohol warmed his body, at least, but his thoughts remained icy. He shouldn't have left Hannah. Even if she was a controlling witch. She needed him right now. And he hated to admit it, but he needed her too. Maybe more. Probably more. He shook his head to lose the thought.

Why did she have to be like that? Even now! They should be together in this! But he was the one who left. Left her… where? In a forest on a hot, dark, cold October morning in July.

Was he going crazy? Would he have left her if they knew where they were? Yes. Without a doubt. But here… She didn't know where to go. And she'd had a shock. Maybe it was the shock that made her so unbearable. No, she was always unbearable. Maybe it was the shock that had made him leave her.

He glanced at the man opposite. Dark blond hair, grey eyes, probably about forty years old. He might have asked this man if he was going mad, because the man looked sharp enough to be able to tell him, except that he wore ridiculously old-fashioned clothes. Like, at least a hundred years old. Victorian or something. If this man hadn't been so surprised to see him, Sean would have thought that he belonged with that bastard they chased through the gate. Another old-fashioned nutter. And a dangerous one at that.

Sean stood up. "I have to go. I have to find my cousin. She could be in danger."

The man nodded, but then held up a finger. He rose as well, climbed the stairs in the back corner, and returned a minute later with a brown heap over his arm. He gave it a good shake before handing it to Sean. "Take this. I don't think it's quite your size, but at least it will keep you warm."

What was *that*? For a moment the emptiness inside Sean was filled with curiosity. It even put a little grin on his face, while he put the coat on. As he ran his fingers across the shoulder cape, he remarked, "This place has been closed for a while, hasn't it?"

The man drew himself up, eyebrows together. "I'll admit it is a little out of date, but you don't seem to have much choice, do you?"

Right. Insult the coat *and* the man. Looked like he would be the same Sean, no matter what happened. Blushing, he told himself—again—not to care if he said a dumb thing. But even the caretaker of a dusty, abandoned factory can have pride in his job. Who was he to judge? He thanked the older man, and turned towards the door.

"You... do know where you are going?"

Fair question, unfortunately. The man had called Nottingham a village, but as far as Sean knew, Nottingham had been more than that since the Middle Ages, let alone by Victorian times. Yet another confusing fact to add to the mix. Partial thoughts and feelings rolled around in his head, none of them making any sense. The only thing sharp in his mind was the image of his mother, lying on the floor, staring into nothingness.

The man's voice floated through the fog in Sean's head. "Forgive me, but you seem to have little direction. How did you happen upon this place?"

A log in the fire cracked, bringing Sean back to the present. "We were following... a man, who led us to the forest."

"Where is he now?"

"I don't know. We lost him in the woods. I was hoping to find him here."

"None have passed by here. But if he led you to Nottingham, he may be from the area. What did he look like?"

Sean frowned. That face would be on his mind until he saw its eyes turn cold. Ever since he'd found his mother's door open, and that face hovering over her dead body, it was all he'd been able to think about. "He had dark skin, black hair, and dark eyes. Tall, about my height. And he wore Victorian clothes, like you, only with a long dark blue coat."

A muscle twitched in the older man's cheek. "Tell me, did he have short hair, or was it perhaps a bit longer than usual?"

"Depends on what you call usual, but it was longer than yours and mine."

The caretaker breathed in through his teeth. "Then you *were* robbed."

Sean's lips tightened. "In a way. Do you know him?"

"There is only one man around here whose hair covers his neck. Unfortunately, he is also the owner of most of the land around here, including this old mill. Which means it will not be easy to regain whatever he took from you."

His words stabbed Sean in the gut. "I'd say it would be impossible. He killed my mother."

The man narrowed his eyes, but said nothing. Not that it would have helped if he had. All he did was fill up Sean's glass again. Sean stared at it, trying to silence the screaming in his head raging to get out. He focused on the face appearing in the liquid. If he didn't find that man, nothing else mattered.

Hannah would have to wait a little longer. Sean sat down again and picked up his glass.

"So he's the boss around here, huh? That should make him easier to find."

"He lives in the castle…"

"Of course he does."

"But you can't go in there."

"Oh can't I?" Part of Sean was hoping the man would get angry—somehow the thought of a fight appealed to him—but his host remained quite calm.

"No. He's powerful. He has magic."

Wait, what? His mouth half open, Sean blinked. First Victorians and now magic? Yes, it would explain the transition from morning to night and ending up in a forest in the middle of Nottingham, but come on! "Magic, right! Like swish and flick? Pointy hats and robes?"

"Don't be foolish! You must be aware that magic is the very reason he is 'the boss around here', as you put it. The only reason, I might add, for he hasn't done much to merit his position." A quick look around. "I really shouldn't tell you this, because one never knows if he is listening, but take this mill for example. He built it for his own profit, but the people in the village required the work, so they came, even without pressure. However, he neglected to take proper care and after a few accidents he had to close it down, leaving all those people without work once again."

Were comfortable chairs the standard for Victorian factories? Maybe they were. How would he know? "What kind of accidents?"

"Oh, nothing too serious at first, just bad maintenance, machines breaking down and all that, but in the end one of the parts snapped under pressure and hit someone in the head. Poor girl died instantly."

"That doesn't have anything to do with magic."

Again his host took the bottle, and emptied it into Sean's glass. "Naturally. My intention was to show you his inadequacy as a leader."

Right. Rubbing his eyes, Sean sighed. Maybe it would be easier to just agree to what this man said. Any information he could give Sean about his mother's killer would be welcome, even if it turned out that the truth was warped by this man's mind.

"So, what you're telling me is, don't go after him or he'll say abracadabra and some demon is going to eat me alive."

Now it was the caretaker's turn to stay silent for a moment and drink his wine. "You have a vivid imagination. I doubt whether he will summon a demon to have you killed, when he can just as easily shoot you, but if it will keep you away from the castle, by all means believe what you will."

"So no demons."

"Not that I know of."

"What then? Does he look in his crystal ball and sing incantations, or does he brew potions from bats' teeth?"

The man pursed his lips. "Again, I don't wish to seem inhospitable, but it is getting rather late and if my advice is not to your liking, sir, then I suggest—"

Sean interrupted him with a gesture. "No, no, I'm sorry. You're right, okay?" *What happened to agreeing with him?* "I'm sorry, it's just… I'm not used to magic being… real, you know? I just have this reaction of," he raised his hands and widened his eyes, "'Ooh, magic, I'm so scared!' But I don't know how else I got here, so I suppose I should listen to you. Can I have some more of that wine?"

His glass was still full, but his host seemed to accept his way of reconciling. "Of course, I'm no authority on the subject, but I believe he uses spells."

"What kind of spells?"

"That's really all I can tell you about it. I haven't ever seen him use any spells, so I simply don't know."

Sean shook his head, his floppy locks brushing his forehead. "No, that's not what I mean. I mean, what does he gain from this magic?"

"Ah, I see." The man scratched his chin. "Well, he is excessively rich, but so was his father before him and his father before that. He is used to getting his own way. I heard he once grew a pig's tail on one of his nursemaids for attempting to bathe him when he wanted to play."

Sean raised an eyebrow. "Yes, truly evil…"

Glaring, the older man tightened his lips. Sean could kick himself. *Agree, Sean, you were going to agree.* He raised his glass in apology, which the other man accepted. Or at least he started talking again.

"Then, when he was older, a girl refused to kiss him and he made her tongue wither in her mouth."

Sean grimaced. "You're making this up."

"I assure you, I saw this girl's shrivelled tongue myself!"

Sean raised his glass to drink, looked at it, made a face, and put it down again. "He doesn't sound so scary to me. What you're telling me is that he's a bad businessman with a screw loose. If all it takes is a rotting tongue to get you people scared, then I'm—"

"Ah, but you're mistaken. Unfortunately, it's not just his powers that the people are afraid of. Sadly, you already know my master is no stranger to killing. He—"

"Your master?" Sean jumped to his feet and glared at the caretaker. The bench he had been sitting on toppled, its clatter on the floor echoing around the hall. "You're *with* him?"

The older man held up his hands in defence. "My dear boy, calm down! I don't condone any of his actions, but neither can I do anything against them. I have been serving the family for as long as I can remember. I'm thoroughly in his grip and there is nothing I can do about it. Believe me, if I could, I would leave. He tried to kill me once…" He shuddered. "But even the village is out of bounds for me. This mill and the castle are all I am allowed to roam."

Sean ran a hand through his hair. Should he believe anything this character was saying? For all he knew, this was the village idiot. Was he even worth listening to? Sean should go and find Hannah. But if this magic *was* real… "You can't leave."

"I can't leave."

"But I came in that door a moment ago, you could simply

walk out." He pointed to the flaked brown door separating them from the outside world.

The man sighed wistfully. "Did I not just explain to you that this man has powers you and I don't understand?"

Hm. "But… haven't you tried?"

"Of course I have!" The man took a deep breath. "I have tried, but I have also given up long ago. I used to know the people in the village, but now I'm sure they have forgotten me."

Sean looked down on the man sitting on the other side of the table. Crazy seemed more and more likely. Who drinks wine in an abandoned factory, claiming they can't leave? And why would some magic man come to his house to kill his mum? Why would anyone kill his mum? He closed his eyes and swallowed. Part of him wanted to believe that the whole weirdness of the situation meant that none of it had actually happened. That he would wake up in a hospital or something, and his mum would be sitting by his bed.

But even in this ridiculous setting it wouldn't stick. His mum was gone. He had seen the blood on her body. The smile gone from her eyes. She was dead. Furiously blinking to try and get that image out of his head, he sank down on the edge of the overturned bench behind him, waiting for his blood to thin and flow again.

"Are you all right?" The man's voice sounded muffled. When Sean didn't answer, he came around the table and put a hand on Sean's shoulder.

The touch brought Sean back to reality. And with reality came an alarming thought. He looked up at his host. "Is the castle close to the village?"

"Right next to it, on top of a cliff. Why?"

"Hannah has gone to the village. What if she meets him on the way?"

4

Sean, you idiot! Well done, this was the absolute worst time to be pigheaded. Now what was Hannah supposed to do? She stared at the path behind her, then at the luring lights of the village. If she could borrow a coat or something, then she could go after him and not be an icicle by the time she found him. It would be a waste to have reached the village only to turn back before she had enjoyed a little warmth.

Then again, she couldn't just leave Sean.

Leave *him*? He left her!

With a last look over her shoulder, she hurried towards the lights. He'd be fine. She would just borrow a coat somewhere and go back right away. He wouldn't get himself killed in five minutes, right? She skidded to a halt. What a horrible expression. Another look over her shoulder. But what could she do now? If she'd even find him by the dwindling light from the phone, she'd still be cold. And he'd still be contrary.

Well, she was mad at him, too! She turned around and passed the first few houses. Pub. Pub was probably better than randomly knocking on some door. But her step slowed at the third house. Something was odd. Rows of low houses lined the street, built from the same dull, grey stones under her feet. But although asphalt would have been more practical, that was not what bothered her. It was the light. It flickered.

Gas lamps. What was this, a living history site? Halfway

down the street she looked over her shoulder again. And why weren't there any people out? Maybe a dead history site then. Continuing without Sean may not have been such a good idea after all.

At least the pub produced the muffled sound of laughter. A sign in the shape of a small, hairy boy with a wide mouth and very close-set eyes told her that the inn was called 'The Monkey'. Hannah shivered at the creepy picture for a moment, but the laughing voices from inside raised her spirits. Good. Happy people would be more inclined to help her. She pushed open the door and the laughing stopped almost instantly. Then the other pub murmur died out. Everyone inside stared at her.

Did the gun show? A quick check. No, it wasn't that. She'd wrapped the weapon in a part of her skirt and held it between the folds. Of course, that did leave her skirt on the short side. But not enough to silence a whole pub, right?

Forcing herself to smile, she took a few steps forward. She'd been right about the village being a living history place. Victorian, by the looks of it, but she had no idea if this was supposed to be early or late. Most of the people were in work clothes. These reenactors were really into it, though. A woman in the corner looked shocked, another beside her was turning into a tomato and some of the men were now trying to look everywhere but at Hannah.

At least with everybody wearing their Victorian clothes, someone might have a normal coat for her. Better say something, though. This silence was getting more and more awkward.

"Hi. I think I got lost..."

At last the barmaid, a large woman in her mid forties wearing a mob cap, came out from behind the bar, grabbed a wide cape and threw it around Hannah, quickly ushering her into a room at the back. The heavy wooden door shut out the whispered conversations starting up. The barmaid stood in front of it, hands on her hips, about as unmovable as the door itself.

A few candles on a side table lit a bed, a couple of chairs

and a large wooden closet. A small window stood out as a dark rectangle in the opposite brick wall.

"What is this place?"

"It's a public house, love. Ain't ya ever been in one before?" The barmaid stole some curious looks at her face, while she took the cape away and tutted. Although her thick Nottinghamshire accent comforted Hannah—she must not have gone too far after all—the intonation was none too friendly.

"Where did you come from? Did someone steal your clothes? You don't look like you were robbed. What's that?"

She pointed a stubby finger to the gun Hannah was still trying to hide, but when Hannah unwrapped the weapon, the barmaid showed no signs of alarm. Even when Hannah told her that it wasn't hers, the barmaid didn't seem to care either way. She brushed imaginary dirt off her apron and tugged on her mob cap, though it looked like it wouldn't budge in a hurricane.

"I'm sorry to bother you. I only came in to borrow a coat. My cousin is—"

"You'll be needing more than a coat if you're to go out there again."

"That's very kind, but—"

The barmaid cracked open the door behind her and called out, "Charlotte!"

Not much of a listener, that one. "I only need a coat. If you don't have one, I'll go and—"

A young woman stuck her head around the door. She had a sweet, pretty face with big brown eyes and a full mouth. Her chestnut curls were tied up, but like Hannah's, they didn't feel inclined and were trying to escape. "Yes, Nellie?"

"Give us a hand here."

The girl came in, not even trying to hide her curiosity. "What happened? Did she say?"

Nellie shrugged and opened the closet. She tugged on her cap again, but all her hair was still firmly in place. If it had ever been rebellious, it had long since turned grey and given up.

Charlotte turned to Hannah, her eyes widening further. "Did they take your corset too?"

"Who? No! I never wear corsets. I only—"

"Looks like it," Nellie grumbled, holding a pale pink corset in one hand and a bundle of white cloth in the other.

Hannah's eyebrows shot up. There was nothing wrong with her figure! Why was Nellie looking at her like that?

"This one belonged to my mother. She was a bit heavier, too. I think it'll fit you."

This was going too far. "No, wait! I'm really not into the whole dressing up thing. I only came in to borrow a coat. My cousin and I got lost in the forest and now he… went to look for help elsewhere. I just wanted a coat so I wouldn't be too cold when I go back to look for him."

Like talking to the wall.

"Perhaps you'd better sit down." Nellie took Hannah by the shoulders and planted her firmly in a chair. Did this woman ever listen? Hannah raised her hand to protest. Unfortunately it was the hand holding the gun. Hannah held her breath, waiting for Charlotte to react. But nothing came. Hannah might as well have been brandishing a baguette.

"Put that on the table, love, I can't help you if you're holding on to things," Nellie said, gesturing Charlotte to give her a hand.

Careful not to touch the metal, Hannah slowly put the gun on the table and pushed it back against the wall, along with Sean's phone. Charlotte gave it a curious look, but showed no concern at all. What was wrong with these people? Didn't they know what a gun looked like? They couldn't have been so in character that they never watched TV? Even then, it wasn't that different from a Victorian gun that they wouldn't recognise it for what it was.

"Thank you, but I really only need a coat. I need to go find Sean. My cousin."

Nellie put her fists on her hips. "I'm not letting you out in that state, no matter who you're looking for. Stand up, we'll get you dressed and then we'll see about any other problems you have."

Sit down, stand up. Make up your mind, I'm not your puppet! Nellie was already pulling on Hannah's top, but Hannah backed away.

"No! I need to find my cousin, I'm not wasting any more time with this nonsense. Please let me leave, I'll find a coat somewhere else."

She turned and reached for the door, but the barmaid was quicker than she looked and parked her broad bosom in front of the exit.

"Excuse me, I'd like to pass, please."

"Not like that, you're not."

Why didn't she realise Hannah wasn't part of their group? Nottinghamshire accent or no, Hannah felt the distance between herself and her hostesses grow by the minute. Maybe a touch of compliance was in order. There was no way she was going to move either the will or the body of this woman without resorting to violence. And escaping through the window seemed like a last resort.

"Fine, I'll put on a dress. Just be quick."

The barmaid gave a short nod and both women went to work. Charlotte pulled a dark purple, cotton dress from the closet.

"This one's pretty, with all the little black flowers. I didn't know you had all these fancy clothes back here."

"They're mostly things people have left behind after their stay. I wanted to sell them, but Bart won't hear of it. They may come back for 'em, he says."

Charlotte caressed the fabric. "Who left this, do you remember? I—" She dropped the dress and stared open-mouthed at Hannah, whose cheeks flushed. Okay, her bra had seen better days, but it wasn't that bad. Nellie looked up from loosening corset laces and stared at her as well, eyes widening. Charlotte reached for Hannah's bra.

"Hey!" Hannah stepped back and held up her hand, ready to slap the girl's hand away, but Charlotte was already distracted.

"You have a tattoo. What is it for?"

"My name is Taylor." More than anyone here needed to know. Hannah absentmindedly rubbed the little spool of thread on the inside of her wrist. A very disturbing realisation formed in her head. This was not an act. They really had never seen a bra before.

She sank back down on the chair. So many questions now fought for her attention, that she couldn't focus on any of them. At the very least she'd gone back in time. No, that wasn't right either. Nottingham was a bustling town in Victorian times. This was not the same Nottingham. But how?

"Are you all right, me duck?" Hannah only heard the question when the barmaid repeated it. Concern softened her features, but only for an instant. When Hannah looked up, Nellie's face went rigid again with mistrust sliding back into place.

"Yes, fine." What else could she say?

The barmaid pulled her up and helped her undress. A crisp white chemise was fine, but when she held up the light pink corset, Hannah protested. Unexplainable situation or no, she was not wearing a corset!

"You won't fit in the dress if you don't wear the corset. So unless you want to wear one of mine..." Not waiting for an answer, she reached around Hannah and hooked up the corset.

It actually didn't feel too bad. The barmaid's mother must have had more or less the same proportions as Hannah. She glanced at Nellie. *She must take after her father.*

"Nellie... Can I have these?" Charlotte held up a pair of dark green shoes with buckles on them. She looked like she was going to lick them.

"If they fit. They've been in there for ages. I'm sure Bart won't notice if you don't parade around in them. Anything for her?" She turned Hannah around and started pulling on the laces.

Woah! Maybe her figure was not so similar to Nellie's mother's after all. Hannah held on to the edge of the table as Nellie pulled even harder. "That's enough! I'm sure the dress will fit now."

Nellie gave her a scrutinising look, but then gave in and tied up the laces.

"These might work." Charlotte showed a pair of black boots, complete with a million tiny buttons.

"Hand me that cover, Lottie."

Another bit of cloth. All Hannah wanted was a coat, so she could go find her cousin. She focused on the chatter between the two women so she wouldn't have to deal with the noise in her head. But concern for Sean still lingered in her stomach.

Charlotte was listing people she thought would love the various items in Nellie's closet. Apparently she had an enormous family. But she wasn't much help in getting Hannah out of here any more quickly.

Nellie finally took her hands off Hannah. "What do you think?"

"Can I have a coat now?"

Nellie scowled at her. "What do you think of the dress."

Hannah sighed. It was quite pretty, but all those black flowers reminded her of the funeral she would have to arrange. A funeral she couldn't even get to if she couldn't find her way back there. And by now it was pretty obvious that 'there' was a long way from 'here', despite the familiar accent.

Nellie deflated. "What's wrong, ducky? Don't you like it?"

"It's not that. The dress is beautiful, thank you. But I really have to find my cousin."

The barmaid crossed her arms and tapped her finger on her elbow. "This cousin, is he dressed?"

Of course, clothes, that's really the most important thing right n— actually, if the light had really been no more than a lamp, Sean would be freezing by now.

"He doesn't have a coat, no."

"*Alrate,* let me see what I can do about that. You sit down here," she pushed Hannah into a chair—which was an odd sensation, since she was now unable to bend her back—"and I'll see if I can get some of the men to come with you."

"That's really not necessary."

Nellie turned and walked out the door. If this woman wasn't going to listen to her very soon, then—

"You're from the south, aren't you?"

What?!

Charlotte sat down in the other chair, all big brown innocent eyes.

"I'm not." Hannah rubbed her temples. Now was not the time to get into the whole north-south discussion.

"It's just that people from the south don't really seem to know about us. From what you read in the paper, I mean. Gosh, I'd love to see London one day. Magics are much less scary there, they say."

Hannah blinked, fingers idly on her temples. *Magics?*

Nellie came in and put a bowl of potato soup in Hannah's hand. "Here, eat up."

Hannah stared at the soup. Magics and potato soup. The words hung like disconnected text bubbles in her head. All she could focus on was finding Sean and then catching this Indian Heathcliff. What she'd do with him once she'd caught him was of later concern. She had stayed here long enough and all this ridiculous talk had only delayed her search for Sean. Putting the untouched soup on the table, she stood up. Time to go.

With a hand already hovering above the table, she froze. The gun was gone. How had she not noticed that before? When she turned to Nellie, something moving across the window grabbed her attention. The glass shattered, shards flying in and tinkling on the floor. But over that sound was the thud of something heavy landing on the table, right next to the bowl of soup. Charlotte screamed.

Hannah ducked and crouched down underneath the window, cursing the unyielding corset. When nothing else happened, she came up next to the window to look out, but it was too dark to distinguish anything.

Whoever had done it was probably gone by now. Was this aimed at her? Or did this kind of thing happen often here? She turned back to the two women, who were standing together, staring at her in shock. Nellie held up a crumpled piece of paper and turned it over so Hannah could read it. In bold black letters it said: 'You're next'.

5

The door flew open and a bald giant sporting a handlebar moustache barged in. A quick glance at the glass on the floor and then at Nellie was followed by an "*Alrate?*" When Nellie nodded, the man took a step towards Hannah.

"You. Out."

"Bart…" Nellie stretched out a hand with the piece of paper. "It's not her."

He looked at the scrap, but didn't take it. "Who is it from? Him?"

"Who?" Hannah squeaked.

"The Baron! Who else?"

"I don't know!" Hannah balled her fists. The women had been friendly, although Nellie had been quick to relieve her of the gun. But this man was downright hostile. Was it just him, or had their hospitality been an act after all? Hands on aproned hips, the giant looked down on her. What was he waiting for? An explanation? Or did he really want her to leave?

Nellie stepped in. "What my husband—"

A knock on the door post interrupted her. A short man with a flat cap pointed his thumb over his shoulder, but from where Hannah stood she could not see into the bar room.

"This youth just came in. I thought he might belong with you."

When nobody reacted, he pulled a bag of bones into view.

"Sean!" In two steps Hannah was across the room, hugging him.

He only seemed to realise it was her after she had already grabbed him, but then he held her tight. "I'm sorry, Hannah. I wasn't thinking," he whispered.

Then he pulled away and held her by her arms. "Something is really wrong here. I met this guy who was talking about magic and he said it was October! And all these people are…" He looked around the room, his gaze lingering on Hannah's dress and his own coat.

"Who?" Nellie took a step forward. "Who did you meet?"

Sean acknowledged her question, but directed his answer at Hannah. "I went to see the light. It turned out to be an old lace mill and there was this bloke there who gave me this coat." He tugged at his shoulder cape.

After a stifled scream Charlotte squeaked, "You went to the old mill?"

Equally horrified, Nellie added, "There was someone there?"

Sean shuffled his feet, glanced at Hannah, then at the men. "Yeah… I think he was a caretaker or something."

Charlotte took in a sharp breath. Nellie put her hand over her heart. The men exchanged concerned glances.

The man with the cap asked, "What did he look like?"

Sean shrugged. "Dunno. Dark blond, greying. 'Bout… that tall." He held a hand in front of his nose. "He tried to be jovial, but I don't think he liked me very much. Mostly, though, he seemed a bit sad."

"Sad. Huh." Cap Man sucked his teeth.

Bart put a ham of a hand on the other man's shoulder. "William…"

Any man would look small compared to the innkeeper, but William was not a tall man by any standard. With that enormous hand on his shoulder, he looked more like a child. A child with very sharp eyes.

"There is no caretaker there. I don't know of anyone alive

by that description. Certainly no man who would venture to the old mill. Might be something, might be nothing, but we stay well away from that place."

Sean locked eyes with Hannah before addressing no-one in particular. "Look, I'm getting a bit fed up with all this mysteriousness. Will someone please tell me what's going on here? Just pretend that I'm an alien or something!"

Charlotte started with a 'But you are…', but Nellie jutted an elbow in her side and took over.

"Maybe if you tell us how you came here? Did you happen to go through a door, or a hole in the hedgerow?"

Both Hannah and Sean stared at Nellie, and she waved a hand, as if that explained everything. After a nod from her Bart left, taking William with him. Charlotte looked confused, until Nellie told her, "They're *others*."

Charlotte let out a long, comprehending "Ohhh…", but Sean looked as lost as Hannah felt.

"Who are others? Sean and I? I've always been myself."

Sean's nod was accompanied by a snort. "True. No matter what others thought. Except maybe right now, because… What are you wearing? Is that a corset?" He tried to tug on her dress, but she slapped his hand, which incited a giggle from Charlotte and an approving nod from Nellie.

"By the way, Sean, this is Nellie and Charlotte. This is my cousin Sean."

Sean offered his hand to the two women, which provoked another fit of giggles. Nellie stopped them by shoving Charlotte with her elbow. Instead of taking his hand, she smiled at Sean and bowed her head. Charlotte then did the same, giving Sean her fullest smile. Sean performed a clumsy bow and a crooked smile and looked at his cousin in utter confusion.

"I think *they're* others."

Nellie sighed. "I'd better explain."

Sean and Hannah took the chairs, while Nellie and Charlotte sat down on the bed.

"We must seem just as odd to you as you do to us, but what you don't seem to realise, is that you probably came through a porthole."

Charlotte beamed at Nellie's words. She looked like she couldn't believe her luck. Even if Hannah and Sean had come through a porthole, which they definitely had not, what would be so great about that?

Nellie continued, "Portholes are like doors, if you will, but to another world. Your world."

"You mean portals," Sean interrupted. "You think we went through a portal?"

"If that's what you call them. People with magic have gone through before, but only for a short time. They say their magic didn't work there, so they came back. I've never heard of people from the other world coming here though. How did you find the porthole? They close when all visitors have returned."

Hannah hesitated. Should she tell them? Sean shrugged when she turned to him, so she bit her lip and said, "We followed someone. A man."

"Yeh, apparently he's the Big Man around here." Sean added.

Nellie narrowed her eyes. "Tall, good-looking, black hair that's a little longer in the neck?"

Hannah nodded. Nellie and Charlotte exchanged glances.

"Naaaah, couldn't be *him*. Why would *he* be in the forest at night? He's always just up there," Charlotte waved her hand vaguely above her head, "Doing whatever he likes to do."

"Oh, Charlotte." Nellie scowled at her. When she returned her gaze to Hannah, caution was back. She seemed to be in a constant conflict. One moment kindness shone through and all was well, the next… there was a darkness about her that Hannah was getting seriously uncomfortable with. Nellie leaned back, physically distancing herself, before she asked her next question.

"Why did you follow him? He is evil. The things that man has done…"

Charlotte sighed. A stark contrast to Nellie, she seemed

lighter than air. "Oh, but he's so handsome! Have you seen his skin? I'd kill for skin like that!"

"Charlotte!" Nellie's voice broke. "He probably has."

Charlotte muttered, "Nothing's happened in years. That black boy who disappeared was, what, five years ago? And they never found his body anyway, so who knows? May not have had anything to do with *him*. Maybe he's not so bad now."

"He murdered my mother," Sean interjected, "*Not* with magic, I might add. Bad enough for you?"

Charlotte drew in a sharp breath and clasped her hands over her mouth. Then she lowered one to her chest and put the other on Hannah's knee. "I'm so sorry! I didn't mean…"

Nellie's lips formed a straight line. Her fingers pressed into her arms. Eventually compassion conquered suspicion. "You poor souls. It looks like he just diverted his killing to another place."

Hannah swallowed. Another world. With magic. If it weren't for Sean's presence, she wouldn't have believed it was real. But Sean was real enough. He'd been shifting in his seat since Hannah mentioned the murderer, which was never a good sign. Sean was getting ready to explode. She couldn't really blame him. Temporarily suppressed emotions were fighting for attention in the back of her own brain, but she shoved them aside. Now was not the time to lose it. Unfortunately, after all these years she still hadn't found a way to prevent Sean's explosions. All she could do was clear the area. In a minute. She had to know.

"If he's killed before, why isn't he in jail? Wasn't there enough evidence to lock him up?"

Nellie let out a cheerless laugh. "Ha! There's no-one here that dares stand up to him. Everybody's afraid they'll end up with limbs missing."

"Are you saying that the police are scared of him?" How could they let someone go free when, by the sound of it, he had killed more than once before?

"The police? Where do you think you are, London? This is

Nottingham. The Baron is the one making the rules, such as they are. He's one of Them, you know. If he turns his powers against you, you're lucky if he only kills you!"

"Them?"

"Magics, ducky, magics."

Ah. Right. Magic. That would explain all the weirdness, but it was a lot to take in. "In… our world… magic is always just a trick. They fool you one way or another, but it just isn't real."

With a sigh Nellie rubbed her forehead with her fingertips.

"Unfortunately, magic here is very real. On the 29th of February 524, our worlds were separated and magic was confined to this side of the Divide, to protect the people on your side. The idea was that everyone without magic would remain in your world. But something went wrong. Many people without magic were separated from their families and trapped here.

"The only way to travel between worlds is to create a porthole, which is something only magics can do. But the use of magic costs energy and power. Since they had only just been banished to a place nobody really knew yet, you can imagine they weren't about to waste that energy on creating portholes for mere commoners, who happened to be trapped with them.

"Later, when everything had settled, magics sometimes created portholes out of curiosity. They'd bring back new fads, things that made them laugh. But no-one's been over since the 1870's. Things were changing too fast, they said. At least, that's what I thought before you showed up."

She tugged on her mob cap. "Fortunately, we haven't seen magic for years, but ten years ago… William out there—and Charlotte, if you tell this to anyone…" She threw the girl a death look. "Has horns."

Charlotte gasped and opened her eyes even wider, while Hannah's eyes narrowed. She tried visualising the little man, but didn't remember seeing any strange bumps under his cap.

"The Baron took William's wife and afterwards just laughed at him, while a pair of goat horns grew out of the poor man's head. It was in that very bar room that it happened. Good thing there were only a handful of people in at the time. We all swore never to mention it again. We sawed off the horns and William has worn a cap ever since."

That was some story. Charlotte obviously believed it. She let out a soft "No!" and stared at the door as if she hoped to see through it and underneath William's cap. Hannah had no such desire. What would it prove? That magic was real? That the Baron was a nasty man?

Sean threw Hannah a tired look. "Victorians, magic and portals. And they all believe it."

Hannah stared at the candle on the table. "Do you have a better explanation?"

Sean's jaw dropped. "Wait, you think they're right? Magic, Hannah! Spells, according to him at the factory. Shazam!"

Typical Sean. He knew everything. "Something weird happened. You tell me how we're not in our own Nottingham if not through magic, or whatever." She cleared her throat. "I'm more interested in how we're going to go back. If he's here and the portal is closed..."

Sean turned to the two other women. "Do you know how to make a portal?"

Charlotte shrugged.

Nellie said, "Only magic can create portholes."

"So we need him to make us a portal. That'll be easy then." Sean leaned forward and planted his elbows on his knees. "Who is he, anyway?"

"The Baron?"

"Yeh, I know he's the boss and all that, but why would he make a portal and come to our world only to... to..."

Hannah swallowed. She stroked his arm, but couldn't finish the sentence for him.

Nellie helped him out. "Normal thought doesn't apply to him. He's a devil, like so many of Them. Magic corrupts."

"He drinks from a cup made from the top of a human skull,"

Charlotte added, "Ada says she's seen it." She nodded fervently, as if that made it all true.

"A nice drink of human blood, no doubt," Sean said.

Nellie's eyes widened and Charlotte grabbed her throat.

Nice one. Hannah scowled at Sean, who went on, "Anything else? Anything that might help us catch him, I mean."

The women were silent for a moment, looking at each other. Then Nellie said, "I don't know that you can. For one, he's never without his sword."

"He uses it as a wand." Charlotte nodded again.

"Okay, so… do you have a sword I can borrow?" Sean asked.

Really? "What are you going to do with a sword?" Hannah gawked at him. "You don't know how to handle a sword, that's ridiculous!"

"You shoot him, then! You've already got the gun."

Actually… She really should ask Nellie for it back. But admitting to Sean now that she'd already lost the weapon wasn't high on her list of priorities. "That's evidence."

"It's not like his body is suddenly going to turn up in our world, is it?" Both the pitch and the volume of Sean's voice were rising. Time to intervene. But Sean-control always worked best if they were alone.

"Nellie… We've taken up so much of your time already—"

The older woman glanced at Sean and stood up immediately. She smiled at Hannah, a sad, motherly sort of smile. "Don't you worry about that, love. Lord knows, in this world we need to look after each other. When you walked through that door, I knew you'd lost much more than your way. You two can stay here as long as you need. Just…" She glanced at Sean again. "Be careful. You don't know him."

Charlotte nodded. "They say he wears his hair long to cover the mark of the devil in his neck."

"Charlotte, tend to your duties." Nellie put her hand on Hannah's shoulder. "I'll make up two rooms for you and bring you some warm soup."

When both women had left, Hannah and Sean stared at each other. The whole situation was too ridiculous for words. Maybe that was why Sean stood there staring, instead of blowing up like she'd expected. Or maybe… Did he blame her? If she hadn't bumped into the door… If she hadn't been angry… If she hadn't left…

"I'm so sorry, Sean! I shouldn't have fought, I should have stayed with her."

"What? No! This is not your fault." He waved a finger at his cousin, then gritted his teeth and pointed upward, arm outstretched. "It's that arse up at his bloody castle! What I don't get is how everybody here knows there's two worlds, but they have no problem letting the mad killers loose in ours, to take the lives of innocent people. How can they do that? There's all of them against one bloke with a wand. Are you serious?"

"You don't know that." She said it more to pacify her own feelings than to calm him down. That didn't often work anyway. "We don't know how big this village is and if that Baron is on his own. Nellie said he's 'one of them', so there must be more."

She picked up the crumpled piece of paper Nellie had left on the table. There must be more to this. If Sean was right, and this Baron really had gone to another world just to kill an innocent woman, then why would he warn her that she'd be next? Why would he target her at all?

"Who cares if there's more? I still think—What's that?" Sean snatched the paper from her fingers. "'You're next?' *You* are next? Who is this guy? Is this supposed to scare us?"

"Sean, getting angry now is not going to help." Would he know she was trying to sound steadier than she felt?

"Don't tell me I can't get angry! He killed me mam! He… I'll…" Throwing his hands in the air, he searched for words, but when nothing came, his hands dropped to his side. He looked at Hannah with damp eyes. "What am I going to do without her?"

She hugged him. *I wish I could tell you.* But she didn't know either. A voice inside her was screaming, 'Anything! Whatever it takes! Get that man!' But none of it would bring Aunt Jess back. So none of it mattered.

They shared another long moment in each other's arms. Then Sean gently squeezed her arm and released her, a watery smile on his face. He took a deep breath.

"They'll never believe this when we get back." He took the butterfly knife he always carried out of his pocket and started playing with it, flipping it open and closed. He often did that if he was stressed or restless.

One corner of Hannah's mouth curled up. At least Sean was trying. She wasn't so sure if she'd be able to let go of her own anger so quickly. Perhaps she didn't show as much of it as Sean did, but despite the feeling of uselessness, her mind was making and rejecting plans to catch this Baron. He may have killed before, but he would not do it again.

Sean flipped the knife again. "I expect one of those blokes with the big beaks to come in any second."

"Those were plague doctors. Wrong century." Then her disdain melted away. "I think. Who knows in this place."

After a little knock, Charlotte came in with a broom and started to clean up the broken glass. Nellie brought more soup and told them to eat. "You'll feel better."

An automatic smile would have to do. With all the questions swimming around in her head—sometimes bumping into each other—there was no room for trivialities like food. Sean ate and talked for a while, but eventually fell silent when she didn't respond.

Nellie had been nice, and Charlotte of course, but from what she'd seen or heard of the others around here, Hannah did not get a very favourable impression. With the look on Bart and William's faces in the back of her mind, even the nice things that Sean told her Roderick had said were tainted. But despite all the other unexplained things, one central, accusing question shone through. How could these people have let that man take her sweet aunt from her?

6

With all that had happened, sleep would have been very welcome, but instead Hannah found herself staring at the dark, eyes wide open. She tried thinking of nothing for a while, but as always when she tried that, after a while she realised she was only thinking 'Go to sleep. Think of nothing. Sleep now.' over and over again.

She sighed and reached for the candle on the nightstand and lit it. By the light of the small flame she slipped out of bed and took two steps towards the window. Nope, not enough layers. When did they invent central heating? She returned to the bed and wrapped herself in the blanket before she hopped back to the window on cold feet.

When she'd cracked open the shutters, she huddled up on the window sill. Letting her head rest against the window frame, she stared up at the night sky. The first time she had seen the sky so full of stars was when she was eight or nine. Aunt Jess didn't earn much working in a tailor's shop, but she took them on a holiday every summer. One time they went camping in the middle of nowhere and spent two weeks playing in a field, building dams in a little stream and looking at the amazing number of stars in the sky at night.

The last time she saw this many stars was in South Africa with Ben. Well, she was star gazing while he was inside on the phone. She hadn't actually seen much of him during that trip.

Poor Ben. If they couldn't find their way back home, Ben would probably be the one to find Aunt Jess. With Sean and her gone, what would be his conclusion? Come to think of it, it might be a while before Aunt Jess was found at all. Ben would eventually start to wonder why Hannah hadn't shown up at any of the usual places, but he would not be eager to find out. Their last conversation hadn't exactly been an incentive for a visit any time soon. And Aunt Jess's house wasn't even the first place where Ben would start looking for her. Poor Aunt Jess.

Her hand reached up to her cheek to wipe away the tears. How could life be so mean to rob her of the best person in the world just when she needed her most? How could so much change in just one day? Only yesterday around this time she was in the pub with friends, having a glass of wine, laughing at something stupid she had done at work. Then at the end of the night Ben had to ruin everything by proposing. And then, today, Aunt Jess… The stars blurred and Hannah let her head fall against her knees.

When she woke up the next morning, the sun was shining outside and there was a fire burning in the fireplace. It looked like it had been for quite some time. Thoughts, feelings and memories flooded in and queued for her attention. She took some time to put them in order, pushing back the ones that were not going to be of use right now. She'd let them in the night before and spent hours crying before she fell asleep. Now her face was puffy, she wasn't any closer to home, and she didn't feel any better.

The smell of freshly baked bread broke through her musings. It made her instantly aware of how hungry she was, not having eaten anything since yesterday around nine in the morning. Though her morning would have been afternoon here, the idea of having lost a day made her even hungrier.

She rolled out of bed and splashed some water on her face from the jug and bowl on a little table in a corner. Getting her mascara off with nothing but soap had been a nice little ordeal the night before, not really helping the puffy eyes. Today would be make-up free. Not that she always wore make-up, but with her face in this state, she would have. Not having the option felt strange. Then again, what didn't feel strange in this place. Hannah tried to get into the dress without putting on the corset first, but that proved impossible. She then struggled with the corset for a while, before giving up, putting on her own clothes and wrapping herself in the blanket. When she was about to go downstairs, there was a knock.

"Hannah? Are you decent?"

Sometimes. She opened the door and hoped her smile was convincing. "Good morning."

"If you want to call it that. It's almost eleven!" Nellie grimaced at Hannah's around-the-campfire disguise. "And you're not even dressed yet! Your cousin's been having a go at my bread for nearly an hour now. About time he had some proper food, I suppose. Come on, let's get you dressed." She entered the room and picked the corset off the bed. "Look at the state of this! What have you been doing?"

Tutting and shaking her head, she hoisted Hannah into the corset and then helped her into the dress and shoes. Normally Hannah wouldn't have stood for someone treating her like a child, but she was grateful for what the woman had done. She and Sean might also have to rely on Nellie's hospitality a little longer, so Hannah let her tut and shake her head until she was done.

"There! That's better. We'll have to do something about that hair of yours, but Charlotte is better at that sort of thing. She'll be in any moment now, so off you go, have some breakfast. If your cousin has left any, that is."

Sean didn't notice Hannah when she came downstairs and entered the bar room. He was sitting with his back to the door at a table near the window, enjoying both an enormous breakfast and Charlotte's flirty giggling.

Bart and William sat at the back, talking quietly and keeping an eye on their unexpected guest. Hannah nodded a greeting, trying not to stare at the man's cap. When she approached Sean's table, Charlotte greeted her cheerfully and then retreated to the kitchen to get her a plate.

Sean flinched when he saw her, but only for a fraction of a second. After that he gave her a gloomy smile and wished her good morning as she sat down opposite him. They had found him some clothes, but they were far too big for him, accentuating the appearance of a lost little boy.

Looking out the window into the busy street, Hannah said, "We'll get him, Sean. It's okay to like someone in the process."

He frowned at his plate, but didn't say anything. They sat in silence for a moment. Sean tore off a piece of bread and used it to clean his plate. Just as he pointed the greasy bread at Hannah and opened his mouth, Charlotte came back in and said,

"It's market day. Are you coming? I mean, I know it's a bit late, but it's nice and sunny out and there's this stall that sells really lovely sweets. I could show you around a bit. I mean… if you want." She was talking mostly to Sean, but with those last words she stretched out her hand towards Hannah. Then, realising her guest had not had breakfast yet, she put the plate down and Hannah ate, while she and Sean talked.

Charlotte was excited to show them the market. Because it was regulated by the Baron, people came from quite far away to buy and sell in Nottingham. Apparently other places lacked his kind of protection, such as it was, leading to miserable quality of products and exorbitant prices for setting up stalls, and making for a pickpockets' paradise.

Hannah tried to listen to the girl's upbeat stories, but her mind kept wandering. On the one hand, she wanted to get out of here as quickly as possible. Though people had more or less accepted them now, this was not their world and Hannah couldn't wait to get back to her own apartment, her own bed and her own stupid job. Although maybe she should try finding a good one this time.

But on the other hand, this was where her aunt's killer was. If she managed to get back to her own world, this madman would go free. For about half a minute she tried to convince herself that the people here would take care of him, but that was too far out there. Then again, if they hadn't managed to overthrow the rule of magics in all those centuries, how could she hope to take on the latest one by herself? But if she didn't, she might never get home anyway.

While her thoughts ping-ponged, Sean had also lost interest in the market. He made a remark about going back to the factory.

"Maybe Roderick knows something about the Baron that might help us."

Charlotte's smile disappeared. "I don't know…"

Bart scraped his struggling chair over the floor when he stood up and came over to them. "Nobody takes care of that building. If someone is living there, he's probably working with the Baron and dangerous. You should not go there again."

"Why?" Sean asked, but Bart marched into the kitchen.

Sean tried again, directing his question at Charlotte. "Why? He was friendly yesterday, though he obviously thought I was weird. I thought he was weird too, until I realised this whole place was weird. Sorry, but..."

Charlotte glanced at William before she answered. "He's not from the village. People here know to leave the mill well alone. And if he admits to being associated with the Baron… All the Baron's servants were dismissed years ago. As long as we don't know where this man came from, I don't think it's a good idea to visit him."

"How are we supposed to know where he's from if we don't go there and ask him?"

Charlotte shrugged, casting nervous glances at William.

Sean grimaced. "Nellie said the Baron hasn't used his magic in years. Roderick said everybody is scared because they know about the magic. I say if he doesn't use it, I'm not going to stand here quaking about what he might or might not do. What's the point of having a skill if you're not going to use it? I never hid my light, no matter what other people said."

"Are you comparing yourself to him?" Hannah interrupted, stabbing a piece of bread with her fork.

"No, I…" He paused, realising that's exactly what he was doing. "I meant I wasn't going to listen now, either. I'll have to see it before I believe it, and probably by then, I'll be back home. Hey, maybe you should come with us."

He flashed Charlotte a smile and had her on his side within a minute.

Hannah meant what she had said earlier. Sean liked girls and they liked him, but he was never a womaniser. Of course the situation was crazy, but if you find something good when everything else is a mess, why not enjoy it?

And that's what she kept telling herself while she watched them smile at each other. They chattered away while Hannah ate, and while Charlotte did her hair. Sure, his mother was murdered only yesterday, but this was nice. So they had landed in some kind of other dimension with no way of getting back, but at least he was enjoying himself. There was a cold-blooded killer out there, who only last night had told Hannah that she would be next, but Sean was just sitting there flirting with the first girl he'd met.

And then Hannah hated herself, because she really did mean what she had said. Maybe she needed a break from her own thoughts. She took a deep breath and got out of her chair. "Shall we go?"

Sean stopped mid-sentence and Charlotte looked surprised, but her smile never faded. She immediately nodded and went to get some coats.

Sean studied Hannah's face. "Are you all right? I mean…" The head-wiggle-and-shrug combination signified that he knew she wasn't all right, but was there anything in particular?

Yes. Yes, there was. "I'm fine."

Charlotte came back with the coats and they walked out into the village square. Hannah had seen quite a few people pass by the window, but as the pub was located around the corner from the square, she had no idea just how big the market would be. Two football pitches? Easily. She had assumed this Nottingham was nothing more than a small village, which in fact it was, but the market was no smaller than the one she was used to in the other Nottingham.

Rows of coloured stalls covered the village square, surrounded by latticework houses and shops where people stood in open doors and laughed and gossiped. Now Hannah could also see what had been shrouded in darkness when she arrived yesterday. A few streets away the village ended where a massive cliff arose. The vast grey stones of the castle that spread out on top of it seemed to soak up the sunlight, leaving it a dark mass looming over the village. Hannah held her hand over her eyes to keep out the sun as she looked up. There were similarities to the Nottingham Castle she knew: a large U-shape with regular, tall windows, decorated with stone scrolls, or whatever they were called. But the two immense round towers on either corner were different. They reminded her more of the gateway at the entrance to the castle grounds in her own Nottingham.

"It's haunted, you know." Charlotte almost whispered it in her ear. The way she peered up showed an apprehensive reverence.

Why not? If you're going to believe in magic, ghosts can join the party. Even in her own world a building like that would have incited stories. Here, it hardly surprised her that people would believe them. Yet another reason for folks to be guarded and scared.

So, he lived in a dark place. Maybe those ghosts were the people he killed, plaguing him. But that would have been a form of justice, and justice had abandoned her. It was up to her to take it back. So would she have to find her way up there, or catch him when he got out? She balled her fists. How could she make plans when she was at such a loss about this world? Coming to the market was a stupid idea. Instead of finding their way back, they were milling about.

Charlotte bought them some sweets and chatted away about several of her family members manning different stalls, as if nothing bad had ever happened. When they came to the end of a row of stalls, Hannah took another sweet from the bag Sean was holding, put it in her mouth and turned towards the sun.

Let it go, Hannah. Just for one minute. There's nothing you can do right now. Someone called out to Charlotte, and Hannah heard her and Sean walk away. She closed her eyes and let the warm light caress her face. *Let go. Concentrate on the sunlight. The sweet in your mouth. No more people around you.* No more plans. No more thoughts cramping the muscles at the base of her skull.

It almost worked. But why were all these people shouting? And what was that other sound? Slowly she opened her eyes, only to see people jump out of the way. A shout. A crescendo of beating hooves. Before Hannah could turn around, someone grabbed her around the waist and lifted her in the air.

She screamed as she lost contact with everything firm but the arm around her waist. Her side hit a saddle. The corset took the worst of the blow, but the air was pressed out of her lungs, stifling her scream. All she could see was the neck of a brown horse, its wild mane whipping her face.

She tried to twist around and face her attacker, but he pressed her down on his legs. The only thing she could think to do was bite him, but he anticipated that. Lacing his fingers into her hair, he yanked her head back. She yelped, clawing for his hand on the back of her head. The pain deepened when he halted the horse and the force of the motion threw her head forward and her cheek caught on a buckle.

When he let go of her hair, she turned to face him, only to see the butt of a pistol coming towards her head. Everything went black.

7

The master came in without seeing Roderick. That was to be expected. When did he ever truly see him? But the writhing, seething girl over his shoulder was new.

Roderick followed the Baron and his unquiet load up the double staircase to the Red Room on the first floor, one of the few bedrooms that were kept in good condition. She was to be a prisoner in style, then. The Baron threw her down on the bed, and she froze. When he retreated, she rolled off the bed and flew towards the door, but she only reached it as the lock clicked, her bound fists hammering the wood. A few last choice expressions left her lips, showing character, if unbefitting her size and sex. Then she turned and slumped her shoulders against the white paint, letting her head fall back, eyes closed.

From his position in the door frame between the bedroom and the adjoining dressing room Roderick studied the newly arrived 'guest'. Something underneath her dishevelled hair and torn dress was familiar. Seeing as she was undoubtedly not from around here, she must be Sean's cousin, but what could have been his master's reason for bringing her here? He eyed a nasty cut on the side of her lower jaw. To be sure, Roderick himself had not always been the most courteous, but bringing a woman to the castle against her will and leaving her in this state? Roderick sighed. One day he would speak up.

Hannah jumped at the sound. "Who's there?"

Roderick took a step forward. "Pardon me, miss. I came in to help you, but you seemed to need a moment to yourself."

"Did I." She stretched her wrists toward him. "I'd appreciate my moment a lot more with free hands."

Roderick hesitated. The Baron had used his handkerchief to tie her wrists, but the fabric touched only the long sleeves of her dress. If he was careful...

"Hold still." He managed to untie her wrists and she thanked him, albeit not very graciously.

The first thing she did was try the door again, but it was still locked. Then she went through the drawers of the small desk near the window. Not finding what she was looking for, she stormed past Roderick into the dressing room and rummaged around in there. Finally she turned to him.

"Do you have a key, or a knife or something, to open the door?"

"I do not."

She growled. If he hadn't been afraid of her reaction, Roderick would have smiled. The sound was more endearing than intimidating.

Her breath formed the most delicate of clouds. Was it that cold? Roderick never felt it. Perhaps he should light a fire. These new arrivals to his world might not make much of a difference to his situation, but at least they kept him occupied.

When he moved towards the ornate cream-coloured mantelpiece, she stopped him.

"So who are you?"

"My name is Roderick. Might I ask you the same question?"

She looked confused. "You don't know who I am?"

Of course he did. "I'm afraid not."

"I think you met my cousin in the factory. Sean?" He nodded and she continued, "So you don't know why he brought me here? Nobody around here seems to be able to stop him anyway. Why didn't he just kill me?"

"Why indeed."

Her mouth fell open and her eyebrows dropped.

"I mean you're right!" Roderick added before she could find something to throw at him. "Your being here is a surprise to me too. But all the power in these parts belongs to him. I have absolutely no say in the matter. I am merely here to do as he commands. And to take care of anyone else inside the castle, though these walls have seen none but my lord and me for longer than I care to remember."

"They told me in the village that there weren't any servants here."

"The people in the village do not know everything that goes on in the castle."

"True. They also say the castle is haunted."

"I've heard that." He risked a sideways glance and a smirk. "You needn't be frightened though."

Her frown gave way to cautious curiosity. "Why is that?"

"I've never seen any ghosts."

He looked around the room. The villagers. They didn't know anything. The last person who slept here had been so beautiful. It was her good taste that paired the carmine of the window dressing and the canopy above the bed with the little red roses on the wallpaper. She brought bedchamber and dressing room together by having the woodwork painted in cream tones and using the same slender furniture.

But that was all too long ago. Its new occupant did not compare. Though this girl was quite pretty, one might not notice her in a crowd. Mainly because she wasn't very tall.

"So you can't help me either," she said. "That's wonderful."

A strong family resemblance—in character, if not in physical appearance.

"I suppose I'll need to find my own way out." She opened one of the windows and looked down onto the village. Slightly paler she retracted her head and made sure the window was closed. "That's high."

Roderick humphed. "It's 130 feet straight down. Don't even

bother with the other sides of the castle. Over there"—he pointed over her head—"is Lake Trent, which goes on for miles. The castle grounds…" He gestured towards the gates, then let his hand drop to his side. "…Are little less than a jungle nowadays. If you're planning to escape, the only way out is through the main gate, which, as you might suspect, is thoroughly locked."

"Don't you have the key?"

"Alas, just as I am prevented from going out, I am also unable to open the gate."

"And there really isn't another way out? The Castle Rock I know is riddled with tunnels, can't we go out that way?"

"If there were tunnels underneath this castle, I would know of them."

She bit her lip and twisted her hair around her finger. She looked adorable and totally inept. "So, are there any weapons in the house that I could use against him?"

A silent laugh escaped him. "Assuming you would be able to find him at a moment when he did not expect nor want you to, and assuming he would not use magic, which is assuming a lot, there are a few swords in the castle and even some pistols that might still work. Those are not the kinds of weapons we fear. However, they are all locked up in his quarters."

"Old pistols may not be something to fear, but the weapon that shot Aunt Jess was modern. If he has one, he probably has more." She took a breath. "Okay, so… get out of this room, find a weapon, escape through the gate."

For a moment she seemed far away, and asked dreamily, "You know, I thought you'd be older. What are you, like forty?"

Swallowing his pride, Roderick ignored her remark. "I'm not at all sure I agree with your plans. You don't seem to realise the power this man possesses."

She raised her chin, eyes coming back into focus. "Instead of hearing about this power, I'd like to actually see it. Then I'll believe it."

That cut on her chin must not have been the only injury she

sustained. How did the girl ever intend to make it out of here alive? "And where would you go, *if* you did manage to escape?"

"Anywhere but here. The village, I suppose. We have to get back home. There's nobody here who will help us, so we'll have to do it ourselves." She threw her right hand in the air. "But that's not going to happen if we can't even talk to each other. Of course, if your man's just going to hang out here, I could try and find him, but the gun is still at the inn. And what if he goes after Sean next?" She looked at Roderick with eyebrows raised, then let out a long breath and grabbed her head with her hands. "Oh, I can't think. My head hurts. And I reek of horse."

Shaking his head, Roderick took her by the arm and set her down on the stool by the mirrored dressing table. Whatever she thought of herself, this girl was no threat. He opened the door to the bathroom on the other side of the dressing room and ran a hot bath.

Handing the girl a towel and some toiletries, he said, "Rest is what you need first. Then you can contemplate whether you want to escape or find out why he has brought you here to begin with."

* * *

Something disrupted her chain of thought. The distinct feeling of being watched wouldn't normally make her very uncomfortable, but she was in a locked room, small enough to see every part of, and she knew there was no-one there. Worse, she was in a bathroom taking what she thought would be a relaxing bath—quite the unexpected luxury—, but she couldn't shake the feeling that someone was enjoying the view. Hannah opened her eyes and looked around the room. Nothing there.

She closed her eyes again, breathed out, and let the warmth of the water soothe her aching muscles. *Let's not get thrown over a horse again.*

But was that really what made her so uneasy? Charlotte's

remark about the castle being haunted shot through her head. No, that was silly, she didn't believe in ghosts. Then again, she didn't believe in magic, but in this crazy place everybody kept insisting it was real. Maybe the same was true for ghosts. But even Roderick had said that he had never seen a ghost, and he had been here for ages.

Bit of an odd character, that one. There was something about him that made her spine tingle. Sean hadn't done him justice with the way he'd described him. But attraction to someone usually went to her stomach, not her spine. And he was not at all worried that he had been locked in here with her. Which might be worrisome in itself.

Maybe he was just glad to have company. If she had been confined to this place as long as he had, she'd probably develop that same kind of fear that had Roderick trembling at the mention of his master's name.

Opening her eyes once more, she stared at the pipes on the wall opposite. They were not going to keep her here that long! If anything, she would—Did that chair just move?

Her skin grew cold, even in the warm water. Eyes fixed on the chair, she reached for the towel above her head. The candle flickered. The cold grew stronger. She had to get out of here! She stood up, water splashing over the sides of the bath, and wrapped the towel around her. Still dripping, she grabbed the candle and reached for the door handle. Then she froze. The chair scraped across the floor.

A scream rose up in her throat, but before it escaped, she forced herself to move. As she opened the door and shot out into the dressing room, she knocked against a man's body. The scream came out when two hands grabbed her around her waist.

"Hannah!"

It was Roderick.

"Calm down, what's wrong?"

Her vision blurred and she leaned heavily on his arms as he led her to the bedroom. There, he set her on the bed and handed her a clean chemise before turning around and raking up the fire.

With trembling hands she pulled the garment over her head and dabbed at her hair with the towel.

"I'm sorry, I must have..."

He turned back to her, knelt on the floor beside the bed and put his hand on her knee. "Tell me what happened."

Still panting and shaking, she moistened her lips. She opened her mouth, then closed it again. Sitting on the bed now, his grey eyes on her, it seemed silly to mention ghosts. "I don't know, I thought I saw something, but maybe it was nothing."

His eyes narrowed. "What did you see?"

He'd believe her. But did she still believe herself? She could have imagined it. She must have imagined it. These people and their silly talk! They'd made her jittery. Not a familiar feeling to her and certainly not one she was happy with. She pulled her knee from under his hand and shook her head. "It was nothing. Just tired, I suppose."

He studied her face in silence, while she dodged his gaze. Then he stood up and turned towards the dressing room, but, to her own astonishment, she said, "Don't go."

Heat rising in her cheeks as he slowly raised one eyebrow, she explained, "I don't really want to be alone just yet." Then she blushed even more when she realised he was locked in with her. He couldn't go if he wanted to.

Without saying a word, he went to fetch the stool from the dressing table, placed it beside her bed and sat down on it. Was he fighting a grin? Maybe she was just imagining things. That chair probably didn't move after all, and he probably didn't grin. There was no sign of it by the time he sat down. But didn't Ben always applaud her observational skills?

Now what? Roderick seemed to be waiting for her to talk, but not wanting to be alone and wanting to talk are two different things. She fidgeted with the bedspread, shivering despite the fire and Roderick's proximity. Draughty old castle.

Finally, he smiled. "Are you all right?" She smirked and he added, "Considering the circumstances. What I meant was, of course, is there anything I can do to aid you in this situation? Perhaps you would like me to dress that wound?"

Hannah put her fingers to her cheek. The cut hurt, but had stopped bleeding. What she wanted to say was 'Get me out of here!' But small talk would have to do. If she could get him to talk, she would simply have to listen, and she wouldn't have to think.

"Tell me about this place. How did you end up here?"

Roderick's face turned dreamy with reminiscence, but he shook it off and stood up.

"You'd better get dressed. The Baron may return at any moment." He returned the stool and opened the wardrobe in the next room.

She heard him rummage around in it and sighed. Better hoist herself back into the corset. Whatever he would find in there, she doubted it would fit without something to rein in the mass.

Corset covered, she walked in on Roderick holding a cobalt blue dress, trimmed with black lace. Her breath caught. The dress was beautiful, but it was more than that. Something Hannah couldn't explain, a feeling, almost like a memory that she couldn't place. Maybe Aunt Jess had worked on a dress of that colour when Hannah was little. Of course, it was ridiculously impractical, but she couldn't resist trying it on.

"That's gorgeous."

He turned and hung the dress back. "No, I don't think you should—"

"Oh, come on! That's just mean, holding out a dress like that and not letting me try it on. Give it here."

There it was again. Or was it? That hint of a smile around his lips.

"No, you really shouldn't—"

She took the volume of soft, slithering material out of the wardrobe and held it against her skin.

Roderick motioned her behind the flowery, painted folding screen.

Why? Why would he do that, when he'd seen her in nothing more than a towel a few minutes earlier? *Victorians.* She slid into the dress. With the corset underneath, it actually fitted quite well, except that the skirt was too long. The large oval mirror was doing its best to seduce her to keep it on.

She broke away from her reflection when she heard a sound coming from the bedroom. She lifted the hem of her skirt and shuffled to the door, dragging a bale of silk behind her.

Keeping her eye on the skirt, so she wouldn't trip over it, she displayed herself in the doorway. "What do you think?"

But it was not Roderick. She recoiled, tripping over the train of her dress, and fell to the floor, her hands behind her to break the fall.

He was taller then she'd thought before. His wavy hair added to the crazed look on his dark face. Filling the doorframe in a charcoal suit, eyebrows knit tightly together, he made no effort to help her up. "That is not yours."

He killed her. He killed her aunt. Her whole body shook with the urge to attack him, make him feel as much pain as he had brought her. Tiny droplets of cold sweat formed on her forehead. She glanced over her shoulder for anything that would serve as a weapon. But even if she found something, could she disregard his advantage in both weight and muscle? Not to mention position. When she tried to get up, her arms started to tremble and she balled her fists. He was here, she had to do something. Show him that she would defy him, that he would have to kill her to break her.

But when he took a step towards her, all her strength left her and she sank down on her elbows. With shallow breaths she stared up at him as he towered over her. He would kill her too. No matter why he'd bothered to bring her here, this was it. Her blood pounded in her ears. She tried to push herself away from him, but her foot only caught the fabric of the dress.

Narrowed eyes full of contempt looked down on her. Then he turned and strode towards the doorway. With his hand on the door frame, he growled over his shoulder, "Take off that dress."

Hannah slowly let out a roiling breath.

Seconds later Roderick came in from the bathroom and, seeing her struggle, helped her up. "I told you not to put that on."

For lack of something better to do, Hannah pulled on her bodice and straightened the silk.

"This dress was my lady Harriet's favourite. Which is why you wearing it would never go down well with him."

Hannah's heart rate slowed to manageable. "Who's lady Harriet?"

"His mother." He let that sink in, then said, "I thought you wanted to escape?"

"Of course. Why?"

"You would be better off with a riding costume."

She could see him thinking. Something along the lines of 'silly female'.

"This dress requires a bustle. Not the most practical attire for flight." He did have a way of making her feel ridiculous.

"I just wanted to try it on."

She said it more to the floor than to him. She'd failed. He had been right there and she had done *nothing*. No attack, no words, no defiance of any kind. Tripped up, literally and figuratively, by a pretty dress. Projecting all her self-loathing onto the blue silk, she skulked behind the screen, and peeled off the fabric as quickly as she could.

He handed her some soft leather breeches and a dark green, tweed suit. Its skirt was again too long, so she flipped over the waistband a few times. It would have to do. As a riding costume, the skirt had a train on the side, for covering your legs when riding side-saddle, but that could be pulled up and fixed with a button on the back. The main advantage of it was that there were only a few normal-sized buttons, and it came with a pair of laced boots with a sturdy little heel. They were a bit big, but she was so glad to be rid of the tiny buttons that she didn't complain.

When she came out, he stood behind her and they both looked at her reflection in the mirror. It wasn't jeans and a T-shirt, but it was better suited for an escape. At least the Baron had left the door open when he stormed out. Something else was on Hannah's mind, too. She caught Roderick's eye in the mirror. "Would you have let him kill me?"

He blinked and laid his hands on her arms. "Of course not."

She wasn't at all sure.

8

Roderick was quite delighted with this member of the family. She questioned him as much as her cousin did, but she was rather more pleasant to behold. If only she was a little less volatile. As if to underline his thoughts, a shot rang out.

Hannah's alarmed face snapped to him. "Was that a gun?"

"Come with me." Roderick led Hannah to the corridor and took a right turn. On his way to the stairwell in the East Tower, he peered into the courtyard, but nothing out of the ordinary showed. Curious. If they weren't shooting at Hannah, it must be—

"Where are we going? Was that him? Who was he shooting at?" Hannah passed him, but went the wrong way at the first corner.

"No, this way. I don't know what happened, I was with you. But if we go upstairs, we can see the gate from the corner tower."

She dragged him along by his sleeve. "Come on! It could be Sean, we have to hurry."

What did she want him to do? Run? He hadn't done that in years. Even when he could still do as he pleased, he was a gentleman, and gentlemen do not run. Gentlemen also have no business in staff quarters such as these. The simple wooden beds and chests of drawers in the rooms off this corridor had been gathering dust for fifteen years without needing him to see to it. But for one time only, he would make an exception. He opened the little window and Hannah leaned out, leaving him no room to look.

"Sean!"

Obviously. But was he the shooter, or—

"Are you all right? What happened?"

Sean's voice, slightly pinched, came from the driveway. "We were just going to see if there was any way to get you out of there, but he must have spotted us."

"With only the two of you? Are you crazy? You're lucky to be alive!"

"Well, excuse me for wanting to help you out! You could have been dead too for all I knew! Aah!"

Roderick bent over Hannah's shoulder. Half covered by the undergrowth on the other side of the road, Sean sat on the ground, clutching his left shoulder. He was accompanied by a pretty, brown-haired girl, who was tending to his wound.

Hannah sighed softly. "I'm all right. How's your shoulder?"

"It hurts!" He glared at the girl, who took no notice and tied another knot, making him squeal.

"Sean, get out of here. If I can see you, he can see you too. Go!"

"No way! I came to get you. Can you get out?"

Hannah shook her curls and wiggled her thumb at Roderick. "Roderick says the gate's locked."

"Well, can't you find a rope, or some sheets or something, to climb down?"

Hannah looked at Roderick, but he made a face and shrugged. With these two anything was possible. They might even make it without getting shot.

"Do you know where I can find a rope?"

Roderick held up his hands. These were lower servants' quarters, how would he know what was kept in them?

While she went through the rooms, Sean and the girl shuffled back into the roadside shrubbery, the long grass and unkempt branches enveloping the two of them. Oh, the exquisite topiary bushes that once grew there. Such a loss.

"Don't worry, Sean, she will be fine," he called to the boy.

"Roderick?" Some of the branches moved, showing exactly where Sean and the girl were hiding. "The people in the inn told me not to go back to the factory. I don't think they trust you much. And now they don't trust me, so thanks for that."

Why had he felt the urge to comfort this boy? Roderick took a deep breath. "The villagers have not had much cause to trust strangers. You'll have to trust yourself. Do you trust them, or do you trust me?"

Arms full of sheet, Hannah pushed him aside and tried to tie her makeshift rope to the window handle. "It's too thick. I can't make a knot."

"Here." Sean checked the other windows, but when he saw no threats, he crept out of the bushes and tossed up his knife.

She used it to cut the sheet into strips and tucked the folded knife up her fitted sleeve. Then she sat on the ledge and swung out her leg. "All right, I'm coming down."

Roderick shook his head. That window handle would not hold her. Rash decisions, a recipe for trouble.

"Wait, let me help you."

He reached out to her when two shots sounded, one closely after the other. Hannah ducked and pulled her leg back in. A bullet hit the window frame, sending wood chips flying towards her face.

Roderick stood frozen. This was getting out of hand. They'd ruin the castle.

Hannah dropped to the floor, motioning Roderick to get out of sight, before shouting out, "Sean?!"

There was no answer. She sat up on her knees and carefully lifted her head so she could peek out. "Sean?"

"Yes! You okay?"

"Yeh, but I don't think this is going to work…"

"We'll get you out, Hannah, I don't care if I have to start a riot!"

She grumbled, but not loud enough for her cousin to hear. "You just be careful! I'll think of something. Go take care of your shoulder, I'll be fine."

"All right, I'll come back with more people later. You be careful, too!"

Loud rustling in the undergrowth marked the departure of Sean and the girl. Subtlety must have died out in the other world.

Hannah ground her teeth. "Why couldn't he just wait for me? Nooo, he had to get himself shot!" She parked her back against the wall and threw Roderick a dirty look. "For all this guy's magic, he sure likes his guns."

Roderick scowled back. "Am I the one trying to climb out of a second storey window, making a show of myself?" He huffed. Now she was making him lose composure. He'd been without company for too long. *Patience, man.*

She rubbed her temples. "I'm sorry. It's not your fault."

He held out a hand to help her up.

With one last look out the window, she took a deep breath. "Okay, so Mister Baron doesn't want me to leave. Then I'm going to find him and he can tell me what he does want. I'm sick of this mystery. If he's going to kill me, let him do it to my face." She walked past Roderick, ignoring his pulled-up eyebrow. Almost ignoring it. "You know what I mean."

She paused halfway through the corridor. "So where is his room, or quarters, or wherever he hangs out?"

Roderick rested his shoulder against the wall. "You're certain?"

"Absolutely."

"In the main building. Follow me."

Passing her, Roderick glanced out the window. The serene beauty of the soft late-afternoon sunlight on the kitchen windows contrasted with the shadows already forming on this side of the courtyard. Even in his present situation, Roderick was still in awe of the building's unforgiving superiority over everyone and everything. The sparkling blue eyes of the new arrival reminded him of better times, so many years ago, when pretty girls had flocked to the castle, just to get a glimpse of its impressive beauty and exquisite luxury.

Roderick dug his nails into his palms as one of the horses stabled on the floor below scraped a hoof. Whoever heard of horses this close to the living quarters in this day and age? It used to be such a lovely state room. But with ever fewer people to enjoy it, the present Master of the Castle had decided he preferred the company of his horses. No sense of propriety. But what could Roderick do against it? What could Roderick do against any of it?

* * *

Down in the courtyard the overwhelming greyness of the three-storey building loomed in front of Hannah. Was she really going to look for a man this dangerous by herself? Okay, with Roderick, but sweet as he had been before, he wouldn't be much help in confronting the Baron. Something pulled on her navel from within. What else could she do, though? Waiting wouldn't help anyone. But would going after him help anyone? There was really only one way this could end: miserable failure.

No, Hannah, don't think like that. No, don't think like that. Glorious victory is what she was heading for. Be your own hero, right? This princess would save herself. She would find him, and… something.

Roderick led her to a door under a semi-circular canopy supported by stone columns. Back inside they passed through several grimy corridors, the dark red carpets giving off mushroomy odours with every step she took. What little light filtered through the dirty windows only lit up the cobwebs in the corners.

Roderick, meanwhile, was happily pointing out architectural features. As if she cared. She nodded and smiled along, but which were pillars and which pilasters was beyond her. *Yes, yes, lovely dirty stuff. Can we please hurry?*

"How can you live here? It's so dark."

"It is not dark! It's… Well, it used to be very lively."

They entered the hall with its grand staircase, and Roderick indicated some once famous paintings, now thought by many not familiar with the castle to be lost. Hannah admired them dutifully, but lingered at the dusty portrait of a disgruntled boy of about eleven years old. His dark eyes underneath black hair were begging her to stay.

"Who's that?"

Roderick answered without looking. "His name… is Victor Pryce. He bears the same title as his father before him: baron of Beeston." He snorted softly. "Right honourable." Then he continued in his normal voice, "You are here because of him."

She took a step backward, her eyes wide open. "That's *him*? But he looks so sad."

"Hm. Must not have wanted to sit still. I can't remember if the artist got away unscathed."

With a last look at the painted boy, she touched the wound on her cheek. If he really was sad in the painting, he'd found a way to deal with it. But therapy would have been better.

They passed the stairs, where a huge, cobwebbed painting of a tree dominated the landing. Roderick halted again. "When his father died, he wanted a dog, so he got one. And another, and another. The villagers kept finding them killed in odd ways." He sighed, staring at the giant tree as if it could pardon him. "I finally spoke up. My one defiance of my master."

He switched his tone and recounted some stories about the various ways the paintings had come into the possession of the Baron. Listening to Roderick talk soothed her, entranced her. His melodious voice dissolved her impatience and his airy way of telling light, amusing stories drove the need for justice to the background.

"So in the end he presented her with the painting, just to be rid of her nagging."

She laughed. Roderick smiled at her. "You may not be here

of your own accord, but I'm glad you came. Your laugh lights up these old walls with the warm glow of long extinguished candles."

Hannah grinned. Smooth talker Roderick. The best part was that he seemed to really mean it. He didn't believe she'd make it out alive, but at least he was helping her. For now. The fact that he'd stayed hidden when his master showed up tainted the carefree way he acted now. But he could have left her to figure it all out herself. Though she wasn't entirely sure he wouldn't leave the moment she got into trouble, right now, having someone with her gave her that little bit more confidence.

With every corner they approached she got more cautious. They hadn't run into the owner of this nest of dust bunnies yet, but that could only mean that a meeting was imminent. Roderick stopped in front of dark wooden double doors.

"His study. If we are to find any weapons, they will be in here."

He opened one of the doors and followed her inside. More darkness. The scant light from the hallway showed curtains to the left. Opening them, she frowned. For some reason, she had expected the light to come in from another angle. But then, the only similarity to home seemed to be a rock with a castle on it, so why would the orientation be the same?

She turned her back to the window and took in her surroundings. Thinking about it, it made sense that more things would be different than the time of year and day, but her subconscious still looked for familiarities. Bottle green, velvet curtains and striped, moss green wallpaper. She could easily imagine them in her own Nottingham Castle, but from what she remembered of the times she'd been inside, there weren't any rooms like this one. They would have made for a comfortable, even cosy space. But here, knowing it all belonged to one man who was bent on taking everything from her, even a quiet study seemed threatening. Better work quickly.

A large, mahogany cylinder desk would probably only hold

papers, so she passed it, but then stopped. A strikingly beautiful woman with wavy black hair, dark skin and piercing eyes looked down on her from the wall.

"Who is that? She's a stunner."

Roderick sighed. "That is lady Harriet. He takes after her. Externally at least. She was as good and as pure as she was beautiful."

"Really? What happened?"

"She died. Seventeen years ago, almost to the day." Roderick looked at Hannah for a second. Then he returned his gaze to the painting. "They say he killed her, his own mother. I was there, you know. I saw her fall from the window, saw her give up the struggle to stay afloat, saw her raise her arm up to the window one last time. I saw her... but I never saw him."

Hannah swallowed, her eyes flicking back and forth between the painting and Roderick staring at it. "She drowned?"

He nodded. "Fell from the window in the West Tower." He pointed vaguely up, behind the portrait.

That poor woman. And poor Roderick. It must have been a traumatising experience for him too. He still couldn't take his eyes off her likeness. Hannah saw the resemblance to the Baron now; the straight nose, the heavy eyelashes, even the look in the woman's eyes. She shivered, gave the painting one last glimpse, and then turned around to search for the weapons, but found none among the books and papers.

Roderick muttered to himself, whispering. "He took her away from me. And what did he ever do to deserve her?"

"What?"

He jumped at the sound of her voice. That man had been alone for far too long.

"Do you know where he keeps those weapons?"

"I'm afraid I haven't been in here in years," Roderick confessed, "But I shall help you look."

Searching through cabinets and boxes of papers, Hannah got more and more appreciative of the digital age for reducing clutter, but after ten minutes there was still no sign of the weapons. She tapped her fingers on a bookshelf. Their luck could run out at any moment now. What would he do if he found the two of them rummaging around in his study? Even if none of that magic stuff was true, he had already shown himself no stranger to violence. Maybe she should ask Roderick to stand guard instead of search.

Roderick moved some boxes that were stacked in a corner. A large chest came into view. He lifted the lid, but almost immediately let it bang shut.

Hannah jumped and turned to the double doors. Still nothing there.

"Sshh! Why did you do that?!" With her hand over her heart she glowered at him. That was all they needed, a tremendous thud to attract attention.

"I'm terribly sorry. It's… I found this." Roderick opened the chest once more and pulled out a scrap of parchment that he handed to her.

"It's just a drawing. Some kind of necklace or something?"

Roderick's hands were shaking, so he tucked them under his arms and began to pace up and down. "No, it's… well, yes, it is a necklace, but the stone… it…" He stopped pacing and raked through his hair. "It's very powerful. It's what provided the family with their magical abilities. It…" He turned and looked at her. "I had not seen it for many years. Please put it away."

A magic necklace. Not even that, a drawing of a necklace. And it got this reaction? That was just begging for an explanation. But it would have to wait, Roderick was too shaken to talk about it now. She folded the paper twice and slipped it into her sleeve. Oh, right, the knife. Looks like she'd managed to procure a weapon after all. But she'd have to get dangerously close to make any kind of threat with it at all. "Did you find anything else in there?"

"No. Look, you're on a fool's errand. Even if you could find a weapon, you cannot find him if he does not want to be found.

Have you looked around? It's a castle, it's vast. Just give it up."

A magic necklace indeed. It made all his courage disappear. Roderick went over to the window and closed the curtains, ignoring her frown. The ensuing darkness in the room only deepened her resolve to find out what had caused this sudden change of heart.

All the way back to the Red Room she pondered his behaviour. Why the change in attitude? Why had he turned so pale, just from looking at a silly drawing? She couldn't make out what was so special about this thing. It was an old-fashioned necklace, far too gaudy for her style, with a large stone in the middle, surrounded by lots of little dangly bits and small connecting chains. But there was nothing scary or even slightly off about it. If it was, as he had said, the source of their so-called power, just looking at a drawing of it should not have made him shudder the way it did. Years of isolation will mess with your head in one way or another.

Still, this Victor was not that old, probably not yet thirty, so Roderick's isolation really couldn't have lasted that long. Maybe it was because he was so scared, that he acted like this. Then maybe she could do something about that. They had reached her room. She was about to speak up when her stomach rumbled.

"Forgive me, I should have been a better host. Let me bring you something to eat."

He left before she could even thank him, so she entered the room and plonked on the bed. No weapons. She'd failed again. At least they hadn't run into the Baron unarmed. When he brought her here, she'd been ready to scratch his eyes out with her bare hands, but after he had caught her in his mother's dress, facing him without any sort of deadly weapon would be undesirable.

Roderick returned with a plate of scones and a pot of tea. Only one cup.

"Aren't you having any?"

"Not now. I have some things to take care of."

What, and leave her alone? Even if he wasn't much of a hero, he was company. And infinitely preferable to solitude. "You keep referring to how great this place used to be. Can't you tell me a little more about that?"

9

Hannah had expected Roderick to decline. If he had things to do for the Baron, he probably wouldn't risk talking to her instead. But she was wrong.

"Ha! I'm afraid I won't be able to stop. For almost thirty years now, I have done nothing but think back to those days." He sat on the chair by the desk, gazing over her shoulder at the red pillows on the bed. "When my Lady Harriet was alive, she loved to throw lavish parties, inviting people from far and wide, thinking up ever new forms of entertainment. The old baron doted on her and gave her everything she asked for and more. She disliked the use of magic, so even though it was his greatest asset, he gave it up for her. They were very happy and the whole region prospered. But then she conceived."

He fidgeted with a button on his sleeve, then frowned at his own fingers, and rubbed his hands on his thighs. "Even before the young master was born, he created problems. My lady was so involved with being in the family way, that she neglected the old baron, who became an easy prey for someone with less than honourable intentions. A chambermaid, in charge of my lady's wardrobe, seized her chance."

Even after all these years, the memory brought a darkness to his eyes. He must have been very fond of the old baron.

"She was a seamstress… and a witch. She enchanted the baron and led him astray. By the time lord Victor was born, his father had been caught in the net of seduction she had woven so neatly. Guilt drove him back to his wife just as much as it drove him away from her. If only the young lord had been stronger, then his mother might have been left with more time for her husband. Unfortunately, the boy grew up demanding her full and undivided attention, continually finding ways to distract her from her marital duties. He was always weak and took a great dislike to his father. Magic was his way out. From that time on, even once good friends stopped coming by, and this magnificent building slowly fell into disrepair."

He leaned back and stared into the fire. Poor man, to be so affected by other people's tragedy.

"Sounds like you and the old baron were quite close."

"You could say that."

"So where is he now? Does he still live here too?"

Roderick glanced at her, then turned his gaze back to the fire. "He does, actually. Lord Victor has made sure he will never leave."

"Just like you…"

He nodded slowly.

"Well then… Isn't there a way I could help you?"

His short laugh was cold, but when he turned to her, his eyes gleamed. "At this moment, my pretty, you are as much a prisoner here as I." He got up and put the chair back. "I admire your spirit, but unless…" Shaking his head, he waved the thought away. "You're stuck. Just try and make yourself comfortable until he decides to let you know why you're here."

She squinted at him. "Unless what?"

"Nothing. Just go to sleep and—"

"Nonono, if there is anything you know that might help us, you have to tell me!"

He glowered at her, eyes turning to granite. "There is nothing that will help us to—"

"Then why did you say 'unless'?"

"Leave it, Hannah!"

"I will not leave it! I have just as much right to find my way out of here as you do, but maybe more of a chance, since he hasn't cursed me. Now tell me what you know!"

Still glaring, his lips pressed together, he came very close and looked down on her. "You have no idea what you're getting into. It would suit you well to listen."

Listen! So she could be stuck as well? He might have given up, but she was not about to. She opened her mouth to tell him so, at a volume he was sure to hear, but he cut her off.

"The necklace."

She blinked. "The what?"

There was the eyebrow again. "The necklace? The jet jewel from the drawing we found." He took a step back and then sat down on the foot of the bed with a sigh. "Here is another story for you. As I said before, the jewel is a very powerful object and with it, someone who knows how to control magic could do magnificent things."

"Such as getting us out of here."

"Such as getting you back to your own world, dear girl."

She gasped. How could she have forgotten about that?

"There is a theory that people from the other world, such as yourself, all possess magic when they come here, so it might work for you."

Hannah wrinkled her nose. The way people talked about magic, its existence alone was distressing, but actually having it herself? She didn't even want to think about that.

Roderick continued, "Many years ago the jewel was stolen by that same temptress I told you about. The only thing known about its whereabouts, is that it was taken west, where Minnie's family lived."

"Minnie?"

"The maid. Her name was Jasmine, but she was known as Minnie. She came from a village called Highlow."

For some reason Minnie did not sound like a temptress at all. But Hannah had already dismissed too much of what Roderick said, so she kept that to herself. One small detail stood out, though. "So it's not here. Then how are we going to use it to get out of here?"

He raked his hand through his hair. "Well, therein lies the difficulty. However, as you so aptly indicated, you have not been cursed. Therefore, we could try to think of something that would never have worked for me. If we manage to free you, you could go out to find the jewel and make your way back to your own world."

That did sound very tempting. "But I can't just leave here. I want that man caught! He murdered my aunt. And how about all of you? I don't want to leave you at the mercy of such a monster!"

He smiled, but almost drooled disdain. "You needn't concern yourself with us, my dear. We have survived until now. Somehow I doubt that the addition of a little blonde woman is going to make much of a change."

"What, a little blond man would have been better?" Apparently his Victorian brain could not find a way to deal with this remark. While he stood there looking puzzled, she asked, "So there is a way out?"

Staring into the fire, he rubbed his chin. "Well... Not directly. I'll have to..." His hand dropped down. "No, Hannah, it's too dangerous! There is no point in risking all that, it is useless to—"

Something in the back of her head flared up, sending needle-pricks down her spine. "Don't make me get angry again!"

He looked her in the eye. "Are you absolutely certain you are willing to undertake this venture? It is fraught with danger, you do not know the land and you do not know where to look for the jewel. May I suggest asking Sean to—"

"Sean is hurt. You saw the way he thinks, walking up that road as if nothing bad could ever happen." And she would do anything to get away from here, from that man. The fact that he had brought her here, but obviously had no use for Sean, had shaken her, mostly because she couldn't figure out why...

"Once I'm out of this castle, I'll go and talk to him, and—"

"No!" There was a force in his voice that she did not expect. "No, you must not do that. There is little time for you to get as far away from here as possible, and since the Baron wants you here, he *will* pursue you." He sighed and came a little closer. "I'm sorry, my dear. I only want you to succeed. I'm afraid that once he realises your direction, he will not only try to retrieve you, but the jewel as well, perhaps even using you to talk to people who might recognise him." He leaned in even closer. There was that tingle in her spine again. "Please be careful, Hannah, I cannot help you once you are outside these walls."

"And I can only help you once I get outside these walls." His concern was flattering, or perhaps not, but staying here was out of the question. "I'll be fine. I've got to get there first, remember? Now what's your plan?"

He hesitated before he answered, weighting her with another dark look. "My lord always takes a bath at the end of the day, before he eats his supper. His bathroom is adjacent to his bedroom and he always leaves his clothes, including his keys, by his bed. You would have to get into his bedroom before he enters it, and hide. Then, when he is in the bathroom, you take the key to the gate – the large one, there is no mistaking it – and you will have to leave immediately, taking great care not to be seen. Be as quiet as possible when you open the door. The lock sometimes creaks a little. By the time you arrive at the front gate, I will have saddled a horse for you."

Seemed workable. Of course, that would mean she'd have to get close to the man she hated more than anything, but had also come to fear.

She rose from the bed and padded to the window. Nothing there but fog. Opening the window didn't help either. It merely sent the mist spiralling.

"I assume you can ride?" he asked.

She nodded. She did okay that one holiday.

"Of course, a side saddle would be more appropriate, but

I'm afraid those have fallen into disrepair. However, I'm sure you will do wonderfully well in a man's saddle."

Was that a quip? If it was, she didn't even mind. More important matters pressed for her attention. She unbuttoned her itchy sleeve and absentmindedly rubbed her wrist. Something thumped to the floor. Oh right, Sean's knife. Picking it up, she wondered when she'd get a chance to give it back to him.

Roderick's hand on her shoulder surprised her. He moved so quietly. There was a lightfootedness about him. And something familiar that she couldn't place. She closed the window and went to pour herself a cup of tea, putting the knife on the bedside table.

Roderick followed and leaned against the bedpost. His eye fell on the little tattoo on her wrist. "What's that?"

"What? Oh." She rubbed it again, which only seemed to make the itch worse. "Nothing. Just a reminder."

He inclined his head. "Sean?"

She shrugged. "I helped him out once, and he said we should get these tattoos. But he kept getting into trouble, so I kept having to remind him that he was on the wrong path. It was actually kind of handy."

That's the thing with addiction, it never really goes away. But she'd been a good buddy. Sean had never lapsed. Buttoning her sleeve, she pushed the knife back in.

"You'll be together again soon." His understanding smile should have warmed her, but instead she rubbed her arms. Sean was alone and wounded. And *he* was out there too. She shivered. Nasty weather.

"I thought you didn't like me." Taking a bite of scone, she studied his reaction. That grin, his eyes on any other part of the room but where she stood, was awkward and boyish, but also a bit sly. It was a very attractive grin. But a grin that hid something. The tingle in her spine every time he came close was becoming almost familiar.

But maybe it was just because she ran into him, wrapped in

nothing more than a towel, only a few hours ago, and then asked him to stay. The man had been alone in a castle for a very long time. He was bound to have some secret thoughts about that.

"You and I, my dear, are very different people." At last his eyes met hers. And they did not let go. Had the room been this hot before? She swallowed her bite of scone with some difficulty, trying to think of something, anything, to say.

"D'youthinkIshouldtakeaweapon?" Maybe she could find a big knife in the kitchen.

After another long moment, Roderick pulled himself up straight. "If it makes you feel more secure. It won't be a match against magic, though." He sighed. "Hannah, you know how I feel about this. Are you sure I can't change your mind and make you stay?" He captured her gaze again, but this time, he only pleaded.

It was almost tempting. Almost. "I have to take care of Sean. The best way I can do that is to get him out of here."

"Then I promise I will do everything in my power to keep the Baron away from you."

She thanked him with a smile.

"Try to get some rest," he said, leaving her to her thoughts.

He didn't want her help. But he was helping her. What about the people in the village? Would they want her help if she could give it? If she found this jewel, and if it really was the source of the Baron's power, would he lose it if she destroyed the jewel? But then she'd be stranded here. And her first concern was Sean. Always.

She lay down on the bed and tried to rest.

At a quarter to seven Roderick woke her up. "It is time. You should enter his bedroom before he does, or risk him seeing you."

She got up quickly, ran a hand through her hair, and followed him down the corridor.

"Any last-minute advice?"

A deep groove appeared between his eyebrows as he took her arms. "Just be careful. Don't talk to Sean first, but go left to avoid the village. Then take the first turn and go west. Get as far away as you can before he notices his key's missing."

With shallow breath he looked her in the eye. Was he going to kiss her? Did she want him to? Before she had time to find the answer to that, he gently squeezed her shoulders and then let go of her.

"Good luck." He looked out a window into the dusky court-yard and nudged her towards the door.

"Roderick!"

He arched an eyebrow.

"Can you get me something to eat?"

She closed the door on his smile and turned around to hide in the sober bedroom. Even after her eyes had adjusted, the dark blue colour scheme didn't make it easier to find a good spot. This side of the bathroom door would be best if he left his keys on the night table. There'd be plenty of room under the bed to hide. Then again, if he left them on that chair by the window, where he'd already hung a jacket, she would have to cross the line of sight from the bathroom twice. Maybe she could hide in that impressive walnut wardrobe? Nope, that was full. No more time. The bed, then? A heavy curtain next to the chair hid a vacant niche. It would have to do. Balancing on the little ledge, she closed the curtain. The niche had looked deeper from the outside. The rise and fall of her chest made the curtain move.

The door opened. She stood as still as possible, trying to breathe abdominally and cursing her corset for not allowing that. With her hands against the sides of the niche she pushed herself back against the wall. Footsteps entered the room. A boot against the door closed it.

A light flickered into life, but it was too dim to be in the bed-room. At the sound of running water, Hannah quickly breathed out and took another large breath, right before footsteps came in her direction. A rustle of cloth. Boots thumping to the floor. Something soft was thrown on the bed. More rustling. How many layers made up a Victorian man's dress? It sounded like a lot to take off. She risked a slow breath. The sounds stopped. Had he heard? Had the curtain moved? Or had he gone into the bathroom?

She clenched her teeth to prevent them from chattering. Sweat broke out on her upper lip. When she reached a trembling hand up to take a peek, the curtain moved with his breath on the other side. Heart beating in her throat, she stifled a gasp. He had been out riding. The smell of horse, fresh air and sweat made breathing even harder. Pressed back against the wall, she still could not escape the warmth of his body penetrating the curtain. *Please don't feel mine.* If he came any closer, he'd know she was there.

Why had she not taken that knife? It would have been so easy to kill him right there! Wait. She did have a knife. Her cheeks flushed. As much as she wanted to, attacking him with such a small weapon would be suicide. Even standing on this ledge she didn't reach his height. Did she even know where to put it to do enough damage?

At last he went into the bathroom. Lightheaded, she pressed her hand against her forehead as she breathed out slowly. As quietly as possible, she took a few deep breaths. She still had to act quickly to maximise her head start. Taking care not to rustle the curtain, she sneaked out of her hiding place.

Now for those keys. She didn't see them on the chair next to her, but made sure they weren't still in his pockets before she straightened and looked at the bathroom door. It was open, light flooding into the bedroom from a gas lamp.

A shadow moved across the floor towards her. She held her breath. He wasn't in the bath. She'd come out too soon. If he came back to the bedroom now…

At the sound of splashing water, she closed her eyes and released a quivering breath. She'd better act quickly now. Being in his room was killing her.

She gritted her teeth. What if she went to the kitchen now, got the knife and killed him in his bloody bath? Wouldn't that make her search for that jewel a lot easier? Her heartbeat reached an impossible speed. Could she really do that? Even to the man who had killed her aunt? Maybe not. On the other hand…

Then again, would she be quick enough to get to him before he could use his magic on her? She had no idea if he would be facing the door. Stupid, she should have checked that before!

Keeping to the far side of the room, away from the light in the bathroom, she inched towards the bedroom door, until she got to a point where she could see him sitting in the bath. His eyes were closed. She breathed out again and released some of her tension. Just as she was about to take a big step and disappear from view, she heard a splash. She froze and looked in his direction, but he had only lifted his hands to wet his face.

The key was on the bedside table. She snatched it and legged it out of the room, without looking back. She'd seen enough of him for a lifetime or two.

Getting to the front gate took no time at all. She looked back up at the castle facade, glinting with the moisture of the fog. Still no sign that he had noticed the keys were gone.

Roderick stood at the gate, holding a familiar brown horse by the reins in an ever thickening drizzle. When she dangled the key in front of him, he gave a little smile.

"Good girl. Meet Allegra. And you'll need this." He put a heavy woollen cape around her shoulders and helped her mount the horse. Then he handed her a pair of gloves, and opened the gate.

Putting on the gloves, she looked down and saw him gazing out of the open gate. She had to hurry, but couldn't help feeling very sorry for him.

"I hate to leave you here," she said, pulling the cape's hood over her curls.

He reached up, but stopped, his hand in the air for a moment, before he slapped the horse's behind and she thundered down the driveway, hoping his lordship felt particularly dirty today.

10

She did it! She was out! No more grimy castle walls. Just… rain. In spite of the weather conditions, she smiled. At least she was away from that horrible man. With a bit of luck—okay, maybe more than a bit—she would be able to free Roderick from him as well.

Left, then right. Don't fall off the horse. She repeated the mantra until she reached the entrance to the castle grounds. A few butterflies fluttered around in her stomach when she passed through. No iron gates swinging closed? No minions blocking the road? Maybe she'd seen too many movies, but you never know.

Left. Allegra knew her way. She automatically kept to the left of the narrow road even before overhanging branches and waterlogged potholes made the right impassable. Still, there should be a right turn here somewhere.

Hannah peered at the forest, but even the third row of trees dissolved into the night. Roderick couldn't have meant a left turn. She'd been riding along the wall around the estate, and when it stopped, a thin line of shrubs was all that separated the road from Lake Trent. According to Roderick, the lake was huge, but on this rainy night all Hannah could see of it was its frothy edge, massaged and fed by the falling drops. Nauseous odours wafted up from clumps of algae in various stages of decomposition.

The road curved along the water's edge, but after an hour Hannah still hadn't seen a right turn. The cape weighed heavily on her shoulders. The wool had soaked up much of the water by now, but at least it kept her warm. She pulled it snug.

Poor Allegra, she had to carry it all. Hannah reined her in as much as she dared. Staying ahead of the Baron was imperative, but she could only go as far as Allegra could carry her, which would probably be further if she eased her pace.

The sound of another set of hooves startled her. She turned in the saddle, but as far as she could tell, no-one was following her. No-one close enough to hear, at any rate. But when she turned around again, the back of a dripping horse and an equally miserable rider became visible through the rain. A man in a broad-rimmed hat sat huddled in the saddle, little streams of rain trickling onto his coat. He looked up when Hannah rode up beside him, and tipped his hat. A friendly smile spread over a face covered in severe burn scars. Even the glass eye seemed to twinkle when Hannah's eyes widened and she took in a sharp breath.

Get a grip, Hannah. Reddening, she smiled back, but then the man's expression changed. His eyes narrowed and the smile froze. Only for a moment, then his lips softened again, but there was something in his good eye that Hannah couldn't place. Recognition? Surprise? Something else too, though. Concern?

Whatever it was, it gave Hannah goose-pimples. She passed the traveller quickly, but when she looked back after a minute, he was still there. He inclined his head, but whether it was a friendly gesture was unclear. Did Victor send him? But Victor couldn't have reached him this quickly, could he? She hadn't seen any telephones, but that didn't mean they didn't exist here. Hannah pushed Allegra to go a little quicker. The horse would have to rest later, when they'd left this man far behind.

When at last she came to a right turn, she closed her eyes for a second. Was this really the turn Roderick had meant? She had expected it much sooner, but this was the first crossroads. With

a sigh she steered Allegra onto the path leading into the forest. The putrid smells disappeared, but so did the light. Allegra
seemed to detect more than Hannah did. She kept walking while
Hannah reached for the bag Roderick had given her, to see if
he'd provided her with a torch or any other kind of light.

The leaves overhead rustled with something other than
rain. *What the—?* A shadow swooped down and hit her in the
shoulder. Hard. Hannah clamped her thighs together to keep
from falling sideways, but Allegra reared and Hannah lost her
balance. She tried to grab Allegra's mane, but it was already out
of reach. Hands clutching nothing but air, she tumbled to the
ground. Pain seared through her cheek when the cut burst open.

What happened? Hannah peered into the darkness, but whatever attacked her blended into the night. Allegra's restless
hooves made sloshy sounds in the mud, but something calmed
her before she could bolt.

A young man chuckled. "That was easy."

Another tugged at the hood of her cape. Then he grabbed
the hair on her neck. "'S a girl!"

Hannah tugged at her skirts. With this Victorian version of
crotchless panties all the women seemed to be wearing, riding
without a side saddle was… interesting enough, even with the
breeches. But Victorians get excited at the sight of a bare ankle,
right? She didn't need two total strangers enjoying the view, such
as it was in the black of night.

"Any jewellery?"

Robbers? In this weather? Hannah clawed at the man's grip.
She tried to stand up, but the man and the weight of the wet
cape held her down. Hannah peered up, but it was too dark to
tell if it was just the two of them, let alone what they looked
like. "I don't have anything of value. If you don't let me go, the
Baron is going to find all of us and then you'll have less than
nothing."

From the sound of it, the first man lowered himself from the
tree, plopping down in Allegra's saddle. The horse snorted, but

stayed put. "Can't have that, can we?"

Hannah felt around in the dark, reaching toward a slightly lighter blob that was probably Allegra.

The second man pulled back his cloak, uncovering a lamp. Hannah caught a glimpse of white blond hair before he let her go and turned towards the horse. The man took his friend's outstretched hand and climbed on behind him.

"So we'll be off then."

"Give him our love."

Allegra jumped forward, but halted four yards down the path. Some frantic whispering ensued. Hannah shed the cape and jumped to her feet, but before she reached the men, Allegra took off. They'd left her the lamp hanging on a branch.

"Thanks for the courtesy!" Hannah cursed. That man with the glass eye. He must have warned them somehow. Why else would they wait on this path in this weather? Shivering, she picked up the lamp and wrapped herself in a cape now covered in mud. She rubbed her backside, that was sore from the fall, and touched her cheek. Wet. Touching her tongue to her fingers, she grimaced. Great. Blood. What else could go wrong? The Baron would catch up with her and she'd be back in that castle before midnight. But at least the rain had stopped.

She dragged her feet along the path until she came to another crossing. A weathered sign pointed towards Ravenshead. The abbey on the other sign had been crossed out. Ravenshead? She knew Ravenshead, but she couldn't have gone that far. Then again, this wasn't her world. Her nose twitched. She'd done it again, let herself be fooled by the similarities. *I hate this world!*

She sank down on a tree trunk beside the path. In her world, Ravenshead was to the north. Did that mean she'd taken the wrong turn after all? She buried her face in her hands. Her eyes stung, but she was not going to cry. This was not the time. Crying wouldn't do her any good. No matter how far she was from anyone she knew, or how little she had left in either world.

Ben's face flashed through her memory. He always made her

feel strong. But he had left her life. Her doing. Her fist clenched against her forehead. Great, now she felt guilty *and* alone. She took a deep breath. She would be strong. For Sean.

She stood up and wiped the wayward tears off her cheeks, flinching when she touched the cut on her face. At least Sean had Roderick to help him out until she got back. With another deep breath, she started for Ravenshead. Come what may. At least she looked like she belonged this time.

Trying not to swing her lamp too much, Hannah reached the first houses. What was it with these villages? Everyone went to bed at eight? The place looked deserted and the gaslight did nothing to brighten it. Staying here might prove a very wrong decision. She was too close to Nottingham to be out of danger. But without a horse, she wouldn't get very far anyway, especially in the dark. She'd have to find somewhere to stay the night.

An eerie orange glow shone above the rooftops on her right. Ignoring the alarm bells in her head, she turned right, where a soft murmur broke the silence. She hesitated. This alley didn't have any street lamps at all. Maybe it was safer to stay on the main road.

But before Hannah could turn, the air was squeezed from her lungs as an arm clamped around her waist. A gloved hand over her mouth stifled her scream. She tried to kick back, but they lifted her in the air, so the only thing she kicked was her petticoat.

"I've got one," sniggered a young male voice over her head. "Little one."

"What's she doing here?" replied a lower, older voice from the side. "Never mind. Bring her along, it's time."

Bring her along? Bring her where? Time for what? Kicking and squirming, she tried to free herself, but her captor just sniggered again and tightened his grip. Sometimes she hated being short. The ease with which this guy carried her along was infuriating!

More figures appeared from the shadows, following the man with the older voice in the direction of the glow. The murmur grew louder and turned into excited talk, mostly of women.

When they halted, Hannah tried one more futile kick and then gave up, panting. The light of an enormous fire in the middle of the village square disclosed the grotesquely carved wooden masks of the men that had gathered in the alley. Wolves, witches and rams were pushing each other out of the way. The man holding her breathed heavily into his demon's mask.

The older man laughed. "Have fun!"

Roaring and howling, the men burst into the square. In fits of screaming and laughter, the women scattered. Some of them guarded small children, but the older children were chased across the square. The demon released Hannah, crowing and growling as he pushed his mask in her face and drove her onto the square. Then he turned to chase some other girl around the fire and left Hannah standing there, heart pounding, not really knowing what to do.

A party. It was just some kind of folkloristic village fete. She put her hand over her heart and waited for her breathing to slow down. Shadows of witches and devils danced across the house fronts, revelling in the blazing chaos of screams and howls.

At the entrance to the alley the older man kept guard. Of average height and rather slim, he wore his goatskins well. He must be the leader. A mask with enormous twisted goat horns covered his head, but he was watching her. She knew it.

Focus, Hannah. She needed a bed for the night. Where could she go? She scanned the crowd and the surrounding buildings, but again and again found her gaze being drawn to the horny man. And every time she looked his way, an overwhelming urge to be near him took hold of her. How did he do that? She tore her eyes away from him. She should go. This unnatural attraction would not help her find a place to sleep.

And yet, she found herself walking back to him. *Why?* She didn't know him. His wooden goat's eyes gave her the creeps.

Her breath grew shallow as she neared him. At the last moment she veered to the side to pass him and enter the alley, but he held out an arm and prevented her passage. His impressive horns pierced the air as he rolled his head.

"Heavy, are they?" She was in no mood to be polite.

Instead of answering, he turned his wooden gaze to the merriment around the fire. When the silence had stretched beyond awkward and into alarming, he broke it.

"Who are you?"

"Hannah Taylor. Who are you?" *Mouth! Wait for Brain for once!* Now what would he do with that information? She planted her hands on her hips and stuck her chin in the air. Might as well stick with the attitude. Maybe it would give her some confidence.

The man rubbed his chest and then scratched under the edge of the mask, but he seemed disinclined to answer her.

"I'm looking for a place to stay. Is there an inn around here?"

Again, no immediate answer. Just as she was about to give up and walk away, he said, "There is no inn around here for miles. Most people don't like to come through these parts. They're afraid of being robbed."

Hannah looked down at her muddy attire.

"Really. So no inn. Any other place where I could stay for the night?"

"I am not the one to ask."

She frowned, sighed and silently counted to ten. "Can you tell me whom I *should* ask?"

After staring at her for another few seconds, he turned around and said, "Come with me."

11

Sure, that's the best idea ever. But what else was she going to do? She sprinted after him and stared up at the horned mask that betrayed nothing of the man underneath.

"Where are we going?"

No answer, naturally. He led her through several dark and winding streets, the whooping and screaming laughter fading as they walked, before stopping on the edge of the village at what looked like a large barn. The wooden slats had once had a dark stain, of which only splotches remained. They also probably once reached to the ground, but now there seemed to be more holes than wall to this place. A witch was standing guard, leaning on her upside-down broom. When they approached, her head kept lifting, tilting back unnaturally far. Hannah swallowed. Below the witch's face was another face. The young man underneath the mask had been leaning on his forehead, the mask pushed back to the top of his head.

"Lucian!"

Before the witch-man could say any more, the Goat held up his hand. "Go join the others, I'll stay here."

Witch-man's face lit up. "Really? Thanks!" He clunked the mask back in place, howled and ran off towards the village square. The Goat, meanwhile, opened the barn door and let Hannah in. Apart from a candle on a round table near the door, the place was quite dark. A few makeshift straw beds were

96

aligned, so there would probably be more out of sight. A temporary camp for this Lucian and his men, whatever they were. At least, she hoped for all of them it was temporary.

As he sat her down at the table, he finally took off his mask. He was about fifty, his hair greying, but his thin, pointy beard still pitch black. In the dark Hannah couldn't quite make out the colour of his eyes, but they were full of plans…

He rolled his shoulders and rubbed his neck. Then he looked at her, gave her a crooked smile and said, "Yes, the horns are heavy."

He filled two mugs with water and handed her one.

"So, Hannah Taylor, why are you here?"

"I told you, I need a place to sleep."

Aaaand he said nothing. Again. So maybe it was obvious that that was not her reason for being here, but most people would at least make conversation. He didn't.

She squinted. "I'm on my way to Highlow."

"This is Ravenshead."

"Then I'm obviously not there yet."

He lifted his mug, drank slowly and then continued: "You came in from the south, meaning you are travelling north. Highlow is southwest of here."

"… Ah." Great. Ravenshead to the north of Nottingham. The one similarity she did not want to be true.

She pointed a thumb at the straw beds. "So can I sleep here? I'll be gone early in the morning, if you'll point me in the right direction."

He stared at her some more. "You can sleep here."

Thinking he would eventually direct her to one of the beds, she waited and stared back.

He sat back, resting his cheek on the knuckle of his index finger. "You remind me of someone. Someone I never wanted to go away."

Oh no. Seriously? Is that what this was, the old ex-wife/ex-girlfriend who never really understood me routine? Wow, this guy certainly was Victorian. Then again, they were still doing it in the twenty-first century, so…

"But you're not from around here."

"No." She yawned, hoping he would get the message.

"How is your mother?"

"Dead." What was wrong with him?

"I'm sorry to hear that, I liked her very much."

That was a new approach. Not one she really saw the point of. "You couldn't possibly have known my mother."

He was unfazed. "Really? Then how about your father?"

What?! "Also dead."

"And how is your aunt?"

Hannah narrowed her eyes. Was that just a lucky shot? "Can I just go to bed?"

"No, I don't think that would be a very good idea." Okay, now he was really getting creepy. "How old are you, Hannah?"

"Old enough to kick your butt!"

He looked perplexed for a moment, then amused. The shadow of a smile darted across the corner of his mouth. "There is no doubt that you are your father's daughter. Even though you look exactly like your mother."

How could this idiot be the leader of any kind of group?

"I'm from… far away and my parents have been dead since I was three years old. I'm sorry, but there is no way you could have known either of them. Now may I please go to sleep?"

He stood up and sauntered over to a leather satchel by the door, from which he took something that looked like a small photo frame. When he came back and handed it to Hannah, it turned out to be a tiny painted portrait… of her.

No, wait. The girl in this portrait had a little birthmark on her cheekbone. Like the one Aunt J——

Hannah threw the portrait on the table with such force that Lucian had to grab it before it could skid off the table and fall. Blood pounding in her ears, Hannah stared at the picture underneath his hand. She swallowed several times before she could speak.

"Where did you get that?"

He remained quite calm. "Your mother gave it to me."

Her chest hurt. *Breathe.* "My m— What was her name?"

"Jasmine, but everyone called her Minnie."

Hannah shook her head. "No, my mother's name was— Wait, Minnie? Minnie the temptress?"

He blinked twice and frowned. "Temptress? No, she was a very sweet and loyal woman. Who told you that?"

Wiping a muddy sleeve across her forehead, Hannah tried to organise her thoughts. Was that why Aunt Jess had been murdered? Because someone thought that she was this sweet and loyal Minnie the temptress? Or could she really be…? No! Nonono, definitely not! She swallowed again and looked Lucian in the eye.

"That is not my mother. I'm not from here and neither was my mother." She got up from the chair. "If you don't mind, I'd like to go and find Highlow."

"No, that is not a good idea. I'm sorry to have upset you, Hannah, please." He gestured her to sit down again, but she remained standing. "Travelling alone at night is a foolish undertaking. Please find yourself a place to sleep. The men won't return until the morning and, if you wish it, I will no longer bother you."

Sleep. Right. A forest full of robbers seemed like a safer place than this. She took a deep breath. It had to be a trick. That's how this guy ended up the leader, because he pulled stunts like this. But if he left her alone, perhaps she could sneak out. "I wish it."

He brought her a spare candle and then left the barn without another word. Hannah sat back in the wooden chair, eyes closed, arms dangling on either side. This crazy place was giving her a headache. When she opened her eyes, the little portrait stared at her from the other side of the table. She picked it up and looked at it again. The resemblance to Aunt Jess was remarkable. Young

Aunt Jess, from Sean's baby pictures. Her aunt had always said that she and Hannah looked very much alike, but this portrait was of a girl even younger than Aunt Jess from the photos. It could have been her… but it couldn't be!

Hannah turned the portrait over. 'With all my love. Minnie'.

Oh yeah, Minnie? All your love, huh? Then what did you give Roderick's old master? Sweet and loyal. Aunt Jess was sweet and loyal. It should have been you they killed, not her!

Again, Hannah threw the portrait away, but this time she meant for it to hit the wall.

A knock on the door. "Are you all right?"

"Fine," she lied. With a sigh she picked up both candles and found a straw mattress in the back that didn't feel too lumpy. She closed her eyes. *Sleep!* Who was she kidding? There was far too much going on in her head. If resentment towards Minnie for getting her aunt killed would make way for a moment, she could focus on something that gnawed at the back of her brain. Why would the Baron of Beeston go all the way to another world to kill someone he thought had been his father's mistress years ago? Apparently he also knew just where to find her, because according to Nellie and Charlotte, he had not been gone very long.

She turned on her other side and stared at the candle.

What if— No. …But couldn't it be that— No! …Seriously though— Shut up!

She sat up and pressed her fingers against her forehead. Sighing again, she grabbed the candle and went over to where the little portrait had landed on the floor. The resemblance was uncanny. She sat down at the table again, placing the candle and the portrait in front of her. But no matter how hard she stared at it, it did not start explaining. Even when she frowned, it had nothing to say. So she sighed yet again, fell back in the chair, stared at the door, and then got up and opened it.

Lucian stood leaning against the barn, one foot pulled up against the wall. He was sharpening a knife, which he stuck in a sheath on his belt when she came out. Again she was mistakenly waiting for him to ask her if something was wrong. Instead he just looked at her and waited for her to say something.

"So… who was she?"

For once his answer came quickly. "She married a man who was once very close to me. We spent a large part of our lives together, but I have not seen her these twenty years. When I saw you, it was obvious. You had to be Hannah." He pushed himself off the wall and came a step closer. "I also know that she was going to raise you as her niece, and start using the other part of her name, pronouncing it 'Jess'."

Hannah's vision tunnelled and she had to sit down. Her stomach turned. She retched, doubling up, and swallowed a few times. *Why?* Why had Aunt Jess never said anything? Why had she lied about being Hannah's mother her whole life?

Lucian sank down on one knee in front of her and placed his hand on her shoulder. Panting, she looked up at him.

"I'm sorry, Hannah. I'm used to speaking plainly. I should have brought this more gently."

"How… why?" was all she could manage.

"Can you stand? Come inside, I'll tell you what I know." He helped her up, led her back to the table, and poured some more water into her cup.

"Your mother and I were great friends. When she went to work at the castle as Lady Harriet's seamstress, she caught the eye of the Baron, but she wasn't interested. He tried to woo her for years, to no avail. Not used to rejection, his lust turned to hatred and she fled. The Baron kept you with him at the castle, hoping your mother would come back for you, but Lady Harriet had promised that she would take care of you, as your mother had become her closest friend. You were only two or three at the time and Sean had not even been born yet."

Sean? He knew about Sean. If Minnie was Aunt Jess, then this sounded more convincing than the temptress story. How could Roderick have got that so wrong?

Lucian scraped his throat. "He then cursed her, giving her and her family the magic she so despised. Sean was supposed to be born in Highlow, but Lady Harriet sent word that it was no longer safe for you at the castle, so your mother and I travelled to Nottingham and she used her magic to create a porthole. Lady Harriet smuggled you out and gave Minnie some of her jewellery to pay for a place to live until she could find work. Then I had to say goodbye to your mother one last time.

"She told me she would change her name in case the Baron ever found out where she had gone. She would raise you as her niece, because if he ever came looking, he would search for a mother and a daughter. I was to tell your father where to find her, but he never did make it."

Hannah had listened without registering most of what he had said. There was too much to take in. But his last words reverberated. "My father… he's here?"

"No." Lucian stared at the floor. "The Baron killed him."

"Oh." That was that then. Not only was her family dead, but they had lied to her the entire time when they were alive. Except Sean. He was her brother without knowing it. For some reason that didn't even change much. They had always lived together. In effect Aunt Jess had always been her mother, and Sean had always been her brother.

But why had Aunt Jess never told them about this? These people, this history… This world was part of them, and they had had no idea it existed. And now that they had been rocketed into it, they were useless in it. If they hadn't followed this Baron, they would have never known why she was killed. Not that Aunt Jess's death made any more sense now that Hannah did know the reason.

"I think I'll go to bed now."

"Yes." He got up, but before he left the barn, he turned. "How is your mother?"

"She's… The Baron… killed her."

He stood very still, the only movement a slight contracting

of a muscle near his right eye. After a few seconds he took a large breath. "My condolences."

Then he left.

For a few minutes Hannah just sat there, not really thinking anything, not really feeling. An automatic move to stand up had her pause. Then she crashed back down on the chair, her head landing on arms flung over the table. All her misery flooded out in long, loud sobs. Aunt Jess, who had loved her and cared for her all her life, had suddenly become her mysterious mother. The memory of her was left with a gaping black hole, where the lies about their family history had been ripped away.

Somehow she ended up on the bed she had been on before. She wanted to figure this out and be logical about it, but her brain had had too much of a shock and shut down for a few hours.

12

Her first sensation the next morning was an intense listlessness. *Don't wake up yet. Go back to sleep. It'll be better.* But the thought of Sean, ignorant of the situation and probably still in danger, motivated her to move. Get the jewel, create a portal, get out of here. Then she could tell her brother what it had all been about. Her brother. How would he react to that?

Not that it mattered. She had always helped him before, and she would continue to take care of him. *So get up already.* Maybe Lucian would lend her a horse so she could get to Highlow quicker.

She sat up and immediately regretted it. Horse riding muscles. The straw mattress probably hadn't helped. She stretched gingerly, wishing all horses to kingdom come. But, like the corset, it was something she would have to get used to. She should have taken it off before falling asleep. *This world sucks.*

Daylight came in through the cracks in the walls and shone in her eyes. She glared at the crack, but at that moment Lucian came in and sunlight flooded the barn, making her squint to see who was with him.

"Oh good, you're up. I thought it would be a good idea to start early."

Various grunts around her told her some of the men had come in during the night, but weren't ready to start the day.

"Start what early?" Hannah asked.

"Our journey to Highlow of course. It's a good two-hour trip."

"You're coming with me?"

Lucian looked at his companion, who nodded. "Yes. We don't have anything planned, I think they can spare me here for a few days."

His friend laughed. "Not for too long though."

"I'll be back soon." Lucian smiled. "Are you coming?"

Hannah scrambled to her feet and peered at the other man, who was giving her curious looks. The kind that assumed a whole different set of events from what had actually happened last night. What he thought didn't really matter, of course, although it was pretty obvious that he couldn't believe what he was clearly thinking! *Well, nothing happened, mister, but if it had, you've no right to be surprised about it.* She straightened her shoulders and walked past him, feeling his stare burning in her back.

"Why are you coming with me?" she asked as she joined Lucian outside, ignoring that same unnatural pull toward him she'd felt the night before. He led her to the horses, that had already been saddled and were ready to go. His goatskins had made way for something equally fetching. Underneath his dark green coat, a burgundy paisley waistcoat looked rather flashy compared to the usual garb of men around here. Beige checked trousers were a little different too, but the absolute eye-catcher was a bright green silk neckerchief, that actually complemented the waistcoat quite nicely.

"Why? Don't you like me?" He returned the question without looking at her, checking the horse's gear instead.

Very funny. She repeated the question without feeling. "Why are you coming with me."

He donned a brown top hat, mounted and sighed. "Because you're Minnie's daughter. If I let you go by yourself, you'd either get lost or robbed. Again. With me by your side you will be safe and at your destination before long and I can return here with a clear conscience. Now let's go."

Again? How did he know—

"That's Allegra!" Eyes popping, she pointed at the horse.

Lucian was unmoved. He looked down on her from his grey horse as if she'd told him grass was green. "Don't worry, all your things are there. I've even added some more provisions."

"But… Those… They… They're yours?!"

A man in green with a band of robbers. Nope, not familiar at all.

"Not if they keep this up. They know the rules. Only nobles."

Hannah picked at a crust of dried-up mud on her sleeve. Very noble indeed. "I hope you usually have more control over your men, because—"

"I can assure you, they have been disciplined."

He turned his horse and was almost out of sight before she had even mounted. Captain Assumptions offered her a clean cape, and helped her up when he saw her struggle. Hannah could have sworn he was shaking his head when she followed Lucian. But she didn't look to check.

They rode in silence for a while. Evaporating rain from the night before created swirls of mist where the hooves trod. Hannah stared at the little vortices fading into endlessness. Was this what she was after? A spiral of revelations leading her nowhere, until her willpower dissolved?

Roderick's tale seemed plausible at the time, until she found out that he had been talking about Aunt Je— her mother. That kindly old victimised father-of-the-Baron had turned out to be a violent aggressor. If his view of his old master's affairs was that warped, what else could he have been wrong about?

A temptress. Aunt J— Her mum could never have been that. Even if she had withheld important information from her daughter. Hannah sucked in the cold morning air through her nose. *She must have had her reasons. She must have thought she was doing the right thing.* Whatever else this world would throw at her, Hannah would find a way back home for her and Sean.

The home their mother had meant for them. It all seemed less shocking in daylight, grey as it might be.

But that didn't change the fact that Roderick's words could not be trusted. Then again, could Lucian's? She looked at Lucian, riding alongside her. He said he was helping her. He said he was helping her because he knew her mother and father and that her mother had given him that little portrait, inscribed with 'all my love'. Why had she done that? Aunt Jess was never a very exuberant person when it came to showing feelings. Could Hannah be sure Lucian had not just stolen the picture? From her father even?

"So… how did she create the porthole?"

Lucian closed his eyes, then smiled at the horse's neck. "You're looking for the jewel."

Hannah let go of a held breath. At least that was real, and not some fabrication of Roderick's imprisoned mind.

"I thought you would be. If I'm not mistaken, you did not choose to come here and you're hoping the jewel will take you back. That probably means that Sean is here too, because the porthole would only close if everyone from the other side returned. Is that true? Is Sean with you?"

"Yes, Sean is here too. He stayed in Nottingham." If nothing else, it might be a good idea to let this man know someone would miss her and come looking for her. Beside the Baron. "So… Do you know where the jewel is?"

Lucian coughed, his gaze fixed on a point in the mist. "It was lost after your mother used it to create the porthole. She must have entrusted it to someone on this side, because taking it through the porthole would have broken its magic, which would have closed the porthole for good. But it was never seen again."

"But you think it's in Highlow?"

"Almost all your mother's friends were in Highlow at the time. It's the most logical place to start."

Hannah peered at him. He was keeping something from her and was not very good at hiding it. *Take what you can.* If he was lying, she'd soon find out. But until they reached Highlow, she didn't need any more from him.

It was only when a signpost indicated they'd neared the end of their journey that Hannah sat up straight to look around. Someone was watching her.

He was there. Again. Hannah hadn't spotted him yet, but his eyes were burning in her back. Or rather, his one eye. With everything Lucian had told her, and certainly after she found out that his men had been the ones robbing her, any thoughts about the burned man had been pushed to the background, but they shot to centre stage as soon as Hannah and Lucian reached Highlow, and dismounted.

Distracted, she agreed that Lucian would ask around. He knew this village and could find his way to people who might know something. Hannah just wanted to find out where that man was lurking. Who was he? Why was he so interested in her?

Lucian, apparently unaware that they were being followed, questioned yet another person, while Hannah scanned their surroundings. There! No, that was a curtain flying out an open window. Hannah shook her head at herself. *Let's not get paranoid, now.*

"No." The man with Lucian shrugged, and went back to sweeping the street in front of his house. Soot billowed up and settled where he'd already swept, leaving the street only slightly less black. This was the fifth or the sixth person who had listened to about two sentences of Lucian's story, realised they were looking for someone and then turned them down. As with the previous ones, Lucian simply gave up and walked away.

A frown and a pout later, Hannah followed him, dragging Allegra along. "Why are they so reluctant to talk to us? They don't even know who we're looking for."

Naturally, he took his time to answer her, searching for someone else to question. His colourful outfit stood out even more in the dingy streets of Highlow. If she had ever thought about Victorian times long enough to form a picture, this would be it:

rows of small houses on streets covered in dirt, an eternal pillar of smoke rising from behind the rooftops. People shuffled about in dirty clothes, blending into their surroundings. Not a smile in sight.

The one-eyed man would have no trouble hiding in one of those alleys. Where was he?

Lucian, ignorant of her jitters, had other things on his mind. "It's what they have been taught, it's all they know. 'Don't get mixed up in someone else's troubles, you have enough of your own.' It's what I believe to be the biggest problem in our society."

What, a robber with morals? Was that a bit of Lucian's philosophy shining through, there? Although it intrigued her, this was not the moment to ask him to elaborate. He had already found someone else to talk to. Opposite a derelict church stood a tiny school building, from which a shiny-cheeked young woman emerged, her dark clothes decidedly less dirty than those of the group of children following her. She looked up when Lucian coughed.

"Yes? Can I help you?"

His charming smile had no visible effect on her, but she kept an anticipating expression even when Lucian explained that they needed her help.

"I'm sorry," she said, "I've not been here that long. You might try Doctor Peveril. His practice is on the main road across the square. Give him my regards when you see him." She turned and started to lead the children along the road when Lucian called after her for her name. "Tell him Miss Elliot sent you," she said over her shoulder. Then she held up her palm, looked at the sky and hurried the children along.

"We should make some haste," Lucian said.

Hannah was already on her way. The sooner they could get off the streets, the better. She cocked an eyebrow over her shoulder, as he followed in her steps. "Obviously."

He failed to hold back a grin. The first drops darkened the stones as they strode along the street, keeping close to the houses in the hope of staying dry.

At least Doctor Peveril's practice wasn't hard to find. They tied up the horses and entered just when icy water really started to plummet. As Hannah's eyes adjusted to the gloomy waiting room, more and more carved and stained wood came into view. The room consisted of wall to wall ornamentation, it seemed. Someone clearly had a fear of empty spaces. All of the seats were vacant, though, and the only person in there was a scrawny woman in a black dress, lighting candles. She would have to light a whole lot more to remove the sense of melancholy that seeped in through the tasselled curtains and settled on the olive green cushions.

Hannah shot a look outside, but if her stalker was still there, he kept out of sight. For now at least, he couldn't get to her without involving other people. Maybe they could ask if there was a back entrance when they had to leave.

"Yes?" The woman's tone was more curious than accommodating, and she made no effort to hide her scrutinising look.

The new cape hid most of the mud on her suit, but Hannah hadn't seen a mirror since she left the castle. Her hair had been rained on, splattered with mud and groped, and she hadn't had time to wash any part of her. She'd slept in a corset on a straw mattress, and spent too much time on horseback. If this bony snob pulled her nose up any higher, Hannah would snap that silly pair of gold-rimmed pince-nez in half and throw them at her.

"Excuse me," Lucian said. "We are looking for Doctor Peveril, we believe he could provide us with some information."

"Information?" She used the exact same tone as before, her voice just a little too high on the end note, like nails on a blackboard.

Hannah rolled her shoulders to get rid of the shivers down her spine.

When Lucian didn't expand, the woman asked, "Are you regulars?"

"No," Hannah snapped. This harpy knew full well that they

weren't.

Lucian gazed at Hannah, than turned his head slowly back towards the woman, his eyes lingering on Hannah another moment.

"We are not," he said. "Would you kindly tell Doctor Peveril that we wish to speak to him?"

"Doctor Peveril is a very busy man. He does not have time for trivialities."

Somehow, all that was wrong with this world seemed to culminate in this woman. The stubbornness, the prejudice, the unwillingness to cooperate in any way! Hannah bit her lip to keep herself from lashing out at the shrew with all her frustration. If only she had that jewel, this was a great person to use magic on. Instead, she slapped at a little white moth that had the nerve to fly too close.

The woman's face drained of colour and she yelped.

What's wrong with her? I'm not going to attack her. "It was just a moth."

"What moth? I didn't see a moth." Her voice was now so high and screechy that it actually did resemble nails on a chalk board, sending more shivers down Hannah's spine.

"It was just a little one, all white and…"

"There was no moth! Please leave!" Pince-nez aquiver, she stretched out her bony arm and pointed towards the door.

Hannah was about to protest, when a dark oak door in the back wall opened and a man with wavy white hair and matching white goatee appeared.

"Miss Jones, I can't hear myself think. What is going on?"

"I'm very sorry, doctor," Miss Jones said, wringing her hands. "These people came in to see you, but they don't have an appointment, and…"

"Thank you, Miss Jones." He gave what could have been a sigh, but if it was, it was well veiled. He waved his hand, beckoning Hannah and Lucian. "Come, come."

Lucian was the first to follow him. Hannah resisted the urge to throw the skeletal Miss Jones another foul look, before she followed as well, and closed the door behind her. No doubt Jonesy would be listening in, but at least Hannah wouldn't be able to see her do it.

The office was much more spacious than the waiting room had been. Not because it was bigger, but because the walls were smooth and painted white. The only clutter in this room was on the doctor's desk, but the gloom from the other room had carried into this one.

"I see," Doctor Peveril began, lifting his hand to Hannah's cheek, "Well, the wound is clean. I don't think—"

He stopped when Hannah took a step back.

"We have come for information," Lucian said. "Hannah here is looking for anyone who might have known Minnie Carroll. I knew her myself, of course, but I've not been back in the village for twenty years."

Lucian had a history in this place. It was only natural that he should explain what they were after, but it still bothered Hannah a little that he hadn't given her the chance to tell her own story.

Lucian knew the people here. Or at least the kind of people. Even Doctor Peveril, who would have lived here when Lucian did, did not recognise him at first. After several sentences, however, he leaned back and narrowed his eyes. While he studied Hannah's face, his answer was directed at Lucian.

"Yes," he said slowly, "I remember. And she is… your daughter?"

13

His daughter? Hannah's heart skipped a beat. 'With all my love', the little portrait said. Could it be…?

Lucian's pointy little beard hopped up. "No." He shifted in his seat. "Doctor Peveril, we are looking for—"

"Well, you are Minnie's daughter, unless I'm very much mistaken."

Before Hannah could answer, Lucian cut in, "She is. But her mother is no longer with us."

Excuse me? I'd like to know more about this father. Hannah tried to catch Lucian's eye, but he kept his gaze on the doctor.

"Who—" she tried, but again Lucian cut her off.

"That is why we are here. Do you know what became of Minnie's friends and family after she left?"

Doctor Peveril thought for a moment, although his gaze continually flicked back and forth between Hannah and Lucian. "No, I'm afraid not. I should've thought you, of all people—"

"Do you know if anyone else from that time is still around?"

The doctor sighed and stared at the floor. "'Fraid not. I mean, of course the people have remained, but none of those would have known her well enough. She left after her mother's demise, and from what I gathered, town gossip and all…" He made an apologetic gesture. "Her friends thought her a bit…"—his eyes flitted from Hannah to Lucian—"hoity-toity, to go and work at the castle. I'm sorry, my dear." He looked back at her. "Highlow has forgotten Jasmine."

Lucian nodded. He was standing at the door saying his good-byes before Hannah figured out that they were leaving. Why? This doctor knew something about her father. He had implied—

"I should've known something out of the ordinary would happen," Doctor Peveril said, shaking Lucian's hand. "We had a visit from lord Victor Pryce early this morning, asking around if anyone had seen a young, blonde woman. I say asking… He was none too happy."

Hannah bit her lip. She had agreed to let Lucian do the talking, but what if he was holding out on her?

"Doctor Peveril, did you know my f—"

But Lucian wouldn't let her finish. He thanked the doctor, and guided Hannah out of the office. Miss Jones, lips pinched, peered at her over the pince-nez. Lucian took Hannah by the elbow, and led her outside.

Once more in the icy shower, Hannah yanked her arm free. "What was that?" she yapped at him. "Don't I get to ask any questions? This is my search, not yours. We're asking about *my* family. *My* mother."

"He didn't know anything," Lucian said with an infuriating calm.

Hannah swallowed, remembering the doctor's words. The most wonderful woman in the world and they had just forgotten her. And look where it left them. In her mind, the village her mother had lived in looked happy and colourful, until the moment she left and took all the Technicolor cheerfulness with her.

Hannah pulled her hood over hair already wet. On the other side of the street was the grimiest pub she had ever seen. Even from the outside it was obvious that no sunshine would come in through those leadlight windows. If there were any sun. At the moment there must be lights on inside the pub, but that was impossible to see. And yet, Hannah was almost sure she saw a familiar, scary face inside. She bit her lips to keep them from trembling. *Don't. Panic.*

"Lucian?"

He was rummaging around in his saddlebag, water dripping off his hat. "Hm?"

"What if the Baron sends someone to find us? Could we defend ourselves?"

"It won't come to that."

Again with the calm. It wasn't Lucian's life on the line. His mother hadn't just been shot. He wasn't locked in some stupid, wet, cold world. He lived in it. He didn't know any better. Fists balled, Hannah concentrated on the rain. Every drop on her face was one on the fire inside her. Drip. Drip. No more worry. Drip. No pain. Drip. Drip. No anger, or frustration, or panic.

The rain didn't work. Whatever reason she could think of to absolve Lucian, in fact only poured fuel on that fire. She'd hit another dead end. All she'd found were more questions. Nothing made sense anymore. How was she supposed to protect her brother if she couldn't even take care of herself? The flames of hysteria lapped at her sanity. Someone was lurking in the shadows, and *he* was being calm! Her voice came out about an octave higher than she meant. "Oh, you have all the answers, do you? If you know so much, how come we're out here in the rain, instead of drinking tea and playing with our newly found jewel?"

Lucian stepped aside and revealed a gun in his bag. "If we run into trouble, we can deal with it."

Hannah glanced at the pub. He was in there. She was sure of it. Waiting to get her. Before Lucian could close the bag, she grabbed the gun, and aimed it at the pub window. She fired, but Lucian's desperate lunge put off her aim and the bullet hit the roof.

"What are you doing?!" Lucian shouted, eyes wild.

Oh good, he'd lost his calm. Maybe they could get some action now. "There's a man in there who's been following me."

He reached for the gun and rammed it back into the bag. "How do you know?"

A sobering question. How did she know? Had she actually seen him? "I…"

Lucian manhandled her onto the horse. "Nobody out in this weather, and you aim at the one place you're sure to hit someone. Are you insane?"

It had seemed like a good idea. Now, she wasn't so sure.

Lucian mounted, and raced them both out of the village. "I thought you'd be more like… your mother. But apparently the resemblance stops where the brain starts."

Lower lip quivering, Hannah kept silent. But the burnt man… he was there! Right? And he'd been following her. Why else would he be here? If she didn't stop him, who knows what he'd do? Besides, she wouldn't actually have hurt anyone.

She wiped her eyes with her sleeve. Who was she trying to convince? She'd just shot at a pub. When had she become that person? She'd felt compelled to do something, to stop letting things happen to her, to take control. Looked like control was one more thing she lost.

What if she had hit someone? Even without killing them, and aside form the obvious consequences, would she have had to pay Doctor Peveril? What was the state of medicine here, anyway? The more she thought about it, the sorrier she felt. Not only for herself, though that was a large part of it, but also for the people trying to make a living here. If they were sick, would the Baron allow them a day off? Not likely. And those poor, grubby children! Wasn't anyone going to do something about these living conditions?

Her tears mixed with the rain while she followed Lucian. Maybe he was doing the right thing after all. She sniffled. What was it about this man? She hardly knew anything about him, and what she did know wasn't particularly positive. He was a robber and he had let her mother be bullied into leaving this world behind with two small children in tow. But that story was far from complete. What about Hannah's father? Was he, or wasn't he?

Hannah studied Lucian's face, but saw nothing familiar. Not

from her own features, nor from Sean's. Would Aunt J—her mother not have gone back, if she thought her husband was still out here? Whenever she'd mentioned Uncle Tom, she'd been so in love, after all those years. Died in a fire, along with her parents. How could she have lived that lie? Uncle Tom never even existed.

"Was she happy here? I mean, before she was driven away."

Again, Lucian didn't say anything, but she had learned to wait for his answers. He reined in his horse, and rode next to her. "She and your father were very much in love. Had been for years before they were old enough to get married. He, your father, his name was Arthur. He was always up to something. He was a farrier, you know, strong as an ox. If he played a trick on someone, they never dared do anything about it, so they just laughed along with a tooth-achey smile. But nobody ever really minded, because he was just such a good man. If he had made fun of you, you could be sure he would buy you a beer afterwards.

"I think there's a lot of him in you, so you probably already know him, though you never met him. He was quick to judge a situation and have his answer ready, too. And like you, he was not always correct in his conclusions. But you could always count on him to help, whether you were a friend or an enemy in need. He always saw the good in people. Even… him." He jerked his head to somewhere left of him.

"What, you mean lord Victor? But he couldn't have been more than a boy then!"

"No, I mean his father of course. The old baron was no less of a villain."

Hannah mulled that over for a while. So, if Lucian were to be believed, this Baron had killed her mother and his father had killed her father. She clenched her teeth, and took a deep breath to calm the boiling sensation in her stomach. Somehow she would get back at that man before she took Sean out of here. If they ever found this jewel.

Hannah shivered. Watery curtains shrouded the trees at the

edge of the village.

"Where are we going?"

"Since you made sure we won't find any answers in the village, I'll have to tap into a resource I hoped not to use. She and I… don't see eye to eye on certain matters."

Hannah pulled up her eyebrows, hoping he'd expand. She still wasn't sure what to make of him. Maybe she could get a clearer view of him if he talked more.

He made a vague gesture. "She is a noble. Nobles are generally not very fond of robbers. And I'm not very fond of nobles." He wrinkled his nose. "But in this case I'll make an exception. Lady Ethel Heanor has always been kind. She used to employ Minnie as an apprentice seamstress. When her husband, Lord Basil, died, her possessions reverted to the Baron, but for some reason he never claimed them and she remains in the mansion. People say she must have some sort of hold over him, but she does not have magic. In any case, we will have to hurry, because Lady Heanor will probably be the first person the Baron will visit after he finds out you've gone to find the jewel. If he hasn't been there yet, he soon will be."

Hannah's stomach leapt. Another person who'd known her mother. She was starting to wonder if she did, herself. Did she know anyone anymore, including herself? Finding the jewel was getting more and more essential, not only for her situation, but also for her sanity.

"What would you do if you had the jewel?" she asked.

"It wouldn't do me any good."

"Why?"

"I don't have magic. I can't use it."

"Oh. Right." He really was trying to help her, then. Not trying to get the jewel for himself.

"What will you do with it?"

Hannah gave a short laugh. "Get. Out. I can't stand this place. No offence."

"How?"

"What do you mean?"

"Do you know how to use it when you get it?"

She shrugged. "Can't be that hard, can it? My mother only used it once."

"And she lost your father." He tried to hide it, but there was pain in his voice. When she didn't answer, he continued: "Magic always, always takes something back for what it gives you. Only short-sighted, greedy people would want to use it."

"And my mother."

He rubbed his eyes with the thumb and forefinger of his left hand. "Your mother did it to protect you and your brother. She saw no other way out."

Hm. "And you did?"

For a split second the corner of his mouth curled up slightly. Then he was stern again. "I tried to talk her out of it, but she would not listen. When she had gone… and after your father died, of course…"—he added the last bit as if it was only arbitrary—"I came back here. But there were too many memories and too few people interested in my return, so I ventured north. Even then, people did not concern themselves with others much, unless they could profit by it. Which is why nobody remembers us."

They left the main road in favour of a path leading into open greyness, two brick gate posts standing guard at the beginning, a large, dark cube looming at the end. The mansion Lucian had mentioned was a solid block of sooty, once red brick, broken up by shuttered windows. Judging from the rust on some of the hinges, many of the shutters had remained closed for years. Someone had made an attempt at growing roses in a border along the walls, but they had not been cared for in a while. Some had died, others had formed a Sleeping Beauty-like hedge, scaling the base of the walls.

The maid who opened the door for them wouldn't let them in straight away. And when she did, the gloomy hallway itself seemed to growl, 'You are not welcome here'. Which is why, when they were shown into Lady Ethel's salon, the light, inviting atmosphere surprised Hannah.

"Ah, I see you've come in through the front door." A plump lady in a plum dress was sitting on the edge of a sofa, pouring three cups of tea. A massive wooden wheelchair was parked next to the sofa. It looked more like an armchair with added wheels. "I hardly ever go out anymore. And when I do, I don't use that dark front entrance. Sit, sit!" She waved to two flowery chairs opposite her. "I never receive visitors anymore either. How nice of you to— Oh!" Her startlingly light grey eyes fixed on Lucian, who blushed. *Interesting.*

"Lady Ethel." He gave a short nod.

After a stern look at Lucian, Lady Ethel turned to Hannah. "Him I know, but I have a feeling I've seen you before, too."

Apparently the association with Lucian did not improve Hannah's chances of gaining Lady Ethel's favour.

"You may remember my mother, Lady Ethel. Her name was Jasmine?"

Lady Ethel gasped. "Minnie! Of course, I should have realised!"

She threw Lucian another dirty look. "So, from the days before you became a true delinquent, when you were still nothing more than a lout."

He tried his stare on Lady Ethel, but hers wasn't any less penetrating, and after a moment that lasted so long it made even Hannah uncomfortable, he cast his eyes down. When Lady Ethel turned back to Hannah, he stood up and strode to the window.

"How is dear Minnie?"

14

When Sean knocked on the door of the factory, he found Roderick in one of the armchairs, reading.

"Good, you're here. I was afraid you'd still be at the castle." He dropped down on one of the benches. "I spent all of last night trying to get people to help me free Hannah, but those boneless cowards won't help me. I hardly slept at all." He slumped over the table, forehead resting on his arms. Why did this world have to exist? There was absolutely nothing positive about it.

Roderick's book thumped on the small table. "Your… friend isn't coming?"

"Charlotte had to work." And she didn't want to come to the factory. Told him Roderick was probably bad news, but she didn't want to come see for herself. Another coward. Who did that remind him of? 'Your friends are no good.' Yeah, he never heard that before. But now those friends Hannah despised would have been an asset. Okay, so none of them would know how to handle a sword, but at least he wouldn't have been alone. Hannah was locked up with a murderer and nobody would help him.

He sat up to face Roderick, who was now standing.

"How is Hannah? Is she okay?"

"She is well, if that is what you mean. She has left the castle in search of an item which may help you return to your own world."

Sean spluttered, eyes bulging. "She *what*? When? Why didn't she come to get me?"

"I'm afraid she left rather hastily. When she learned about this object, she wanted to retrieve it promptly. She told me she did not think you capable."

Of course not. Here he was thinking she needed him for a change, but she wouldn't even let him try. Sean felt his cheeks heat up and frowned.

"Because of your wound, that is," Roderick added quickly.

Hm. Sean rubbed the fresh bandage on his upper left arm, but the frown remained. "So she just left?"

Roderick nodded.

Throwing his good hand in the air, Sean started pacing. "Typical. Typical! She's always doing that. Has to be the one who'll save us all. No thoughts for the rest of us, just 'look at me! I'm a hero!'. So where did she go? I'd better go after her if she wants to stay alive."

Roderick hesitated. Didn't he want Sean to know where his own cousin went? What had Hannah been telling him? 'Because of your wound.' Sure, that was it. Not because she would never trust him with anything.

Roderick rubbed his chin. "She left for a village west of here. But you won't catch up unless someone would be willing to lend you a horse."

Sean flinched. "A horse? I wouldn't know what to do with one. Where did Hannah get a horse?"

"She took one of my master's horses."

"What, she stole a horse?" A crooked smile stretched across his face. What do you know, there was hope for her yet.

"I don't think she would see it that way."

Sean laughed. "No, of course she wouldn't! Ha! Hannah the horse thief! Not so righteous now." He folded his arms across his chest and grinned at Roderick, who curled an unsure lip. Well, how could he know? All those times Hannah had berated Sean for not following all of society's stupid rules. And now she stole a horse. From a baron! Something good had come out of this world after all.

His stomach somersaulted. She was still out there, in danger. Breaking rules is easy if you have someone protecting you. Mum had always been there for him and Hannah had been Brainy Smurf beside her. But she'd caught him when he fell, and now he had to catch her. He had to. If only to hold it above her head for the rest of her life if he succeeded.

"So, what can I do to help her?"

"I sincerely doubt whether you would be able to find her. Like you, she has no knowledge of the surrounding territory, and although I told her the name of the village, she could easily have mistaken her way."

"Then why did you let her go?" But he waved the question away. "Never mind. She wanted to go, so she went. And all we can do is hope for her safe return, I suppose. Or maybe I could find someone to take me to this village. That's not as terrible an idea as storming the castle."

"I do not think you will find many prepared to offer help when you tell them he has already gone after her," Roderick said, "Although I may have slowed him down some by slashing his saddle's girth."

Sean gave him a thumbs up, which he acknowledged with a slight inclination of his head.

"I have to find her, though. This is the second time he's picked her over me. She may not be so lucky to escape with her life next time."

"If I may," Roderick interjected, gesturing him to sit down, "I do not think he wants to kill her. He has had plenty of opportunity to kill or otherwise harm her earlier. As a matter of fact, I believe he very much wants to keep her alive and bring her back."

"But why Hannah? What's so special about her?"

"My dear boy," Roderick said, "You may not have noticed this, but she is rather good-looking. Either of you would have sufficed as an apprentice and a companion, but she is rather more capable of providing him with an heir."

Sean was halfway out the door before Roderick could stop him.

"Hannah does not want you there."

Sean froze. A frown formed as his gaze slowly shifted from the door to the floor. Even in a strange world she didn't think he'd be worth having around. Hannah the hero. No room for sidekicks.

Roderick ushered him back to the table, and found a bottle and two glasses. Sean stopped him before he could open it.

"Roderick, it's nine thirty. I'd prefer some water, if you don't mind."

Roderick pouted at the bottle, but switched it for a bottle of water.

Sean drank a glass and a half in silence, watching Roderick take tiny little sips. Then he put his glass down.

"I don't care what she said, I can't just let her run off like that."

"My boy, she is far away by now. She is on my master's fastest horse and he, with some luck, will have fallen off his. The best you can do—all any of us can do now—is wait for her return with the jewel."

If she would return. One day she would find out that she was not invincible. Today could easily be that day.

"Jewel? That's what she's after?"

Nodding slowly, Roderick said, "I told her about the theory that people from the other world would automatically acquire magic in this world. Controlling it with an item such as this jewel would give a person tremendous power. It was part of a story. I should never have mentioned it. But she would not let go of the thought that the jewel would take you home, so she went for it."

Sean shot another look at the door, but then filled his glass again, emptying the bottle.

"Maybe wine isn't such a bad idea after all," he grumbled.

Roderick jumped up. "My master's cellars are even better stocked than his study," he said, ambling back to the counter.

Sean stared at his glass. "Yeah? What does he keep in his study, the sherry?"

Roderick looked up in surprise. "No. Really, your world has the strangest customs. Books, of course. Books on magic in his case."

Sean stood up so violently that he tipped over the bench, the crash startling Roderick into dropping his glass.

"Can you get to them?" Sean asked. "You said yourself that people from the other world have magic—"

"It's only a theory."

"—so maybe I could learn to use it too."

"No! Dear boy, don't even think it. Magic is an evil practice. No good can come of it."

Sean shook his head. "I would only use it to help Hannah, and get us back home. You said yourself that this jewel of yours only works for people who know how to control magic, so I have to learn. Your baron is gone, you have to take me to his study!"

Roderick sulked, "He is not *my* baron. And I don't like this idea. Magic is not something you toy with."

"I won't toy with it. Not if I learn it correctly. You have to get me some of these books."

Roderick's eye wandered to the office above the dining hall, where he'd gone to fetch the coat Sean now used. Sean stepped over the fallen bench, and ran up the stairs, leaving Roderick calling after him. No, he wouldn't stop. If there was something there that could help Hannah, he would use it.

The office had windows on three sides, looking out over the dining hall, the work floor and part of the mill yard. But Sean was only interested in the large mahogany book case standing against the one wall without windows. He stretched out his hand, but then hesitated. If this worked, it would give him an awful lot of power.

Kinda scary. With great power comes great… awesomeness! His fingers caressed the beaten leather on one of the spines. It sent a tingle through his fingertips. He quickly piled books into his arms and inched his way down the stairs, hardly able to see where he was going.

When he reached downstairs, his wounded arm grazed the railing. He grimaced and dropped the books, clutching his arm. Roderick came to his aid, setting him down in the nearest arm chair and unbuttoning the sleeve of the shirt Nellie wouldn't let Sean leave without, to inspect the bandage. He paused when he came to the tattoo of a sewing needle near Sean's elbow.

"I had a problem once, and Hannah helped me out," Sean answered the unspoken question. The needle was more fitting than he wanted Roderick to know. "I was grateful, so we got the tattoos. But then she never let me forget it."

Roderick checked Sean's arm, but the wound hadn't opened. When Sean buttoned his sleeve back up, one eye on the pile of books he had to sort through, someone knocked on the door. Since it could only be Charlotte, Sean concentrated on his buttons while Roderick let her in.

"Hey," Sean muttered, still a little miffed that she hadn't joined him this morning. But then the answer came in a much lower voice than Sean had expected.

"Ey'up."

Sean's mouth dropped open, and he whipped around. Charlotte was there, but she had brought someone along. He was quite heavy-set, not too tall, but very muscular. At this moment, however, he seemed rather powerless, scuffing his shoe and flexing his hands into fists.

"Ben!"

Sean's brain was both frozen and working at full speed. One half kept repeating 'that's impossible', and the other was whipping up questions, some of which came out. "What are you doing here? How did you get here?"

A half smile hung around Ben's lips. He brushed his hand

over his head, but his frizzy black hair was too short to get dis-
arranged.

"I followed you. That is to say… When I got to Hannah's
place, she wasn't home, so I thought she might be at your mum's.
But when I turned the corner, I saw her running away, which I
thought was odd, so I followed her, only she was too fast and I
lost her. I walked around for a while… but I couldn't find her,
and then I spotted that open gate. So when I went through…
That was so bizarre! Anyway, I tried to get back, but I must have
just walked around in circles, because I only arrived at the village
a few hours ago."

He babbled. Sean had never seen him babble before. Ben
always knew exactly what to do and when to do it, as if he'd
been planning it all along. Even in unexpected situations. But
apparently an alternate world was a disturbance beyond the
reach of even Ben's calm competence.

"Can you believe they call it Nottingham?" Ben asked. Only
then did he notice Sean's bandage. He frowned. "You're hurt.
What happened?"

Sean could not stop staring at him. Ben. Here. He blinked.
"A lot. Mum was shot. Hannah was kidnapped, but she escaped
to find some kind of magic thingy and now I'm going to learn
magic."

It was Ben's turn to stare. "Did you hurt yourself with the
magic?"

"No!" Sean frowned and gestured over his shoulder. "He
shot at me, didn't he! That bloke from the castle, the one who
shot me mam!"

Right. That sounded odd, even to Sean. He introduced Ben
and Charlotte to Roderick and told them to sit down, so he
could explain. Ben sat down in one of the comfortable chairs
across from Sean, as did Roderick, but Charlotte placed herself behind Sean's chair, keeping an eye on Roderick at all times
while Sean recounted the events of the last few days.

"So Hannah's on a horse and you're playing Harry Potter?"

Ben rubbed his neck. "And neither of you has a clue what you're doing."

"At least I've got the books. Hannah just went off, looking for something she's never seen in a country she doesn't know. How stupid is that? I think we should look for someone who knows his way around, and go find her."

Shaking his head, Roderick raised his hand. "I agree to some extent. I had wished to keep this from you, but I do not place much trust in a positive outcome of Hannah's quest. With a generous amount of luck, she may return here safely. However, others with more knowledge of the history and the territory have sought this object in vain before. I suspect that it will take her some time to realise that she, too, will be unable to retrieve it."

Sean spread his arms, fingers wide. "There! Thank you! So we should go and find her, right?"

"I have told you before, it will be nigh impossible to find her and very well possible to get hurt, or worse, yourself."

Sean's knee started to bounce. "We have to do *something*! The way I see it, the only other thing to do is to learn magic and see where that takes us."

Roderick sighed. "Magic is unpredictable, especially if you do not know what you are doing. It can take away things you're not prepared to lose. You could not possibly hope to learn enough to wield the power of the jewel before Hannah's return."

"Ben?" Sean stretched out a pleading hand.

Ben only shrugged. "I don't know, man. This is all way too weird for my tastes. Magic? I mean, do you know anything about it? At all? I still think we should just wait for Hannah to come back. If she's found the thing, then we can discuss using it, if not, there's really no point, is there?"

Wait for Hannah. Looked like they had more faith in Hannah than in him. Even in this world, she had to have things her way.

One more person to try. "Charlotte? You know what magic can do. And you know me. I'm not the Baron. I can use this thing for good. Just to get us out of here."

White-knuckled hands clasped together on the back of the chair, Charlotte looked like she was going to cry. "But you'll have no time to practice. You could get hurt."

Roderick cut in before Sean could answer, "Magic is a thing of the mind. If you have the knowledge, you also have the skill. It depends more on willpower than strength or dexterity. But I still say we should wait for Hannah."

Sean clenched his teeth. Apparently his willpower was questionable as well.

"How long are we going to wait for her?"

Roderick poured them all a glass of wine. "Again, as I have told you, taking action now is useless. We have no way of knowing where she is, or whether she is in need of our help. I tried to tell her too, but, like a true woman, she did not want to listen."

Sean sat down, took a sip, and rubbed his face with his hand.

"Look," Roderick continued, "I understand your desire to take action. All too well. There have been many times when I could bear it no longer and have undertaken foolish attempts to alter my situation. But I have had to accept the futility of any such efforts and the inescapability of my fate. I find it rather disheartening to have to watch another make the same mistakes."

"Besides," Ben added, also taking a gulp of wine, "what help could *you* give her?"

Sean narrowed his eyes. A fine thing to say for someone who had been found wanting. He opened his mouth to defend himself, but Charlotte put her hand on his arm to cut him off.

"He's right. You're hurt. It would be even more dangerous for you to go off aimlessly."

Her words lay heavy in his stomach. Even if she was right, did she have to take their side in this?

Ben stood up. "I hate to be trivial, but I need a toilet."

Roderick went with Ben, leaving Sean with his thoughts.

15

Charlotte tapped his hand. "You know what you need? A nice walk. You've been in here all morning, while outside the sun is shining. Your friend Ben went out ages ago, you should follow his example. Well, don't go out by yourself. I told him that was stupid. Come take a walk with me."

"There's no sun, it's drizzling."

"Well… then… pretend the sun is shining."

Pity he couldn't find out just how sweet she was. But Hannah was more important right now. Seemed like he was the only one who thought so. Even Ben was remarkably passive in this. What right did they have to tell him not to act? But what could he do without their support?

He sighed, but got up and followed Charlotte out the door. "Where are we going?" Not that he cared. But she had a way of always happily commenting on everything she did, or anything that happened around her. It was a refreshing change to the people back home, who either didn't care, or presumed you already knew.

"I thought we could go to the windmill. Best thing to stop you worrying is to meet new people. George, the miller, is a very good friend of mine. He's more… open than the other people in the village. They tolerate you because Nellie took you in, but George suspends judgement until he knows you better. I would really like you to meet him."

Sean shrugged, hoping his facial muscles were making a smile he didn't feel. "Okay."

She smiled back, but raised her eyebrows. "Oh… kay. Huh!" She giggled and then started running, yelling to him over her shoulder. "Come on!" He grinned, shook his head and trudged along. She threw her head back, crossed her arms and, foot tapping, waited for him to catch up. Then she took his hand and dragged him off.

By the time they reached the windmill, their hats and coats were soaked. They stopped underneath the balcony to get rid of the worst drips. An orange-haired little boy sat with his back against the red brick, eating carrots.

"Hello Georgie, is daddy home?"

Georgie nodded, but Sean wasn't interested. Red bricks, brown balcony, white cap and sails. "It looks the same, except for that house attached to it."

"The same as what? I thought you had never been here?"

"No, I mean… The Nottingham where I'm from, there's also a windmill. And it looks exactly like this one."

"Oh." She glanced up, but didn't comment. She never answered when Sean told her something about his world. At first he thought she didn't want to seem ignorant, but that wasn't it. She was scared. Anything to do with magic, or things she didn't know, she shied away from. And yet she was the only person in the village, including Nellie, who didn't stare at his back when he walked past.

He followed Charlotte around the mill, where she knocked on the door of the miller's cottage, and entered before anyone had answered.

"George? Ah, there you are!"

In a wooden chair by the fire sat a burly man with dark orange hair and slightly lighter coloured mutton chops, whose features softened the moment he recognised Charlotte, but hardened again when he saw the stranger accompanying her.

"Saw Georgie at his favourite pastime," Charlotte chatted

away. "How are you, George, anything you need?" She kissed his cheek and wandered over to the stove to pour herself and Sean a cup of tea. "This is Sean, George, he's… new here. He says there's a windmill near where he lived too."

The miller's face lit up and in a glorious deep voice asked, "Is there now? Do you like mills?"

Charlotte, on the other side of him, nodded fervently.

"Err, yes, I think they're… fascinating," Sean lied, but if the miller saw through that, he didn't let on.

"A fine fellow, Lottie, a fine fellow. What brings you here on a day like this?"

Charlotte started off on a ramble about her family again, and the miller chimed in here and there. Family stories, just what Sean wanted to hear. He looked around for something to occupy himself with, but the cottage was quite small and the miller apparently led a sober life. How did the man not get bored out of his brain? A few more minutes of family fun and Sean couldn't stand it any longer. He opened the door and went outside with a casual "I'm going to check the, err…"

The drizzle had turned into rain. He kept close to the wall of the mill, and with no idea where to go, he ended up next to Georgie.

"Hi." What did one say to a five-year-old? Was he five? Weren't they always?

Georgie said nothing, but offered Sean a large carrot.

"Thanks. Mind if I sit down?"

"No." The little boy stopped chewing while Sean sat down, but started again when no conversation followed.

Sean stared at the carrot for a while and then took a blunt little knife from the basket of carrots. This intrigued Georgie enough to once more stop chewing.

"I saw this on the internet, let's see if it works." Sean started carving the carrot. "The blade is a little wide for this, but we'll see. Do you have a little one?" Georgie sat up on his knees and rummaged around, handing Sean a perfect baby carrot.

Rubbing his chin with the back of the hand that held the knife, Sean grinned at the gleam in the child's eyes. "Hm. I think it went in this way…"

He made a few more cuts and then held up a little flute. A blissful greed spread over Georgie's face.

"Do you want to try it?"

Georgie nodded eagerly and snagged the carrot flute from Sean's hand. After two toots he produced a little yelp, sprang to his feet and ran towards the cottage.

Sean sniggered, took the leftover bits of carrot and stuck them in his mouth. Then he stood up as well and strolled back to the cottage.

"That was very sweet of you." Charlotte took his arm as they were walking through the mist, following the path through the woods back to the old factory. After playing with Sean some more, Georgie had wanted to come too, but when Sean promised him he could come by some other time, the child had let him leave, happily tooting away.

Sean shrugged. "Just passing the time. At least the kid didn't talk about mills."

"George didn't either!"

He flashed his crooked smile. "No need to get so defensive! I only said the kid didn't!"

She made a face, pulled on his arm and strolled along, chatting away. Sean watched her brown curls bounce up and down as she walked. She accepted him. Or at least she seemed to. George had even called him a fine fellow. Not that that meant much from someone who hardly knew you, but it was nice to be treated without suspicion. If Hannah didn't make it back, Sean would have to find a job. Maybe George could use a hand. It'd be an honest job. Wouldn't that please Mum! Wherever she was…

Charlotte was on her umpteenth story about someone he didn't know. How could she be so absorbed by such trivialities?

He smirked. His mother had accused him of that exact thing not too long ago. She wouldn't do that anymore. Now he would just hear it from Hannah, but if *she* said it, it sounded less true, somehow. It's so much easier to do what you like if someone else will be the responsible one.

But now, even Hannah had gone. As many times as he had wished for that to happen, now that it had, could he live up to his own expectations? Someone would have to learn how to create a portal, no matter what the others said. That Baron wasn't going to do it for them. It was up to Sean to find out how. Could he really excel and show everyone they'd been wrong about him? Would Hannah even notice? If she came back with the jewel, she might not even realise that he had taken the trouble to learn how to use it.

But had Hannah managed anything by now? How would they even know if something had happened to her? What if she realised she had magic, too? Would she decide to stay here? It's not like she had a fiance waiting. He snorted.

No, she would be too eager to start running Sean's life now. Wouldn't she love that! But what if *he* decided to stay? If he had to start being responsible, why not here? If Hannah couldn't find and kill this Baron, then he would. After all, it was *his* mother. It might not be too bad living here after all, none of the usual temptations...

His gaze wandered to Charlotte. *Oh. She stopped talking a while ago...*

"Are you all right?" she asked now. She really was rather sweet.

"I'm fine." He put as much reassurance in his smile as he could.

"So, do you know what you'd like to do if you have to stay?"

Oh, that's what she had been talking about. "I'm quite good with computers. But that's not going to get me anywhere here."

Charlotte frowned. "Really? How? Do you know how to talk

to them?"

Shaking his head, Sean gave a laugh that sounded more like a sigh. "We're almost there. I hope Roderick is in."

"Hm."

"You don't like him much, do you?"

She hesitated. "I'm not sure. His clothes are awfully old-fashioned."

How would Sean know? But that was not the reason for her cautiousness. She liked clothes, but she wasn't that shallow. "If his clothes are a reason not to like a man, you wouldn't have liked me, the way I looked when you first saw me."

Charlotte rubbed her arms. "Yes, but he reminds me of… At least, they told me about… Well… Not to trust anyone we don't know. But if you think he's a good man…"

"Just because he lives in the castle, doesn't mean that he's in league with… him." He made a vague gesture towards the castle. "Sometimes you just have to trust someone."

Her luscious lips curled. "I trust you."

That made him laugh. "You hardly know me."

"I think I know you better than you know Roderick. Here." She reached into a hidden pocket in the folds of her skirt and pulled out a necklace of a few amber beads on a brown cord. As she placed it around his neck, she said: "I made it myself. That's my hair."

Gross. Fortunately, he managed to hide that reaction. She looked so adorably proud, that he took it in his hand and examined it. It was actually quite finely and artistically made. His thumb slid across the braided pattern, but then he let go of the necklace and moved his hand to the hair that fell over her shoulder. Her cheeks lit up and she giggled, eyes flitting from him to the ground to the trees and back. He'd never had that reaction before. The intense sweetness this girl radiated was intoxicating. And she seemed to adore him for no particular reason. What was that, simple naivety, or did she want something in return for this trinket?

She bit her lip, still alternating looking at him and anywhere else. Something in his stomach jittered. Did she really just want to give him something, no strings attached?

"Thank you, Charlotte. It means a lot to me." He leaned in to kiss her, but she giggled again, turned, and fluttered away. *Now what?* Funny girl. Could someone please give him a guidebook as to how to behave towards her? Still, it would be interesting to find out the slow way. He would almost want to stay just for that.

They reached the factory around noon and were greeted by Ben, who had brought some bread, cheese and a vegetable pie, as well as an abundance of apples.

"Thought you might like some lunch."

"You and your apples." Sean grabbed one off the table and rubbed it against his shirt. "Where'd you get them, with no money?"

Ben pulled up one corner of his mouth. "It's amazing how fast you can find friends in this place."

Was that sarcasm? From Ben? That would be a first. But then, he had taken the wine Roderick offered him at ten in the morning. Sean bit his apple and studied Ben's face, but Ben didn't seem to be aware of it and cut a chunk off the pie. Roderick came into the dining hall from the other side. Had he arrived earlier, or was he coming in just now? Sean had been meaning to ask him how he got to the castle and back, but something always prevented it. Sean opened his mouth, but Roderick spoke first.

"Any news?"

Why did he look at Ben when he asked that? Did Roderick now think that Ben was the more important player, too? Ben didn't even acknowledge Sean before he spoke.

"Nothing of importance."

"Nothing *at all*," Sean said in a sharp tone. Ben glowered at him, but he glared back. Ben was all right, usually, but this was not about him. Hannah had shown him the door after all, but for Sean nothing had changed. She was still his cousin. "This is ridiculous. I'm sure there's more we can do than wait."

"Like what?" Ben snapped. "What do you think *you* can do?"

Cheeks flushed, Sean balled his fists. "Hey, what is your problem? Why are you even here? You ought to—"

The rest of his sentence was lost in the thunderous sound of rocks falling and crashing into each other in the courtyard.

16

Three heads turned in the direction of the mill yard. Sean was up first, running through the door Roderick had just used, into the mill yard at the centre of the building. One corner of the yard was covered in a cloud of dirt and dust, almost obscuring the fact that part of the facade had come down, leaving a gaping hole in the side of the building.

Coughing, eyes watering, Sean stopped abruptly to avoid the falling detritus. Ben, right behind, bumped into him. Roderick followed, his face drained of colour.

"That was where the entrance to the castle was. I shan't be able to return."

Sean looked at him and back at the pile of rocks and rubble that appeared under the settling dust. "Don't worry, we can clear that, if we work together." He went over and started pulling on a large block of stone, but as soon as he moved it, a new wave of debris came tumbling down.

Roderick seized his arm and yanked him aside.

"Thanks," Sean wheezed. The remains of the wall crashed down in front of him. He would have been buried under them if it weren't for Roderick. He gripped his arm. Blood was seeping through the bandage, staining his shirt.

"Oh, I am sorry, my boy."

"For what, saving my life? This"—he pointed at his arm—"really doesn't matter."

The three of them stared at the destruction—Sean clutching his arm, Roderick open-mouthed.

"How did this happen? The building has shown no signs of deterioration these many years."

Ben cleared his throat. "There were some blokes in here before. Before you arrived, I mean. But I didn't think anything of it. I don't know everyone. I thought they might be your friends."

"I have no friends." Roderick's shoulders drooped. "Nobody ever visits. They think the building is haunted, like the castle."

Ben put his hand on Roderick's shoulder. "We'll get you some food, at least."

Sean nodded, but something was missing. Remarks on the ghost stories. "Where's Charlotte?"

When had he last seen her? Sean rushed back to the dining hall, but found it empty. The others dragged in, not looking very upset.

"The noise." Roderick shrugged. "It probably frightened her. Allow me to take a look at your bandage."

"It can wait. She wouldn't have left if she thought I was in danger." From what he'd seen in the last day and a half at least. He couldn't be that wrong about her. This was odd. He took his coat off the chair he'd left it on and headed for the door.

A familiar voice sneered, "Oh, you're an expert on her now?"

Not losing any momentum, Sean narrowed his eyes. Ben had changed. Sean wasn't sure if it was Hannah's refusal to marry him or the fact that he'd found himself locked in some place he never knew existed, but Ben had never been this caustic. Sean threw him an icy look and rushed out.

With long strides Sean paced along the path back to the village. The slate sky still threatened rain. Something was wrong. How could Ben not have noticed that? Wasn't he supposed to have some kind of policeman's instinct or something? Instead, he made snide remarks and moped around eating apples.

Sean had reached the edge of the village. Shouts echoed through the streets, where people huddled together—some pointing, others hiding, a few of them pressing bloody cloths to parts of their bodies. More blood. Sean touched the bandage on his arm. His life seemed to consist of blood and violence ever since Mum—

The smell of smoke hung in the air. As he approached, its source became visible. One of the houses that lined the market square had been set alight. The idiot was still dancing around in front of it, torch in hand. His stupid wooden devil's mask made him look even more moronic. He probably never considered why he had destroyed someone's property. Never thought about the people who would now have to find another place to sleep for the night.

Why did nobody do anything about it, though? No buckets of water. No balled fists even. The people that didn't hide huddled together and didn't seem interested in stopping one dangly bloke armed with nothing more than a torch. They couldn't possibly be scared of his mask…?

Two women stood shoulder to shoulder, looking on with their hands over their mouths. Maybe they'd know more.

"Who is that guy?"

They barely looked at him, shaking their heads and staring at the fire.

A teenage girl answered his question. "He's one of them."

She pointed to a group of wooden-masked men on the other side of the square, who held up a variety of weapons, including a pistol aimed at a greying, pot-bellied man. The man's face had turned a bright pink that spread all the way under his hair. Sweat trickled down his cheeks, to the great amusement of the man holding the gun. Another two masked men appeared from within the shop, carrying a bag full of what Sean presumed were stolen goods.

This was why he'd only ever taken from big companies. No violence, no real losers. The people in this village had enough to deal with. Didn't those asses realise that?

The burning house was separated from the rest by alleyways

on both sides. It creaked ominously, and bits of burning thatch came sailing to the ground. It wouldn't be long before it collapsed. If Hannah had been here, she would have known what to do. *She's not. Who needs her.*

Sean turned to the girl. "We have to do something, we can't just stand here!"

The girl recoiled and shook her head. She wouldn't be any help. Then one of the women screamed. Letting go of the other woman's shoulder, she pointed at the attic window of the burning house, left hand still clasped over her mouth. A frightened toddler's face appeared in the flaming window frame, its chubby cheeks smudged with soot.

Several other people now gasped and screamed, but they remained rooted in their spots. A thought flashed through Sean's brain. Had there been people present when his father had been trapped in that fire? People who did nothing?

Cursing, Sean ran past the buffoon with the torch, who now stood gawking at the window, his victory dance of stupidity cut short by its horrific consequences. Before Sean reached the entrance, the blaze inside slowed him down. *Impossible. A window?*

Then he saw her. Charlotte, in the alley. A chair in her hands ready to break the window. But flames licked the beams above her head. Charring. Consuming. Sean veered towards her and dove at her waist. Part of the overhanging roof crashed down where Charlotte had stood moments before. Not a second later the rest of the house gave in.

Through billowing blackness the house breathed out a flow of orange cinders that burned Sean's skin, and robbed him of his breath. He got up on his knees, and stretched out his hand towards the pile of burning wood and plaster. No hope. The frightened little eyes were gone. The child was lost.

Charlotte laid a hand on his shoulder and pulled him backwards, away from the searing heat of the pyre.

The darkness took on a red tinge as Sean balled his fists. Eyes narrowed to slits, he sprang to his feet. Through the smoke, he hurled himself at the young man with the torch, who dropped to the ground after the first punch in his stomach. Sean ripped off the wooden mask, but before he could do any more damage, the man's friends hurried over, leaving the shop they had guarded. One of them grabbed Sean's arms, but he could get a good kick at that white blond mop before they caught his legs. Panting and straining against the masked bastards, Sean called them everything he could think of while they helped their friend up.

A young woman stumbled out of the abandoned shop. She looked at the smoking remains of the house, her face frozen in horrified shock. A gurgling cry escaped her lips, and she fainted.

The pink-faced man caught her and put her down gently. "Both of them?" he asked another man, who had come out with the woman. The man nodded.

Sean howled. He jerked his arm free, but someone knocked him out before he could use it.

Sean woke up in his bed in the inn. Charlotte slept in a chair next to him, but she woke up when he moved. Bits and pieces came back to him. The fire. Someone carrying him to the inn through the rain. Someone else applying some kind of salve.

A dull pain in his neck shot up to his head when he tried to get up. *All right, I'll stay still.* The crisp white sheet felt cool against the right part of his neck, which burned as though part of the fire had lodged itself in his skin. Charlotte put a reassuring hand on his arm. He pulled it away.

"Thank you," she said. Her whisper hardly registered.

"I could have saved them."

She cast down her eyes, then shook her head. "No, we were both too late. We would have burned with them, had we entered."

"Who were they?"

"A boy of three and a girl of five. Their mother left them for a minute to pick up a package. She hasn't yet woken up."

The dull pain was now throbbing against the base of his

skull. He closed his eyes. "Why didn't anyone do anything?"

"What could we do? None of us has any weapons, because the Baron doesn't allow them, but attacks like these never happen! They have never dared to come here before. They must have found out the Baron is gone."

"So they're not his men?"

"No, they belong to a group of robbers who normally operate around Sherwood Forest, although I thought they only preyed on rich travellers."

Sherwood Forest? He slowly opened one eye to look at her. Apparently she wasn't joking. Another jolt of pain shot through his brain. Was there any upside to this place? Then he opened both eyes and frowned.

"I *could* have saved them. If I had used magic."

"No! Sean, no."

Why did it please him that the mere mention of the word startled her like that?

Her eyes were wide open, pouring all her fear into his. "Don't say that. Magic is only ever used for personal gain. Nothing good can come of it."

"Then it's about time someone tried to use it for the good of others." He put his hand to his head. "As soon as this headache goes away, that is."

"I'll get you a glass of water." And with that she left the room.

The bar room filled with applause when Sean entered that night. No smiles, no whoops, only people clapping for Sean, making him wish he had stayed in bed. "Why?" he whispered over his shoulder to Charlotte, who'd come to collect him.

"You stood up to them! Because of you they went away. Of course these people are grateful. Even under the circumstances."

"But why was I the only one?" he continued, but she had already left to help Nellie out. Nellie's husband, the bald, mustachioed man who had shown Sean in on his first night, led Sean to a table and put a big glass of cider in front of him. Several people slapped his back, or wanted to shake his hand, making Sean grimace with pain in his neck and shoulder. He tried to smile, but the whole scene left a bitter taste in his mouth.

Just when he was about to ask a total stranger why he had not been more courageous himself, the door opened and a man came in, followed by a scruffy little dog. Although he was a giant of a figure, the intense sadness in his eyes diminished his size considerably. He searched the room, locking eyes with Sean, and came over. Slowly, the noise in the bar room died down.

"I want to thank you for what you tried to do. I…" He lowered his gaze and could say no more.

No introduction was necessary. This wreck of a man must be the father. "Charlotte did as much as I did." Although Sean didn't want to keep the man from his wife any longer than he had to, it would have been unfair not to mention Charlotte. Nobody else seemed to care about her efforts. The man turned to Charlotte.

"Then I thank you too. And so will Mary if… when she wakes up." He swallowed, turned back to the door and rushed out.

Charlotte hugged herself and bit her lips. Sean watched her while the sounds of people talking and even laughing became louder again. She seemed out of place. She seemed to be the only one who really cared what happened to those around her. All the others were too busy leading their own lives to be interested in what happened outside of their little bubble. Their village had been attacked, but the attackers were gone and they had survived relatively unscathed, so now it was time to breathe a sigh of relief and get back to surviving daily life. How could they forget that little round face in the attic window? How could he forget it? How could he forget that he had chosen not to enter that house after all?

His stomach turned. Without touching his cider he left the room to go back upstairs. He doubted a single person noticed.

<h1 style="text-align:center">17</h1>

Hannah hesitated, not knowing how much to tell. She glanced at Lucian, but he had left her to deal with Her Ladyship. Did that mean Hannah would be able trust her? According to a person whose trustworthiness she wasn't certain of to begin with. She couldn't even trust her own mother when it came to this place.

How is dear Minnie? Lady Ethel waited for an answer with eyes so pale, they seemed to be almost transparent. Although there was patience and kindness in them now, that colour was unnerving.

Hannah sighed, making a decision. "My mother is dead."

Lady Ethel clasped her hands together in her lap with a soft 'Oh!'. She seemed sympathetic. She was also Hannah's last chance. If anyone in the village remembered her mother, the chances of them knowing anything about the jewel were very slim. Better get to the point.

"Lady Ethel, my mother took us to the other world when we were very little, but now the Baron has killed her and the only way we can go back is by finding the jewel. Do you know where it is?"

Lady Ethel blinked twice and frowned. "We?"

"My brother Sean and I." Odd to introduce him as her brother. But nice too.

"Minnie took you and your brother to the other world… how?" Then she threw her head back and let out a long, understanding sigh. "With the lost jewel! Of course! I never did believe the rumours. Turns out I was right. Well, there you go. I've been proved right more often, you see. Once, when my John was still alive, we—"

Her expression told Hannah she was about to elaborate on how right she had been then and probably on several other occasions.

"Lady Ethel?"

"Yes, dear?"

"I'm afraid we don't have much time. Lord Pryce is looking for us and could be here any moment. Do you know where my mother might have hidden the jewel?"

She thought for a moment. "How much do you know about what happened?"

"Depressingly little." Hannah gave her all the information Lucian had given her. Roderick's version seemed less trustworthy, poor man. She told Lady Ethel about her mother fleeing from the advances of the older baron, never telling her own daughter who she was, and about her finally being shot by the younger baron.

Lady Ethel listened without interrupting, her back straight, hands in her lap. When Hannah finished, she tutted. "Such a shame."

"Thank you."

Lady Ethel offered Hannah one of the teacups and took one herself, which she held up at chest height. "Ah, yes, that too, of course, I am sorry. But I meant what happened to the older baron. He used to be such a nice man, you know. Well, after he met Harriet, that is. I knew them quite well, since we were neighbours, as it were."

Lucian snorted from his place by the window and she glared at his back. "But let me start at the beginning. As you know by now, some families in this world possess magic. Or perhaps I should say that magic possesses them. But not all of those families have been magics for the same amount of time. The

Pryces though, they are very, very old. From when the two worlds were one, even."

This was news to Hannah, and she raised her eyebrows. But Lady Ethel continued without expanding, only stopping for a tiny sip of tea. "Yes. I don't recall the legend exactly. There was a love affair and a madwoman and they ended up cursed. And as with all magics, they are both appalled by and drawn to their abilities, unable to keep from using it, although they know it will cost them, and cost them dearly."

She sighed and looked at a painting on the wall to her right. "I saw that struggle in my husband as well. It's why we never had any children. He didn't want them growing up with the same inescapable temptation."

Another sip of tea. *I should drink mine.*

"The Pryces were not so conscious about their inheritance. One of them tried to break the curse by transferring it to an object, a jet stone. It took him years to gather the necessary knowledge, and when he finally managed to curse the object, it took all his power and killed him. But the curse on the other family members remained. The older baron grew up with parents more interested in money and alcohol than in him. What they did teach him was that he should learn to use his magic well. It was a part of him whether he liked it or not, so he had better turn it to his advantage. He did. He bought every book on magic he could find and tried the spells on the villagers, for entertainment."

"That can't have made him very popular." Hannah put her empty cup on the coffee table, and hoped she'd be offered another.

"Don't interrupt, dear. Would you like some more tea?" As she poured, Lady Ethel glanced at Lucian. He hadn't touched his cup. Lady Ethel returned to her upright pose.

"Well. And then he met Harriet. Oh!" She smiled and put a hand on her heavy chest. "They were such a handsome couple. And the parties! We never missed one. They were a delight."

"I'm sure." Lucian's voice was just loud enough to be heard.

Lady Ethel huffed and glared, but otherwise ignored him. "They were so much in love. Obviously, she wasn't from around here. Well, you've seen the young baron, his complexion isn't half as dark as hers was. She hated magic, but she loved him, and he gave it all up for her. His parents were gone by then, so he could do as he pleased. Hence the parties. After such a youth, he turned out to be so charming! I remember one time—"

"Charming!" Lucian swung around, bitterness distorting his features.

Lady Ethel drew herself up to her full insignificant height, her pale eyes spitting fire.

"Stop interrupting!" she threw at him. "Do not display to me, Mister Quimper, your high moral fibre."

Jutting his beard forward as if it were a weapon, Lucian took a step forward. "*I* do not live off other people."

"Indeed? I myself have on numerous occasions escaped with barely more than my life. If there is one way of living off others, Mister Quimper, then—"

"Excuse me!" Hannah threw herself almost physically between them. If this went on much longer, Hannah would join in and give them a piece of her own mind. She wasn't often the calm one in these situations, and it wouldn't last very long. "I'm afraid we do have to hurry, Lady Ethel. We wouldn't have come here if there was any other way of finding the jewel before the Baron catches up."

When the buxom noblewoman turned back to Hannah, her expression softened. She passed the parties and went on with her story.

"It all changed when she was expecting their first child. With her family far away, she turned to me for guidance and to Minnie for friendship. We both were happy to give it, but we could not have foreseen the jealousy that grew in the Baron. He demanded his wife's undivided attention. Even if she had given up our friendship, he would still have come to resent little Victor. Unfortunately, he also made it very difficult for her to see anyone else. The parties stopped and she became very lonely. I still have her letters somewhere…” Her voice trailed off, and her gaze rested on a bouquet of pink dried flowers in the corner of the room.

A heavy-ringed hand waved that thought away. “While she became a prisoner in the castle, he made sure he got his fun elsewhere. After the child was born, things took a turn for the worse. Victor took up all of Harriet’s time. And the Baron had never learned by example how a father should act. Bored and disillusioned, he broke the last of his promises and returned to magic.”

She sighed. “After that, her letters got scarcer and I’m not sure about the details.” She looked at Lucian, who had calmed down and was listening to her, resting on the windowsill. “I know Minnie got married and had a little girl—you. One of Harriet’s last letters says that for some reason the Baron became obsessed with Minnie. She had been a friend to them both before, but had rejected first his friendship and later his advances. Then he cursed her. At some point though, she disappeared. All sorts of wild stories started to circulate about how he had killed her and her child. It would have been his first killing. Although it made sense, because more deaths followed soon after, I never really believed it. Looking back on it, I don’t know why I never connected Minnie’s disappearance with the loss of the jewel. The few servants that were left working at the castle made sure that that became common knowledge soon enough. The Baron had lost his jewel, seen by many as the source of his power. They were quick to hope for an end to his reign. Some of them even tried to take him on, hence the killings.”

Lady Ethel took a tiny bite from a biscuit. “The rest of what I know is hearsay. Harriet’s letters stopped and we were no longer welcome in Nottingham Castle. When Victor was twelve years old, she died. Whether he killed her or not, I don’t know. She was determined to keep her son from magic, but he would have been the first to withstand its allure. And with a father like that…

"After her death, though, the Baron became more or less a recluse. He dismissed the few remaining servants and let his twelve-year-old son deal with the affairs concerning the lands. Years later Victor decided to build a lace mill. Some said it was a whim, others said he wasn't content with the wealth he possessed, but it created work and so they went. For two years they endured accident after accident, one more serious than the other, but after a young girl died, he closed it down."

She nibbled the biscuit again. "That was six years ago. People were just beginning to breathe freely again, but now… another death. And in the other world, too." She tutted and shook her head.

Hannah waited for more, but she was done with her story. Hannah tried again.

"Do you have any idea where she might have hidden the jewel?"

Lady Ethel stared at her. "Obviously not. I just told you I never connected the two occurrences."

Hannah wanted to cry. Sitting through the entire history lesson hadn't brought her one bit closer to finding that blasted jewel and getting out of here.

"But," Lady Ethel continued after pushing the last bit of biscuit into her mouth, "can't you feel it?"

Feel it. Hannah raised an eyebrow. "Feel it?"

"If you are Minnie's daughter, and you most certainly are, then the curse rests on you as well. The Baron would have needed the jewel's power to curse anyone. So, since you have been cursed with the jewel, you should be able to feel its lure."

Hannah stared at Lady Ethel, then at Lucian, who raised both eyebrows, then back at Lady Ethel. "I don't feel anything."

"Then you'll have to concentrate more. Whoever or whatever curses you is linked to you. My husband inherited magic from his mother and could feel her call long after she had been buried. The Pryces are linked to each other, but also to the jewel. You have been cursed with the power of the jewel, so you should feel it. Close your eyes."

This was silly. But with those pale eyes on her, how could Hannah not obey? She closed her eyes. The only sensation she got was being very aware of two pairs of eyes on her. *Concentrate more. Open yourself to any kind of pull.* Her first thought was for Sean. If she had a link to anyone, it should be him. And it was easy to imagine him as well. Look, there he was, all—Hannah gasped and opened her eyes, expecting to see Sean as close as he had been a second before. Of course, he wasn't there, but she could still feel his presence, his essence almost. Beside her. Practically inside her.

"What is it?" Lucian looked worried.

"Just… Sean." Her hands were shaking. Sean was never going to know this. He would tease her blind if he knew the powerful reaction he had caused.

Lady Ethel nodded. "Yes, I told you you would have a connection to your family. And to the Pryces. Try again, try to go around your brother this time."

Hannah closed her eyes once more. It took her a while to muster up the courage to let this strong sensation wash over her again. But now, when Hannah saw Sean, she knew what to expect. After a while she could put her anguish over him aside, and search for something else. And something came. Her mind's eye clouded over and a chill made the little hairs on her arms stand up. Orange flashes pierced the dark, growing ever colder. Did someone laugh? A nasty, derisive laugh grew louder, but Hannah could see no-one laughing. The sound echoed in her ears, close enough to almost feel it. Hannah opened her eyes, and the laugh was gone. Lucian and Lady Ethel exchanged a dark look. Hannah's teeth were chattering, and she rubbed her arms to try and regain some warmth.

"Did you see it?" Lucian asked. Hannah shook her head.

"Where is it?" asked Lady Ethel.

Hannah pointed over Lucian's shoulder. "That way".

Lucian let out a breath, glancing over his shoulder, out the window. "Good, we'll go there." Pausing, he addressed Lady Ethel. "Could Victor track Hannah this way?"

"I should say so, yes. The bond may not be as strong, but he should certainly be able to feel her."

"Then we'd better leave straight away," he said, bowing ever so slightly to Lady Ethel.

"Oh, but you must take some food. Mary?" The maid stood and left the room. "I'm sorry you couldn't stay longer, dear. If you do remain, remember to visit. It's always just me and her." She gestured to the knitting the maid had left behind.

Smiling, Hannah confirmed that she would, and Lady Ethel clapped her hands. Despite her harshness to Lucian, it was hard not to like the vivacious woman.

"Would you mind lending Mary a hand? Make sure she packs enough cheese. She's always so frugal with the cheese. I'd like a word with Mister Quimper."

Lucian's cheeks flushed. *Again!* "I'm not sure that's possible, milady. Lord Pryce has not found us yet, but every minute we stay will bring him closer."

"Let him come." Lady Ethel stuck her little round chin in the air. "I'm not afraid of him. He's left me alone all these years, but in the end, what can he do to me that won't be welcomed?"

With all the emotion already coursing through Hannah's body, she thought it best to step away from the pain in that last remark. If everything went wrong and she had to stay, she'd make a point of visiting again, but right now Hannah had to practice a little self preservation.

In the corridor, she took a right, passing rows of portraits. Now that she knew how to find the jewel, she wanted to get to it as quickly as possible, and take herself and Sean back home. But she was grateful for Lady Ethel's generous offer of a hamper.

She glanced at the paintings. Nobody here had thought of a new fashion in all those years. Corsets and capes all the way.

A portrait at the end of the corridor caught her eye: a dark blond man in burgundy suit threw the viewer a dapper look. It almost made her smile, but Hannah had seen that look before, be it slightly less presumptuous. The portrait was of Roderick. Hannah halted, put her hands on her hips and took a closer look. It could have been painted yesterday, he looked exactly the same. Then Hannah looked at the nameplate. Roderick, Lord Pryce, baron of Beeston.

18

How could she have let herself be fooled like that? She wanted to scream! She wanted to abandon all plans and race back to her brother. But instead she found herself limp and unable to take independent action.

Lady Heanor's maid packed them a hamper full of goodies, which Lucian eyed suspiciously, but loaded onto his horse nonetheless. He then more or less loaded Hannah onto her horse, and set them both off in what was apparently a northerly direction.

All this, Hannah barely noticed. After the initial shock she'd been angry at herself, angry at Roderick, angry at Victor and again angry at herself. When that passed, she was left with bewilderment and a profound worry for Sean.

He didn't know about Roderick. Once again, he had befriended the one person sure to pull him down. This time, however, Hannah had been fooled as well. This time, Hannah had to get *him* out of a bad situation because *she* had made the same mistake. All those times she had belittled her brother for not being able to tell a good person from a bad one stung her memory.

'He is still in the castle,' Roderick had said about Victor's father. In her eagerness to believe anything bad about Victor, Hannah had immediately assumed that he had him locked up somewhere. How could she not have seen that they were working together?

Switching the reins to one hand, Hannah rubbed her eyes. There were no woods in this direction, mostly meadows that gradually became patchier, dotted with rocks and fens. They passed a small flock of ragged sheep, whose frayed wool immediately reminded her of her brother. The urge to run back to him was so strong, that she wanted to turn her horse around there and then. Only the memory of her last action on impulse prevented her from doing so again. Even if riding back to Sean shouldn't have immediately dangerous consequences, it was probably better to think this over first.

But thinking meant stalling, which meant going with Lucian for the time being. Finding out about Roderick had shaken what little trust she had in Lucian as well. But what were the alternatives? Running back to Sean, only to risk facing the Baron there with no more means of defeating him than before? Going for the jewel by herself, now that she knew how to find it? The last time she depended on no-one but herself, she immediately got robbed. More than that, she really wanted to be able to trust someone, anyone, in this intensely lonely place. And that was exactly what worried her.

A pang of longing for her own world made her stomach cramp. Was it this place that made her unable to read people? Why couldn't they be more like Ben? Trustworthy and predictable. Another pang, but this one was different. Definitely guilt. It was time she accepted that what happened with Ben was exclusively her fault. Inconsiderate and selfish. Great. Inability to read others gained her insight into herself. Why couldn't it have been something positive?

She had been horrible to Ben. He had become such a familiar face during all the holidays together, all the time spent after work together, and all the dinners at Aunt Jess's—Mum's—, that even she hadn't seen Hannah's feelings change. He'd become more like a brother than a boyfriend. One she maybe kissed a little differently.

She had loved their holidays together, the donkey safaris, the mountain climbing, the horseback riding and the archery. But getting married? His proposal had done one good thing: show her that this was not what she wanted. At all.

Though he was perfectly sweet, perfectly reliable and not even boring, she kept thinking: *Do something naughty. Come on, do something unexpected for a change.* She wasn't going to marry a man whose every move she could predict!

But her ignorance had cost her a dear friend. Hannah pulled her cape snug, trying yet again, but this time knowingly, to deflect anything that made her look bad.

The grey sky had begun to darken. Did Lucian expect her to ride all through the night? She was still a bit jet-lagged and didn't feel very tired yet, but a flight-by-night was not very appealing.

"Do you think it'll be far away?"

He turned his head towards her, but then got distracted by something behind them. "I shouldn't think so, no."

How would he know, anyway? "We'd better find it before Sean does anything stupid. What is so interesting that you can't look at me?" Hannah turned around in the saddle, but the only thing she saw were some riders in the distance.

"It's probably nothing." He cast another glance over his shoulder.

"Who are they? Do you know them?"

"Hm. It looks like they're Lord North's men. He's one of the Baron's neighbours. They have been known to demand payment for using roads, even outside of the lord's territory." His hand went to the flap of the saddle bag containing the pistol. He had reloaded before they left Lady Heanor's.

Hannah looked back once more. The three stocky men in brown bowler hats advanced quickly. Lucian took her horse's rein and pulled her to the side in order to let the horses pass. They slowed, obvious thunderclouds over their heads. One of them clutched his arm, another had a black eye. Rather recent too, by the looks of it.

Lucian nodded a greeting, but Hannah couldn't help staring. Who had they been fighting? Each other? Didn't look like either of them won. They glared at her, and for a moment Hannah thought they would stop, especially when Lucian lifted the leather flap. Then they accelerated and rode on in silence.

"No toll today." Hannah whispered at Lucian when there was enough distance between them.

He gave her a little smile, but kept his eyes on the men. "Looks like the kind of damage my boys would do. Or might have done if they were around."

Hannah squinted at him. Was that a slip of the tongue, or a deliberate hint? Looks like they weren't as alone as Hannah had thought. Now all she had to do was decide whether that made her feel threatened or protected.

Around her, night was falling, covering heather Hannah was sure concealed marshland underneath. Protected sounded good, for once. She had tried so hard to be wary. But his calm control invited her to trust him. Apart from robbing her, which he had apologised for, he had tried to help her. He had even taken her to see Lady Ethel, in spite of their mutual dislike. And now he was helping her find the jewel, which wouldn't be any good to him because he didn't have magic. *If* he was to be believed.

She wanted to believe him. What he said seemed to make sense, and he did have Aunt J—her mother's portrait. If she could get him to talk, he might have some of the answers she so desperately craved.

"Why did you never ask how I got here?"

He moved in the saddle. "Will you tell me now?"

Hannah gave him a redacted version of stumbling through the portal after Victor had killed her mum, being taken to the castle and escaping after Sean had been shot. She clenched her fists around the reins when she got to the crucial bit. "But why didn't he kill me?"

Lucian's usual pause lasted even longer after that question. Hannah's horse shook her head, as if she didn't know either.

"I'm not sure." That was useful. "There is one other thing you should know. It's the reason why your mother left when she did. You already know of her condition at the time. The Baron... has reason to believe that the child is his."

Hannah's eyes widened. "I thought you said she didn't want him!"

"She did not."

"Oh." Hannah swallowed. "I see." Yet another thing her mum had had to bear alone all those years. "So Roderick thinks Sean is his son? But he already has Victor, so what does he want with him?"

"As far as I know, the Baron was unaware that Minnie was with child when she left. But it must have been an easy calculation when he met Sean and realised he was Minnie's son. I really don't know what he would want with him, but it might have been the reason to spare your lives."

Hannah let that sink in for a few minutes. If it was true, then Sean had saved her life without even knowing it. And what was she doing to save his? Wasn't it more important to go back and warn Sean about this than to find some old jewel that may or may not have the power to take them back? Roderick could be hatching plans for Sean while his guard was down.

Hannah halted her horse and closed her eyes, concentrating on her brother. When she saw him, he stretched out his hand and smiled, but it was a very sad smile. At least he was still there, though. Hannah tried to tell him to hold on. Did this bond have any telepathic qualities? Sean probably wasn't even aware of it at all. Why would he be looking for her voice in his head? If that's how telepathy worked.

With considerable difficulty, Hannah pushed thoughts about him to the side, and tried to concentrate on the jewel. Knowing what to expect, she opened her eyes quickly after sensing its pull. That nasty laugh could go bother someone else.

Lucian had stopped as well and was waiting for her.

"Still that way." Hannah gestured ahead into the gloom. Even right in front of her, Lucian had become a silhouette against the granite sky. The sloshing of hooves on the wet road continued on.

Just a little further. They could be almost there. The pull Hannah felt from the jewel was a lot stronger than the one Sean exerted, though she wanted Sean's to be stronger. Did that mean that the jewel was closer? She patted her horse on the neck and let it walk on.

Five minutes later Lucian halted at a vague pale splotch in the darkness.

"This is the best shelter we'll find around here, I'm afraid. You seem to be leading us to the coast. If we go that far, we'll find some more inns, but these parts are mostly inhabited by sheep."

The coast? they hadn't gone that far, had they? This travelling by horse must be faster than Hannah thought. Then again, there didn't seem to be many similarities between this world and hers, apart from some place names and their relative location to each other. This Nottingham could be much closer to the coast than Hannah was used to. Clearly those Dividers only had a faint idea of what they were doing.

She dismounted and trudged towards the pale shape, leading Allegra by the reins. A weathered cross on the door was covered in dirt and cobwebs.

Trying the latch and finding it wouldn't give, Lucian put his shoulder to the wood. The door flew open, and he stepped inside to light a candle.

Hannah found herself in a small chapel. The whole space couldn't be larger than about a hundred square feet. An old wooden cross still hung on the wall opposite the door, but the single kneeler had been cast aside, broken.

"Heavy heart," she remarked.

"Organised religion is a thing of the past," Lucian remarked when he saw her staring at the sorry kneeler. "People still believe, but they have better things to do than to talk about it."

He went outside to unsaddle the horses, and shoved a blanket in her arms upon his return.

Hannah hesitated. The blanket reminded her of the person who put it in there. Why had he sent her for the jewel? If it was really this powerful, why had he not gone to find it himself long ago? Or sent his son after it? Maybe he just wanted her out of the way. But then why had Victor come to Highlow looking for her?

"Shouldn't we keep moving?" she asked. Not a very pleasant prospect if he agreed, but anything to hasten her return to Sean. And if she was totally honest with herself, the appearance of Lord North's men only made it more clear to her that the Baron could catch up to them any moment. Lucian and the apparent proximity of his men made her feel slightly safer, but she doubted they would really be a match for the Baron. They'd have done something about him if they were.

"Travelling at night is not something any sane person would do around here. Or even an insane person. The landscape is different from here on. It's too easy to lose your footing and end up in a bog. Local people with lamps have been known to disappear that way. We're probably safe for now, but we need to get moving early in the morning."

Lucian settled himself on a blanket in a corner. An insect was drawn to the candle flame, but came too close and sizzled.

"There is no moth!" Hannah couldn't help herself. Her imitation of that harpy at the doctor's office was out before she knew it.

Lucian gave a bark of laughter. "It's not entirely her fault," he said with a smile. "Superstitions die hard. Those little white moths are harbingers of death, according to most people you'll talk to. We see them in the forest all the time. Then again," he added with a sigh, "we see loved ones die more often than we like, too."

Hannah sat on her own blanket. "So, you really live in the forest?"

"We move around, mostly." He opened the bottle of wine from Lady Ethel's hamper and took a swig. "But the forest provides the best security."

Hannah took the bottle when he offered it, but studied him again before she drank. She still couldn't see it. Neither the ruthless robber nor the defender of the poor seemed to be a role that would fit him. He didn't like the nobles, but didn't speak too favourably of the common people either.

They ate in silence for a while. Had it only been two days since she inadvertently left her own comfortable world? And now she was hiding in a chapel with a criminal. Hannah took another sip of wine for warmth.

"Why don't you have a normal job? I mean, how did you become a…" Hannah gestured up and down his figure.

"That is not important."

Oh great, no answer again. This would be a long night. Hannah stretched out on the floor and tried to find a comfortable position. No luck.

Lucian stroked his beard. "I do what I do because the people around me need someone to take care of them."

"Oh, so you are doing it for them. How noble."

Hannah yawned. Although she was tired from riding all day after a night of too little sleep, she was reluctant to close her eyes. She'd tried focusing on the Baron to find out how close he was, but he must have found a way to scramble his signal. Nothing came through. And the more she focused on the jewel, the more space it seemed to take up in her mind. The last few times the cackling had started only a few seconds after she'd closed her eyes. She feared it would soon be there without her even focusing. No wonder Mum had left the bloody thing behind.

"I'm sorry, I didn't mean to be sarcastic," she said. "I just thought the nobles would take care of them."

He raised an eyebrow and huffed.

Okay, maybe not the Baron, but… "Lady Ethel really cares

about what happens to the villagers."

Leaning back against the wall, he nodded. "True. She is one of the few nobles who does. Unfortunately her influence is minimal, as the lands all belong to the Baron. And he at least meets with representatives from the villages under his authority every month. Most just collect the taxes. So I try to give the people back a little."

Hard to believe there were people acting worse than the Baron. "Aren't you afraid they'll use magic on you?" Look at her, talking about magic as if it was as common as sheep.

He showed a boyish grin, which looked attractive, but didn't seem to suit him at all, especially in the candlelight. "I know what I'm doing."

I bet he does. "Don't you have a queen, or a king, or something, to keep the nobles in check?"

He laughed. "We are... between kings at the moment. But they are never much good anyway. They are either someone like Lord North, or a puppet. North is actually a contender for the crown, I believe, as is Lord Pryce. Titles mean less than possession, especially of land."

"Who's Lord North?"

"One of the Baron's neighbours. Technically we are not on his land, but this area belongs to a very old Viscount with no direct heirs. It's common knowledge that Lord North will take possession as soon as the Viscount finds eternal rest."

"Can he do that?"

Lucian shrugged. "He is the most powerful of the neighbouring nobles. Legality doesn't mean much to someone like him."

Such a wonderful place to live, this. Hannah yawned again. It must only be nine, if not earlier. How could she be so tired?

"The people must really love you."

The smile tightened. Rolling himself up in his blanket, he mumbled, "Good night."

Hannah lay staring into the dark for several hours, putting

off the eerie laughter. Every so often she glanced in Lucian's direction. He was going with her, solely because he knew her mother once. Was he the friend he said he had been to her? Lady Ethel had called him a lout. Hannah couldn't imagine her mother being friends with a lout. But she couldn't have imagined her lying, either.

And what about this father business? Lucian said the Baron killed him. Hard to grieve for a father you've never known. But what if the doctor was right and Lucian was… Would she be happy or sad to have found him? Would it explain why she'd wanted to be close to him since she first saw him?

At long last she dozed off.

19

No matter how much everyone else seemed to think Sean was some kind of hero, one person was not impressed. Ben had stalked into the breakfast room when Sean was already done eating, and had found a seat at another table. Halfway through his meal, he picked up his plate and joined Sean.

"I hear you got into a fight."

"A fight?" Of everything that happened yesterday, a fight did not stand out to Sean.

Ben raised an eyebrow. "You don't remember attacking someone on the village square?"

"Wha…" Sean stuttered. Was Ben accusing him? "He was a… He'd… He…"

"Uhhuh." Ben shoved a forkful of egg in his mouth.

He was. Ben was taking the side of the devil-masked idiot. What had Hannah ever seen in this guy? "Are you serious?"

Ben leaned in, staring Sean in the eyes. "Why are you still here? Why are you such a loser, waiting for Hannah to get you out of trouble again? These people here,"—he gestured around him—"they have no idea. They think you're something, because you went for some guy who didn't see you coming. You were just acting out your anger, and they took you out in no time at all. They could have killed you, you know. Then what kind of hero would you have been?"

He was right. Sean did not feel like a hero at all. Heroes succeed in what they're doing. Sean had just… been there. Instead of looking for Hannah and finding a way to get back home, he had gone after Charlotte, whom he only knew a few days. He had told Hannah he would get her out of the castle, but had he really tried? Or had he been too easily persuaded by the defeatist attitude of the people in the pub? He had let himself be convinced that they had neither the means nor the courage to storm the castle. That he should wait to find out what the Baron wanted with her. That he should wait until his arm had healed a little. Was his wound really so bad that he couldn't have stood up for his own cousin?

Ben huffed. "You know, I don't care what you are going to do. I am going to find Hannah, so we can all leave this sickening place. You just stay here and wait for us." He threw down his fork as he got up and left.

Rubbing his arm, Sean watched him go. He searched for something to say in his defence, but found nothing. When Charlotte entered with another client's breakfast, he still sat in silence. She came over to ask him if there was anything he wanted, but when he said nothing, she brought him some tea and left him in peace.

Peace was not the right word though. Stirring his tea, Sean stared at the man in the corner eating his breakfast. Had he been there yesterday? Had he done anything at all? Any of these people, what had they done?

He should just tell them what he thought of them. Bunch of cowards. Was it his fault the children had died after all? If one of *them* had acted sooner, there wouldn't even have been a fire.

The tea was cold before he caught Charlotte staring at him from behind the counter. He gestured her to come closer.

"Why did you leave? Yesterday, at the factory. Why did you go without telling me?"

Her eyes opened wide. "I did tell you. I saw the smoke, and said I was going to check. But you were talking to Ben, you must not have heard me."

She blushed and smiled, returning to polishing glasses. Sean didn't remember her saying anything. Had she really done so? She hadn't made an effort to make sure he knew, in any case. And now, even she had returned to the order of the day, as if nothing had happened.

Sean balled his fist under the table. "Why are you all so passive?" he burst out.

Charlotte hurried over, and sat down opposite him, putting her soft little hand over his. "People die. Bad things happen. There isn't really anything we can do but clean up afterwards. But we hope. With every new thing that happens, bad or good, we hope for something to change. You're here now. You've given us hope too. And Hannah is looking for a way to help us, we all hope that she will succeed."

Hannah the saviour again. "What good is that? You can hope till snow turns green. For all you know Hannah has found a way back to our world and you'll never see her again. Why don't you do something?"

What was that look? Pity? Hurt? No hope, that much was certain.

Hoping for Hannah to come rescue them. *Of course, that's what she does, isn't it?* Come to the aid of people who were silly enough to get themselves into trouble. In a world without magic she just might have managed it too. And they probably would have given her a statue. Wouldn't she have loved that.

But here, she didn't have a clue what she was up against. Or perhaps by now she did. Who knew if she was even alive.

The fact that that was a worrying thought surprised him. And then the surprise surprised him. Of course it was a worrying thought. She was like his sister. She could take the blood from under his fingernails, but she also made him laugh. Why had he not worried about her more? She was always so confident, but this time she really did need his help.

He got up and stomped out without saying goodbye, not noticing the scruffy little dog that followed him.

Sean stared at the old books lying on the table in front of him. One way or another they were going to get out of here. And no other way would work unless they used the one that involved magic. Just once. That was all they needed. If they did it right. And how were they supposed to know what to do if no-one would look into this? Who said that they were right and he was wrong? Just because they were afraid of it.

He leaned forward, opened one of the books, and sniggered. This one was illustrated.

When Roderick came in an hour later, half the books were scattered across the table, earmarked or opened and face down. Sean looked up.

"Where have you been?"

Raking a hand through his hair, Roderick sat down at the other end of Sean's bench. "Attempting to reopen the passage-way. It's damp and narrow, but it allows me more living space than my master realised when he cursed me. At least, it used to." He sighed. "Where's your friend?"

"Gone after Hannah," Sean said, returning to his reading.

"No, I meant your pretty friend. I was under the impression that you two had become quite inseparable."

"We're not." Sean did not look up, but stopped reading. If she was only going to nag him about this, he didn't need her around. One girl telling him what not to do was bad enough. A replacement was not necessary.

"Is that one of the Baron's books?" Roderick asked in one of those I-know-it's-none-of-my-business-but tones.

"Yes."

"But I thought you said…"

"Yes!" Sean snapped, slamming the book shut. "I know, magic is not the answer. But the portal is closed. If we want to go back home, we will have to use magic. And I'm going to make sure we can."

Taken aback, Roderick blinked. Then his eye wandered over

the titles in front of him. Most of the books Sean had put aside were introductions, but there were also a few which assumed more expertise on the subject.

"Just how much do you think you will learn in the few days your cousin is away?"

Sean shrugged. "It's not like I have anything else to do."

Roderick pursed his lips. "I wouldn't say that…"

Sean glanced at him. Roderick had been in that castle alone for too long. There's a time for everything, and this was not the time for sweet girls. Sweet, yes. And… decorative. Decorative but meddling. He gave his head a small shake.

"So I've been reading a little bit already," he said instead, "and it seems like it's all about some form of control over the elements. So you were right, no demons to worry about."

"You didn't attempt any of it in the village, I hope?"

The village. Every time Sean remembered it his thoughts turned black. He hesitated. "No. They'd probably lock me up before I could turn to the dark side."

Roderick tapped his finger on the table. "The dark side…"

Roderick slid closer to Sean. A low growl stopped him before he reached his side. Sean turned towards a small scruffy dog cowering under his chair and shushed.

"Where did you find… it?" Roderick wrinkled his nose and pointed at the little quivering bag of bones.

"Apparently it was the kids' dog. It stayed outside the pub all night and followed me as soon as I came out. Can't get rid of it."

"The… kids?"

Sean related the events of the day before, trying to keep a neutral tone, but his voice broke when he remembered the toddler's face.

"And now this creature has decided to constantly remind me of what happened." He scolded the little dog. Stupid animal. Why hadn't it stayed with the kids' parents? Did it think he needed comforting? If it did, it wasn't working. Instead, it made him seriously uncomfortable. He wished it would go away, but couldn't get himself to throw it out. *But don't think I'll name you or anything.* The dog nudged his ankle and settled down, still casting a suspicious eye at Roderick, who returned the look.

"I am sorry, my boy." He sighed. "How could my master have let this happen?"

Sean threw him a look of disbelief. What would the Baron have against it? He had tried to kill his own servant. Why would he care about some village children he didn't know? Sometimes what went on in Roderick's head was beyond Sean.

Perhaps it was easier for Roderick to believe there was some good in his master. But the longer he stayed in this world, the more useless Sean felt. He'd wanted to show the world he could be the responsible one, but so far he had made zero difference. Would the machine really stop working if this tiny cog jumped out? Even in his own world he'd always felt more like a spare part.

The only thing that could set him apart might be this magic thing. He opened his book again, but it took considerable effort to let go of enough bitterness towards the villagers to be able to read anything.

About an hour later he looked up and pushed the book away. This one was boring. Who needs magic to communicate over long distances if you've got a phone? He stretched and looked around, then remembered, and felt under his chair. The little dog yipped when he grabbed it and put it on the table in front of him.

Roderick had been dozing in a chair by the window, but he now opened one eye.

"You people should take more trips into our world. We've found other solutions to some of these problems."

Roderick smiled. "Old magic. Even here it is sometimes made redundant by new discoveries. But there are still some diamonds among the coal."

"I thought all magic was bad?" Sean grinned. Maybe Roderick

saw some good in magic after all. "Come here, I want to see if I can conjure something up."

He put his fists on his hips and considered the little creature in front of him. "I wonder if I'm going to need a wand. The book didn't say."

"Do remember, my boy, that there is no guarantee that you will be able to use any of this. There may not be any truth to what I've told you."

But Sean was in no mood to listen. He pointed at the dog. "According to the book, I need to…" What was it again? Stepping aside, Sean reached for one of the books he'd read earlier.

Roderick shot up. "You're not going to—"

But Sean waved his concerns away. "Don't worry, I won't hurt him. I just want to see if this works."

Roderick frowned and leaned back in the chair, crossing his arms over his chest. "I can understand your curiosity and your eagerness to try your power, but do you really think you will be able to achieve anything at all after reading half a book and never seeing magic in action before?"

Sean tried to keep the dog still, but it kept licking his fingers, until he took a step back. "Now, stay!"

Wagging its thin tail, the dog stood on the edge of the table, waiting for Sean to come close again. Sean held his hands up to calm the dog down, then realised he needed the book that was left on the table behind Dog and had to calm it down again. Book in his left hand, he read a few words and then stretched out his right towards Dog. Shifting from one foot to the other, he looked at the book and at Dog in turns and grinned.

"Okay, so…" Hand still stretched towards Dog, he fixated on the little creature's face. *Concentrate. Give the subject your order. Visualise.* Finding out that that was what the ancient book wanted him to do had taken him a while. *Don't think about that. Concentrate.* For a full minute he stared at it, but other than that its tail stopped wagging, nothing happened. He dropped both hands, closed the book and laughed.

"Right. That doesn't work."

Roderick shook his head. Looked like the Victorian version of an eye roll. But he had moved to the edge of his seat. He must believe Sean was capable of something after all. Well, after a bit more practice, probably. Sean turned back to Dog and rubbed its chin.

"Try holding it." Roderick's voice sounded tense.

Sean raised his eyebrows. "Does that help?"

"It might."

Sean scratched his own chin, shrugged, and picked the dog up, holding it in outstretched hands. Trying to get it to stop licking his fingers had no effect, so he took its little head in his hand and turned it to face him. After about twenty seconds the animal started to squirm, trying to pull out of his grasp.

Sean set Dog back on the table and planted his fists on his hips, pout to one side.

"I don't think..."

But Dog shook his head, then reached over his back and started chasing his tail.

Sean cried out and pointed at him, grinning widely at Roderick. "That's what I wanted him to do! Look, he's really doing it! It worked!"

20

Sean Taylor, dog master extraodinaire! Now who's a spare part? He eyed the dog as it ran around in circles on the table. This was unreal. Roderick rose from his seat and advanced towards the table, a deep ridge between his eyebrows. He poked the little dog in the side, to see if it would stop, but, if anything, the animal only put more ferociousness into its action. Clearly not ordinary canine behaviour.

Roderick put his hand to his mouth and shook his head. "Unbelievable."

Sean still wore his biggest smile as the little creature snapped at its tail and finally caught it. He yelped, but attacked it again. Sean's smile melted away. Growling, the dog dug its teeth into its own tail.

"No. No, stop." That was a little overenthusiastic. Sean shoved his hand under the dog's belly and whisked him off the table, but as soon as it hit the floor, the animal continued snapping and attacking his tail. Why didn't it stop? This wasn't Sean's intention. Had he done something wrong? He checked the book again, but found nothing. Roderick wasn't any help either. His hand was still covering his mouth, but for some reason his eyes seemed to be smiling. Did he think this was funny?

"Stop, Dog!" Sean picked it up again, and peered in its eyes. "I command you to stop!"

But when he let go, determination took over, and with the

next bite Dog took off a piece of flesh. The creature whimpered and licked its tail, drops of blood spattering the floor. For a moment, it seemed the curse was broken, but the next, Dog spun round again, snapping and growling with a sickening fierceness.

Panic turned Sean's stomach. *How do I make it stop?* Was it his fault? Or the dog's? Eyes wild, Sean stepped toward the little dog and shoved it with his foot, soft at first, then harder when it still wouldn't listen. The little thing would kill itself. He couldn't let that happen. Whether it was his fault or not.

"Stop! You stupid… stop!"

A little voice slit through the pounding in his ears. "No!"

Sean stiffened, then glanced over his shoulder at the horrified orange-haired boy in the door frame.

"Georgie!" Sean cried out. "Georgie, I didn't hurt him! Look, he's—"

Tears streaming down his face, the little boy launched himself forward and scooped up Dog.

"He's bleeding!" he hissed at Sean, clutching Dog close to his chest. Dog shivered in Georgie's arms, finally seeming to calm down. Sean tried to touch the boy's shoulder, but Georgie shied away and bolted for the door. On the threshold he turned around, felt in his pocket and threw something at Sean before he ran off. It hit Sean in the chest and dropped at his feet.

Shaking, Sean took a deep breath. Relief that the dog had finally stopped hurting itself was quickly followed by concern. If Georgie told anyone what he'd seen, would they believe him?

Sean picked up the carrot whistle he had made Georgie the day before, and frowned. "I'd better go after him."

He caught up to Georgie not far from the factory. The boy didn't want to speak to him at first, turning his back to Sean to protect the little dog cowering in his arms.

"Georgie, please talk to me. I really didn't want to hurt him. He was biting his own tail, I was trying to get him to stop. Please believe me. Look, there's blood in his mouth. Doesn't that show you he did it himself?"

Georgie looked, and bit his lip. If he believed Sean's explanation, he might be persuaded of Sean's innocence. But with any critical thought at all, that blood could easily have come into the dog's mouth when he licked his wound.

Sean let out a breath when Georgie asked, "But why did he do it?"

"I don't know." It wasn't an actual lie. "But I was only trying to help him. Do you believe that?"

Georgie nodded and sniffed.

"Georgie, I'm going to ask you not to tell anyone what you saw me do. Will you do that?"

The boy frowned. "I mustn't lie."

"I know, I know. But you thought I wanted to hurt him when you saw it, and now you know that's not true. And if you tell someone else what you saw, they will think I'm a villain too. Do you think I'm a villain?"

The little head shake wasn't entirely convincing.

"So you won't tell anyone?"

That shake was more determined.

"Look, I've been reading about magic, and you know what? Maybe I can make your little friend better!"

He shouldn't have said that. Georgie shrieked, his face scrunched up as he clamped the dog against his chest. He stumbled backwards, then took off towards the windmill.

Sean watched him go. Great. Now they weren't only afraid of magic, they were starting to be afraid of him.

* * *

In the course of Sean's studies over the past hours, books had scattered over several of the long dining tables, and even over a couple of the comfortable chairs. Roderick eyed the volume Sean had been using. Sean had chosen it quite well. It dealt with the basics of learning magic, explaining its structure first, and then starting with some exercises in its first stage, manipulating animals. Roderick had read this when he was about ten years old, but Sean had not had the advantage of growing up surrounded by magic. Yet what he had accomplished on his first try had been astounding.

Roderick smiled, remembering. That first reaction to magic. The excitement of trying something new, and finally succeeding, was mesmerising. Playing with something so full of promise, so full of potential. First as a means to do good, then as a source of power. And Sean had given him an impressive display of power. Raw power, in dire need of restriction and guidance. A little spark of hope drove away some of Roderick's fatalist darkness. Guidance, yes…

Hadn't life been amusing? Death wasn't nearly as much fun. It literally and figuratively took the magic out of existence. Life had lost its challenge. All these years he'd wondered if he'd have been better off with an alternative afterlife, although he'd never given it a second thought when he was alive. What is the point of living if you can't enjoy it? And who enjoys thinking about death?

And then life after death turned out to be real. Instead of better, it turned out to be like ordinary life, only limited beyond even the life of a normal person. No magic, but no freedom either. No satisfaction. No pleasure of any kind. Where was the fun?

But now, finally, he had begun to hope. Fun was as yet too much to look for, but Roderick had relished his long-forgotten ability to manipulate, even without magic. Perhaps these largely other-worldlings had not been the greatest challenge, unused as they were to the advantages of this world, but they turned out to be entertaining and full of potential nonetheless. If there was another way, then perhaps he would have taken it. But in this life, or death, as the case may be, Roderick had learned to put himself first.

Memories of times when he had changed people's minds,

just with some words and a few simple gestures, filled his mind. With power came an air of authority, making it easier to turn their will to your advantage, which in turn created more power. That power was almost within his grasp once more and he was hungry for it, so hungry. At last he would be able to eat again and not feel the same emptiness afterwards, to drink again and actually get drunk. To touch, and take, and feel satisfied.

Brushing his finger over the books, Roderick looked up when Sean entered. It would take a considerable amount of restraint on Roderick's part to lead Sean through these first steps and not skip ahead, now that the boy had shown such ability. But control was imperative. He'd managed quite well up till now, and this next move was critical.

Sean plonked down in a chair, and Roderick enquired after the boy and the dog, a social obligation Sean would surely appreciate.

"I don't know," was the answer. "I don't think he believes that I never intended to hurt that dog. Ah well. Stupid mutt has found a new master."

Lost in thought, he pulled up his knee, and bit on one of his fingernails.

Tapping the table with one finger, Roderick considered Sean's demeanour. The boy was shaken by this first experience of his power. An expected reaction, but one that needed to be pruned.

"Of course you didn't mean to hurt it. You didn't even know if you had magic at all." He paused and waited for Sean to look at him. "But you do."

Sean pulled up one corner of his mouth and huffed. He stared at his shaking hands. "Yeh. Great."

"You could make a difference."

Too soon. Sean threw his hands in the air and made a face. "Oh sure, I could make all the dogs eat themselves. Gather round for the spectacle of the century!"

"No, no, no, I don't mean that. You'd have to practice, naturally, but do you not see? You could stand up to the Baron."

"Oh come off it. I'm trying to get away from here, I'm not going against a man with years of experience in this. I'm going to look up how to make a portal and that's it. As soon as Hannah comes back, we're out of here, and that'll be my contribution to this whole mess."

He rubbed his face with both hands, and bent forward to take the book from the little table, but Roderick placed his hand flat on the cover. He caught Sean's gaze and held it.

"Do you think Hannah will let you leave once she knows you have the power to help the people here?"

Sean frowned. "She might, or she might not. I don't care what Hannah wants. She'll listen to me for a change. If I'm able to create a portal, she'd be mad not to go through."

Roderick did not answer immediately. He held Sean's gaze a few moments longer and narrowed his eyes, wondering how much to tell him. Would he take kindly to the truth?

Sean mistook his silence for something else. He turned away and raked his hand through his hair. "Look, I'm sorry, all right? I like helping people just as much as Hannah. And apart from that bastard in the castle, everyone has been really nice." He stared out the window. "Honestly, if I could help you out… you know… set you free or something… I would, but I have to focus on getting back. We don't belong here."

Not entirely true. The time had come for some enlightenment. Roderick rubbed his chin. How would the boy take it?

"You're right, of course. You should concentrate on your own situation, and we should find our own way out of ours. Still, you will have quite a way ahead of you. Manipulating animals is only stage one. You will be attempting to manipulate the elements, which is the very highest form of magic. Not even the Baron can do that. Your mother only succeeded because she had the jewel."

Observing Sean with an intensity he hadn't felt in years, Roderick paused. It took a moment for his words to sink in. Even then Sean's foggy look did not clear. He blinked a fair few times before realisation struck, but the fog only thickened.

"Wh… my mother made… you knew my mother? How? Why didn't you say so?"

Roderick sighed. "I'm sorry I kept this from you, my boy, but I wanted you to know me better before I told you. Your mother was born in a village not far from here. When she grew up, she came to work in the castle. That's where… I fell in love with her."

Sean's eyes widened under his frown. He opened his mouth to say something but Roderick cut him off, leaning towards him.

"Unfortunately, I was already married, so we had to keep our love a secret. When Hannah was born, the Baron got suspicious. For several years he made your mother's life miserable and in the end she decided to flee. She broke my heart, but the Baron kept me from ever leaving the castle again. I did not even know she had a second child until you knocked on that door three nights ago. You see, lord Victor… is my son."

Sean gasped, the ridge between his eyebrows growing deeper. "You're his father?! *You're* the old baron? You lied to me! You…"

"I'm sorry, Sean." He twisted his intonation to make the name resemble 'son'. That felt… interesting. "I never said I wasn't him, but with all the stories the villagers must have told you, I knew I could not tell you straightaway. Even now, when you've spent so much time with me, you believe their stories instead of what I'm telling you."

Sean still leaned away from him, frowning. What stories had they told him?

"Ask yourself this: when they told you those stories, they talked about the Baron. But who did they mean?" He watched Sean closely. If the villagers had been precise in their stories, this would be the end of their relationship.

Sean stared over Roderick's shoulder, thinking back to what he had been told. Then he returned his gaze to Roderick. "That was all him?"

Roderick held back a smile. "They may have remembered

some of the things my father did, but my only crime was that I loved your mother more than I loved my wife."

The frown slowly disappeared from Sean's face, but he narrowed his eyes. "Is that why he killed my mum?"

"I'm afraid so. He searched for the porthole for years, until I had begun to hope he would never find it. But then he did." He cast down his eyes and rubbed his forehead.

"So… you're saying… Hannah is my sister?"

Roderick nodded.

"And you're my…"

Roderick kept nodding. "I'm so sorry, my boy. For… everything." He paused. "Was she… was she happy?"

At last Sean relaxed. "She was. She never talked about the past. All she ever said was that Hannah's parents and my father had died in a fire."

Roderick sighed. "In a sense, she was right. She took my heart, my life with her when she left. But if she had not, you would all have died. She made the right decision choosing your lives over mine."

He sent a watery smile Sean's way. *Come on, boy.* How much more would he need?

Mouth open, Sean stared at Roderick for a full minute. The cogs seemed to be turning, but not much came out. "I wonder why she said Hannah was my cousin." Then the light went on and he looked at his hands. "Is that why I can do magic?"

Excellent. "Yes, it is. But to tell you the truth, most people have to practice for quite some time before they achieve anything at all. Your power is… extraordinary." Something Roderick had not expected at all.

Sean snorted. "Not very good at it, am I?"

Roderick ventured to put a hand on Sean's knee. "It was the best first attempt I have ever seen. You simply need to learn to control it. Trust me, I know what you're going through. Although I was much younger when I started and I had examples to follow, I remember what it was like to feel that power blossom. That one thing that makes you stand out from those around you."

"Everybody says that magic is bad. Even you said that!"

"Because it is used by people with bad intentions."

Sean looked at his hands again, resting in his lap. "Do you think I could use it for good?"

Roderick stood up and put his hand on the boy's shoulder. "If you learn to control your power, you could do great things." He meant it too, which was an odd sensation.

Pity Victor was never like that. Had to find his own way. And that's exactly why Sean would be the more powerful. Where was Victor now? Gone to find a girl. A girl who was out looking for something he had been too lax to retrieve long ago. But away from the safety of his castle, so many things could happen.

Sean, however, reminded Roderick of his younger self. Eager to make this power his own, to use it as he pleased. And he still had ideals. Though Roderick had never been troubled by them himself, he had seen them in others. His wife had been full of them and he had seen them in Victor too, long ago. Sean was young. He had been away from his home for so long, it was only natural that he should try and better this world. He would find his way eventually.

"I don't feel it." Sean interrupted Roderick's thoughts.

"I'm sorry, you don't feel what?"

"I don't feel like this is where I belong, even if I am from here. I don't think I should be the one to help anybody, especially with something that everyone hates and distrusts. None of the people here want to be helped by magic, they're too scared."

Roderick squeezed Sean's knee lightly, then walked a few steps into the room. "Perhaps you're right. Perhaps the people here do not wish for your help. I have found myself alone only too often, wondering why I tried at all." He turned to look at Sean. "Perhaps you should not waste your time on them, but concentrate on making your way back to the other world. If that is what you truly want. Sean." Again he twisted the intonation of the name, which had a clear effect on the boy.

"Will you help me? Even if I only want to take Hannah home with me? Oh, and Ben."

Roderick pretended to think for a moment, then said, "Of course I will." At the moment, the boy was completely worthless. The other world had left him with no practical skill at all. But he had shown great potential. With some proper training, he might be able to put all that power to good use.

He went over to the cupboard and pulled out two glasses and a bottle of wine. "Thirsty?"

Sean grinned. His excitement had him hopping from one foot to the other. No sense of decorum. "So when do we start?"

The plop of the cork underlined Roderick's answer. "Now."

21

The book snapped closed, and Sean took a deep breath. Roderick's revelation had made him even more eager to perfect this new art. Because as things were, he wasn't going to help anyone. But if he got better…

"This stuff is amazing. Can you do all this?"

Roderick read the title of the book Sean had been engrossed in for the last hour, and coughed. "There were limits to what I could do, even before Victor… took my power away. To control the elements, one must possess immense power and ability. Very few have ever achieved it."

Sean cast down his eyes, stroking the book in his hand. "Hm, not something I should strive for, then. Too bad, it sounds wicked."

"Sometimes a little wickedness is needed to achieve greatness. You were surprised by the force of your own magic. Why should you belittle yourself so?"

Sean snorted. "Well, you know, Hannah…" He held up his hand instead of finishing his sentence. Would it be wise to let Roderick think his daughter was a bully? It might make her seem less sympathetic, but it would also make Sean seem weak. Especially with the way Roderick viewed women.

Pretending to read earlier, Sean had mulled over everything Roderick had said. This land, with all its fear and distrust, was rightfully his. He was the son of a baron! There had to be some potential in that. And Roderick had been impressed with his magic. If he could learn to harness it, Victor was history. Right when he'd thought there was no way he could change anything, this opportunity had come his way. A chance to show everyone that he *could* make a difference. And if that left him with a castle and a pile of money, all the better.

But then of course, there was Hannah. They still hadn't heard from her. Or even about her. Which probably meant the Baron hadn't found her yet, which was good. But Roderick had touched on something bad, too. What if she realised they had magic, and she wanted to outshine him yet again? All this work might be for nothing.

A vision of a scruffy furball biting its own tail appeared, making Sean wince. Would Hannah have done it wrong? If he were to accomplish anything, he needed to get better at this quickly. Everyone learns from mistakes, right?

Still, what other mistakes could follow? He needed a teacher. Someone with experience. Who could help him avoid bloody tails. Who knew Victor's weaknesses and could help Sean defeat his mother's killer. Who wouldn't mind seeing his son as the new baron?

It would take quite a lot of convincing to get the villagers on his side. But that would be much easier if he were the boss. Right? He'd thought that if he had to stay, he might start as a miller's apprentice, but baron sounded a lot more attractive. And he could always go back to the other world if things didn't work out. By then he would know how to.

There was only one problem. Hannah. Of course he wanted her there. But not in the seat of power. Which meant *he* had to be the one on his father's good side.

His father. What was Sean supposed to do with a father? Be happy he had one? He always knew he had one. Now that he turned out to be alive, Sean didn't know him any better than if he had stayed dead. Good thing Roderick didn't expect hugs and kisses, because Sean wasn't nearly there yet.

"What would you like to try out first?" Roderick asked, to break the silence. "Is there something you need right now?"

Sean raked a hand through his hair. "Yeah, a new portal. But since Hannah isn't back yet, I'll have to stick it out a little longer." He looked around for inspiration. "I don't think I really need anything. Nellie said I could stay at the inn until Hannah comes back and we can go home. That is, until Georgie tells everyone that I kicked a dead kid's dog, of course. Then everyone will hate me. I wish I could make sure he kept his promise." His gaze crossed Roderick's. "Could I do that?"

A twinkle appeared in Roderick's eyes. "You would be attempting second level magic, but there is no harm in trying."

No harm in trying to shut up a little boy... Sean shushed the little voice. It would only be temporary. Once he'd mastered magic and people had seen the good he would do, Georgie might even have forgotten what he saw. And if he hadn't, people wouldn't mind as much as they would if Georgie told them now.

Roderick got up and browsed the stack of books on the table.

"Ah!" He took one and handed it to Sean. "This one should help you out."

Sean pulled a face. "Roderick, you know all this stuff. Can't you just tell me? You saw what happened with the dog. Do you know what I did wrong?"

Roderick hesitated, then gave a slow nod. "I think so, yes."

"Then teach me. You don't have to pretend you don't know how anymore, even if you can't actually do any of it."

Fingertips tapping the side of his leg, Roderick paused. His gaze drifted over the books, but he still didn't speak. Then he put on his warning face.

"In the wrong hands, magic is a power to be feared. In your hands, magic is an immense force, that will strike awe into anyone who beholds it."

How was that a warning? Sean waited for the 'Use it wisely' or something, but apparently, that was all Roderick was going to say.

"So where did I go wrong with the dog?"

"You panicked. Your order still stood, but the force of it became greater with your willpower. You sincerely wanted the dog to stop, but you hadn't given it that direct command yet. So the force you put into wanting him to stop only flowed into the command of chasing his tail. It's not a difficult mistake to correct, but these subtleties make all the difference. The power is always there, and like I said, in your case that is quite some power, but using it correctly requires concentration and presence of mind."

"Okay. So, keep a cool head. Right. Anything else?"

Roderick shrugged. "It all depends on what your goal is. You've read the basics: magic controls or manipulates mostly the living world around us. Plants would be the lowest form, but they have no instinct or thoughts to change, so they become elemental.

"Next up are animals. Naturally, man is master over all animals, so this requires the least power.

"Human minds are relatively easy to change, making that the next step.

"Then there is the human body. Most magics have some degree of power in this, but it is also the extent to which most magics' power reaches. The Baron had a talent for it, though, and loved to show off his prowess.

"Only the most powerful magics ever get to manipulate the elements, partly because this also requires a degree of scientific knowledge. In order to change the consistency of a lifeless object, one needs to know the elements of which it consists."

What do you know, school biology and chemistry lessons came in handy after all. "And where do portals come into all of this?"

Again, Roderick hesitated, wringing his hands. "A portal is… The Divide… Our worlds are separated by magic. Portals break through that magic, and in essence lift the spell, if you can call it that. Very locally, of course. It means that creating a portal itself does not in fact take all that much strength. It's the passing through it and losing one's magic that drains a person."

"So… I could already do it?" That would be too easy. Wouldn't it?

"Probably…"

"Then why did mum need the magic thingy, the jewel? You said it was elemental magic, but now it's only lifting magic? And why did you send Hannah after it? You knew she didn't even need it!"

"No. No, that isn't exactly true."

This had better be good. Sean's breath shortened. Father or not, if he had sent Hannah into danger for no good reason…

"You may be my children, my blood, but I didn't know you. Living in the other world with no knowledge of this one was the future your mother chose for you. The fact that you appeared here by chance made my old heart sing, despite the desperate circumstances, but I couldn't break your mother's wish. I did not want to tell Hannah about her powers, for fear she would choose to stay. But I also told her *not* to go after the jewel. And yet she went."

That sounded like Hannah all right. Now what? If he could create a portal, all he had to do was wait for her to come back and that was that. Home. Safe. No revenge. No power. But the portal would stay open until they both returned. He could simply go home with Hannah now, and come back later without her.

"Roderick, if you teach me how to make a portal, I won't use it now. For one, I'll have to wait for Hannah, but I also don't want to leave you alone again. Besides…" Ugh, this was harder to admit than he'd thought, still feeling justified about it. "I have to apologise to Charlotte for being cranky with her this morning. Please trust that I won't desert you, and show me how to do this."

Roderick's shoulders drooped, but after he had looked Sean in the eye for far longer than Sean deemed necessary, Roderick sighed.

"Your mother took the jewel mostly to deal a mental blow to the Baron. But I think she also hoped to avert any negative consequences."

"What do you mean?"

"Magic is delicate. Use it wrongly and it takes from you what you don't deserve."

"That won't apply to me. I have nothing in this world, so if I use magic, I can only gain."

Roderick pursed his lips, but a twinkle in his eyes negated the reprimand his mouth was supposed to make.

"To make a portal, all you do is will the Divide to lift. Most choose a specific spot to create their porthole, because it is invisible in itself. The door to a cupboard would do, if you don't intend to use the cupboard in the meantime. For that reason, some use a naturally formed doorway or hole in a tree or shrub."

Piece of cake. Sean loped to the factory door, placed his hand on the door frame and concentrated.

"Sean, no!"

"What?"

Roderick closed his eyes in a pained expression. "Everyone who now uses that door from the other side, will end up in your world. You'll have to go through and come back in order to make it disappear."

Oh.

"If it worked."

"You'll know soon enough."

With his hand on the doorknob, Sean hesitated. He had been so sure this was why he would need to learn magic. But was it? Somewhere along the way, things had changed. This whole horrible other world now showed potential for more than just revenge. Maybe he didn't want to leave at all anymore.

The thought scared him into opening the door and stepping through as quickly as he could. Warm summer night air enveloped him. To his right, familiar lights beckoned. To his left, Green's Windmill was lit from beneath, the field in front of it a grey stretch of silent emptiness. How many times had he played there? Picnicked there with his mother and Hannah?

He turned back around. Home was straight ahead. A couple of streets, that was all. He could arrange everything, so that when Hannah would follow him through the portal when she got back to the factory, all she had to do was walk those two streets and he'd have everything ready.

For her to take over.

He reached for the door and stepped through.

Roderick looked utterly relieved. "Good. Now close it, and we'll try again."

"In a sec." Sean stumbled to a chair and crashed down.

"Ah. Yes. Like I said, it takes its toll."

Before Sean could answer, there was a knock on the door. Roderick bowed Charlotte in.

"Your presence brings beauty to my crumbling prison."

Cheeks colouring, Charlotte gave an awkward smile when she entered. She brought a large basket with her, which she put on one of the tables.

"Sean said you couldn't return home, so I brought you some food." Giggling, she sent Sean a sideways glance. "I told Nellie it was for a picnic."

Sean smiled. Oh dear, she'd done something naughty. She probably surprised herself with her own audacity. And here he was, acquainting himself with the specifics of manipulating the human mind.

The smile faltered. Manipulating a dog into doing something it didn't want to do was one thing, but human beings? Then again, weren't people manipulated all the time? Wasn't this just some kind of advanced marketing ploy, or really strong propaganda?

But he'd gone too far, even with the dog. Ethics aside, was he ready to move up to humans?

Charlotte's smile had disappeared, too. With a soft 'bye' she headed back out. Sean jumped up as Roderick opened his mouth.

Sean waved his unsaid remark away. "Yes, I know. With magic I could make her change her mind. Well I don't need magic for that."

He dashed out and grabbed Charlotte by the shoulder. "Charley! Charley, come on."

Tears brimming in her eyes, Charlotte planted her hands on her hips under her cape, making her look like she was about to take flight. "You should be ashamed of yourself. You come into our world knowing absolutely nothing about us. I keep telling you that you're a good man and you'll do good things, but all you do is criticise us." She took a breath. "I thought I'd bring you lunch. See if you'd calmed down. But you can't even smile at me anymore. Maybe I was wrong. Maybe I shouldn't hope for anything from you."

As much as that stung, it meant that she at least had had some confidence in him. Maybe he could still resurrect it.

"Charlotte, I'm sorry. I shouldn't have said that you're too passive. I was wrong, okay?"

She didn't answer and kept her gaze to the ground, but she stopped pulling away.

"Now can we please go back inside? I'm freezing!"

Another scowl apparently sufficed, because she headed in. She did not sit, but pulled her cape close.

Sean came in too, closing the door. "Oh come on, Charlotte, I said I was sorry. Here, you're cold, come sit by the fire." He pulled up a chair, then put his arm around her and gently sat her down. Squatting in front of her, he looked up at her face, but she stared into the flames, back straight. Okay, so maybe she was a bit angrier than he would have thought, but it still shouldn't make a difference. Roderick had left the room when Sean went after Charlotte, so there wasn't any hurry.

"Charlotte, look at me."

She glanced at him, then blinked and turned her gaze back to the fire. Sean reached up to touch her cheek, turning her face towards him.

"I shouldn't have said those things, I didn't mean to offend you. I'm sorry I criticised your friends and family..." Okay, just a little white lie. "...But when you mentioned Hannah, that really hit me. I'm worried about her." At least that was true. A little. "But when you said that you were hoping for her to rescue you, that hurt."

He lowered his hand to stroke her arm now that he had her attention. "She has always considered herself my guardian, getting me out of trouble before I even had the chance to get in. I've always been told to be more like Hannah, to trust her, to follow her. And now that I finally had a chance to show someone—someone I care about—that *I'm* worth something too, she tells me she's relying on Hannah."

Eyes watering, Charlotte slid off the chair, and dropped to her knees beside him, wrapping her arms around his neck. "Oh Sean," she sobbed into his shoulder, "I'm so sorry."

He held her tight and stroked her curls. Nothing like a little personal revelation to get to a girl's heart, whether you meant it or not. He had used more outright lies in the past, this one wasn't even all that untrue. Then again, this girl was a lot more interesting than some of the others. He rested his chin on the top of her head and held her until she calmed down. Then he pulled her onto his lap, and they sat on the floor gazing into the fire for a while.

"Hey," he whispered.

"Hmm?"

He lifted her chin and kissed her. When he pulled away, a delightful blush accompanied her smile. His second kiss was a little more excited, and she giggled.

"Sean!"

"What?"

"You know!"

"No, what?"

She giggled again. "You can't—"

"What, no good?" he asked in mock horror.

She rolled her eyes. "No…"

"No?!" Smirking, he nudged her shoulder. "Don't *you* tell me no too. I've heard it too often already."

She laughed, but then her features softened. When he kissed her again, she didn't resist. He pulled back to look at the reflection of the fire dancing in her brown eyes. "No?"

"Yes," she whispered.

"See, it's not that hard." He took possession of her soft lips, his hand on her back, pressing her against him. When he felt her muscles relax, he slowly slid his hand to the small of her back and bent over to lay her down, but she immediately broke away.

"No!"

No surprise there. He held his head close to hers, resting his forehead against hers, and produced a crooked smile. "What did I just tell you?"

A nervous giggle escaped her lips. "But—"

"Don't you trust me?"

She cast a sideways glance at the fire before looking back at him. Her voice was a little unsteady. "Yes?"

His grin widened. "There you go, you're learning." He had held his hand on her waist, slipping it up with his next kiss. Just when he felt her surrender, a knock on the door echoed through the room. Grunting, Sean let go of Charlotte to get up and open the door.

George the miller filled the doorway. He was carrying Dog, its little tail wrapped up in a bandage.

"Sorry to bother you. Miss Charlotte." He inclined his head towards the girl, who was just visible behind the chair. Her cheeks glowed, but George took no notice. "Georgie tells me this is your dog, but he doesn't want to say what happened to its tail."

He shoved Dog in Sean's hands, ignoring its whimper. Sean released the animal, and it darted straight for Charlotte.

"I'm sorry if the lad has been misbehaving. I'll get it out of him yet. Evening." George tipped his hat and turned.

"Hang on!" Sean stretched out his hand. If George would make his son talk, Sean would turn from village hero to village villain before they even knew he was dabbling in magic. And though he wasn't particularly satisfied with his hero status, the other option was far worse. "I'll come with you."

He went back in for his coat, an apple, and a struggling Dog, and blew a kiss at Charlotte, who would just have to accept it for now. She did look a bit forlorn, but this was more important. He'd make it up to her later.

After sitting so close to the fire, the cold outside struck him even harder. For one short moment he hoped Hannah had found shelter, then he went back to planning what to do when he got to Georgie. Time to put into practice what he had read that afternoon. He went over the technique in his head, but he realised it probably wouldn't work if he couldn't hold Georgie, like he had held Dog. Dog had been happy to be held, Georgie wouldn't be. That was if old George would even let Sean near his son. But then old George didn't know what Sean had done. Yet.

A little out of breath, Sean arrived at the mill. George's long strides he could easily match, but a slight anxiety squeezed the air out of his lungs. Suppressing the little voice that told him to come clean, he wondered out loud what could have happened, and said he would try to calm Georgie down. The miller only nodded and opened the door. Dog jumped from Sean's arms and ran for cover.

Georgie was in a corner, playing with a doll made of wheat stalks. When his father came in he looked up, but a shadow fell over his face as soon as Sean appeared.

"Go away!"

His father frowned. "Georgie!"

He wanted to say more, but Sean interrupted him.

"Georgie, I won't stay long, I just want to talk to you."

"I don't want to talk to *you*."

The miller took a step forward, but at an appeasing gesture from Sean, retreated to his chair.

Sean crossed the room and squatted next to the boy, grabbing him by the shoulders. *Don't do this. It's wrong.* He would make it right later. Georgie tried in vain to shrug him off. Sean held the boy in silence until the child looked up at him. Sean held his gaze for a few seconds and then let go.

"Do you know what happened to the dog?"

Georgie balled his little fists and turned pink. The frown that hadn't left his face since Sean entered the room deepened, and he opened his mouth, but the accusation Sean had expected did not come. Instead, Georgie sat there with his mouth open, jutting his chin forward. When no sound came out, the expression in his blue eyes turned from angry to puzzled to desperate. He tried again, tears forming and finding their way over his cheeks. Then he looked at his father, backed away from Sean and ran towards the miller.

"Daddy!"

Sean breathed out. So many things could have gone wrong. First he thought nothing had happened, then the spell might have been too strong. But it looked like the boy was still able to talk, just not about what had happened to Dog or to him.

Excellent, this magic stuff really wasn't all that difficult. At least, the actual process of it wasn't. The reaction to it required more of Sean's strength. But sacrifices would have to be made.

Georgie had climbed onto his father's lap, crying into his little fists. In between sobs a few words became clear. "Daddy, I can't... He's... I want... But... I can't..."

"It's all right, Georgie," Sean said. Could he really be this mean? "I'm not angry. If you want,"—he looked at old George when he said this—"the dog can come and live with you?"

George, not really knowing what to do with the shaking boy on his lap, nodded.

Sean got up. "I'll be back to check on it later."

"No!" Georgie sprang up, standing perfectly still in front of his father's chair. He glared at Sean with red eyes. "Go away. Don't come back!" Then he started shivering and fell back into his father's arms.

Sean swallowed and opened his mouth, but there was nothing he could think of that would help either him or the kid, so he walked out, back to the factory.

He didn't want the dog. He'd send Charlotte over to check on Georgie. She could deal with…

He sank down on one of the rocks lining the pathway. How could he have done that? How could he deliberately have prevented a little boy from telling the truth?

Realising he was tugging his own hair, he lowered his hand and stared at it in the diminishing light. Should he go back and undo what he had done? That would ruin any chance of staying in the village. He'd be regarded as an enemy, 'one of them'. They might not even let him stay in the factory with Roderick. Then how would he ever find Hannah and go back home again?

But could he really leave Georgie in this state? The poor boy had done nothing wrong. Of course, it would only be for a while. He could undo his actions right before they left. After that it didn't matter, even if he did come back. Why would Georgie tell anyone what happened if he had already gone home?

Sean took a deep breath and stood up, continuing on his way back to the factory. Charlotte might have an answer. She was good with people. But she was so against magic, that he couldn't possibly tell her he was using it. Especially since he was good at it.

That made him smile. He was, wasn't he? Sure, he had some skill with computers, but anybody could learn that. This was special. This set him apart.

Entering the factory, he was greeted by Roderick and his eternal glass of wine. But after Roderick's earlier confession, Sean saw this man in a different light. Perhaps not yet as a father. There was too distinct a lack of scenes like the one he'd just witnessed in his memory. No dad had taken him on his lap when he was sad. It had always been his mum. The mum that had been taken from him. The mum he was still waiting to avenge. And the wait was getting to him.

Taking the glass he was offered, his eyes searched the room for Charlotte.

"She left," Roderick said, taking a sip. "Quite upset, I might add."

He gave Sean an accusing stare, but Sean plonked down in a chair and took up a book from the little table. Sipping his wine, he opened the book at the midpoint. He'd make it up to her. No worries.

Now, a chapter on stage three magic, manipulating human bodies.

22

Lucian was leaning against the door frame when Hannah woke up. It must have been after sunrise, but a mass of thunder clouds kept the sun from brightening up the day.

Hannah moved and wished she hadn't. A dull pain in her hip drowned out the soreness in every other part of her body. Another day on horseback. Yip. Pee. She reached for the saddle bags in search of food. Lady Heanor had been generous, but they'd eaten most of the provisions the night before. She found some bread and used Sean's knife to cut off a small piece of cheese.

Lucian started to pack up. His blanket was already neatly folded, and now he grabbed her bags to take them outside. Hannah munched on the last of the bread, flipping the knife closed and pushing it up her sleeve. Her stomach grumbled, not happy with the amount of breakfast she provided.

Visions of bacon and eggs plagued her. On special occasions Mum would take them into town for a full English. If only she had known then that Aunt Jess was her mother. Hannah could picture them, sitting at breakfast, wondering what was the occasion. If Aunt Jess had told her that she was her mum, would it have made a difference to their lives?

Oh, get a grip, this was no time for tears. Hannah groaned as she sat up, rubbing her shoulders and glaring at Lucian, who looked far too chipper.

"Come on, darling, I've saddled yours as well. Time to go."

"Don't darling me," Hannah mumbled, hoisting herself onto the saddle, still wrapped in her blanket.

"Your mother never was one for mornings either." He grinned and stroked the dark grey horse he'd been riding.

He wasn't wrong. Sean had always mocked the way Mum and Hannah needed about an hour to really wake up, while he was all ready the moment he opened his eyes. Like this annoying person riding next to her, blowing happy little breath clouds into the morning air. Only adding more grey to an already barren landscape.

Where were they? The closest place Hannah knew with hilly moors like these was the Peak District. But Lucian said they were drawing closer to the sea now. Spiky rock formations stabbed upwards through the grass. A solitary tree showed muted autumn colours. Here and there ancient stone walls were crumbling, unable to support the skeletons of thorny shrubs that had fought bravely for an existence in these inhospitable surroundings, but given up long ago.

The wind picked up, and Hannah pulled her head closer inside her blanket roll.

Lucian stretched out his right arm and rubbed her back. "Still this way?"

With a sigh Hannah closed her eyes. "Left, we need to turn left." Opening her eyes again, she looked ahead for a turn or a crossroads.

"Actually…" The thought woke her up a little more. "I'm not sure I want to find this jewel anymore." She'd spent most of the night worrying about Sean. Somehow the jewel seemed to be in the way more than it would help. Every time she focused, dark mists were spreading over his image, even before Hannah wanted him to disappear. The horrid laugh that accompanied the lure of the jewel seemed to come from Sean now.

Lucian turned his head toward her, silent as usual, waiting for an explanation.

"It's Sean. He… I…" What was it, exactly? He needed her? She'd always thought he did, but in this place, what could she actually do for him? "I think… maybe we should look for the jewel together."

Lucian narrowed his eyes. "You want to go back to Nottingham, risking the Baron finding us, to pick up your brother and bring him back here?"

"Yes. No." *Well done, Hannah, that's telling him.* "He's alone. He doesn't know who he's dealing with."

"He's an adult. Don't you think you'd only be putting yourself and him in danger longer than necessary?"

He was probably right. Which was even more frustrating. "Stop telling me what to do!"

Lucian straightened. "I merely asked."

"Oh, very psychological of you," she bit at him, clutching the reins. Wait, he had no idea what that meant. Bloody backward world!

"Is it very different?" Lucian asked, as if he had read her thoughts. "Your world?"

Hannah looked up. Was that some genuine interest? Up till now, he had only wanted her to know about his world and all its shortcomings, like he wasn't interested in her life at all.

"What I miss most right now is laughter. I haven't heard anyone utter a carefree laugh since I came here. There are always things you can worry about, but most people have a job that pays for their home and their food. Even if they don't, the government helps them out with the basics. It's what they're supposed to do.

"But most people work during the day, then go home and spend time with family and friends. Enjoying themselves. Having fun. Shopping, gaming, going out. Browsing the internet. Oh yeah, we have electricity. It's like…" How do you explain something that's so common and you don't even remember how it works exactly? "The power of lighting in wires. We control it to make machines work that make our lives easier. Leaving more time for fun."

That sounded like everyone in her world was always happy. Well, compared to the people in this world, they seemed to be. In Nottingham, everyone was suspicious and always under threat from the Baron. In Ravenshead, people lived off the generosity of a robber. And in Highlow… That place was so depressing, she didn't know how people could even live there. Part of her wished she could do something about it, but it had taken her own world an industrial revolution and two world wars to get from this to where they were now. There had to be a better way. But with magic as a giant obstacle, what good could she possibly do?

Lucian took it all in without comment.

"Your world sounds a great deal more pleasant than ours," he said at last. "This world would greatly benefit from a leader who could steer us in the direction of your world. Your mother did well to keep you there."

There was that pain in his eyes again. It was always there when he talked about her. He must have loved her very much. Hannah gritted her teeth. If this man was her father, why didn't he just say so? Or was he ashamed of what he had become? She could simply ask him, of course, but he'd already told her her father was dead. Maybe she could get Sean to ask. If she ever saw him again.

She tapped a thumb against the saddle. The irregular pattern caught Lucian's attention, but he only asked if they were still going in the right direction. Sometimes when Hannah closed her eyes the jewel pulled her in a different direction than the one they had been following, once even leading them back the way they came. Hannah wasn't sure the whole thing worked at all. But Lucian darted happily about, then on this side, then on that. Well, not exactly happy, but she wished he'd stick to one side already.

"Have you thought about how you will use the jewel yet?"

She had. Lucian had said that magic always takes something

back, but it seemed to her that the only thing she could lose was Sean. And if she didn't use magic, she could lose him just the same. Eventually the Baron would catch up. Maybe, through Roderick, he already had. Was that why the laughter came from Sean? Had she lost him already? *No.* She refused to believe that. It was not too late.

"No. I have to find the thing first and take it back to Sean. Then I'll worry about how to use it."

"To go back."

"Exactly."

If she'd use it. Part of her still hoped they could find a way out of here without using magic. But a small voice, seemingly even further away than the back of her head, had started nagging her to try it out. If she found the jewel, they might be more powerful than the Baron. They could get their justice. But the voice was still small enough to push aside.

"You could come with us."

His smile was genuine and grateful. "Only if I can take every single innocent person with me. If not, then I still have a purpose here. But thank you for offering."

Must be great to have a calling. Joining the police had always been Hannah's dream. Helping people, making sure they stuck to the rules and were on the right track. It sounded perfect. But they were probably right to reject her for lack of resoluteness. She'd been terribly upset, thinking she was resolute all the time. But as soon as she realised she undid almost all the decisions she made at a later stage, her confidence had taken quite a blow, and she'd been unable to make any decisions at all for a while. And just when she'd thought refusing to marry Ben was the first good and resolute decision she'd made in a while… As soon as they got home, she would start to do things differently. Stop looking back and start thinking about the future.

Hannah closed her eyes and thought of Sean. Still there, still with a sad smile, holding out his hand. But that scary laughter that could only come from the jewel was getting stronger

all the time, and it seemed to drown out Sean entirely sometimes, leaving nothing but darkness drenched with an evil laugh.
Quickly, Hannah opened her eyes.

The air had gradually become more salty and the landscape
more rugged, rolling grass hills making way for more of those
jagged inky rocks.

Lucian rubbed his chest. Again. He had been doing so since
lunchtime, and now it was already getting dark.

"Are you okay?"

"Excuse me?"

"Are you all right? Are you ill?" Hannah tapped her own
chest, and he shook his head.

"No, just a little… burning." He raised his arm and pointed
at the contours of a tall white building some miles away to their
left. "I think we've almost reached the end of our journey. The
abandoned lighthouse of Westerquay could be a good hiding
place for a jewel."

Hannah nodded, not wanting to try to sense the jewel again.
They had reached the coast. How much further could it be? But
that added another worry to the tightening band around her
lungs. The more she thought about it, the more convinced she
became that this man was her father. If they found the jewel
now, would she ever see him again? She could wonder for the
rest of her life. But if she asked him now, would he tell the
truth?

Hannah swallowed. "So if we find it there, will you go back
to the forest?"

"I'll make sure that you get safely to where you want to go,
but yes, after that, I will return. I have to."

At least he was determined. But did he really think that he
was making any difference? Wasn't he just lucky to have escaped
the Baron and people like this Lord North for so long?

"Why do the people in Sherwood follow you?"

He grinned. "What, you don't think much of my natural
leadership?"

Hannah gave him a sideways look. *Hmpf, too easy.*

His mouth softened into a pensive smile. "I give them something, and in return they listen to me." He gave her a curious look. "I'd like to give *you* something, but first I'd like you to listen to me as well." He paused, but when Hannah didn't say anything, he shifted in the saddle and continued. "I give the people around me a little bit of wealth that we manage to take back from those who've taken it from us. But I also give them something else. I give them hope. Hope that something will change. Hope that more people will stand up against the way things are and have the courage to do something about it. To stop putting themselves first and think of others. You can't survive all by yourself. At some point you will need others. If not friends, then at least allies, and you won't get them if all you rely on is you."

Hannah smiled at his sudden outburst of passion. "Do you really believe something will change?"

"I *must* believe that, mustn't I? If this is all there will ever be, the rich getting richer and more powerful, and everyone else having to bow to their every whim, then what is life worth? People concentrate on surviving instead of living, they trust and believe in no-one but themselves. That is a very lonely world."

He clenched his fist around the reins. "Magic should belong to all people. Then we would be governed by people with the right abilities."

Hannah wasn't so sure about that, but this was not the time to burst his bubble. "Why would you want everyone to have magic when you've been telling me that it's a bad thing all this time?"

"Everyone knows that magic is dangerous. But we would be able to decide things for ourselves and not have to fear it from the few in power."

"Maybe you're right." And maybe not.

He stopped his horse and dismounted. They were on a stretch of relatively level ground a few hundred yards across, the road meandering through patches of spiny grass, along the steep rocky coastline towards the lighthouse. From there it curved inland, passing several rock formations before sloping upwards into the mountains and disappearing from view.

"We're not there yet. Why are we stopping?"

He gestured at her to come down as well. Hannah frowned, but obeyed, leaving the blanket draped over her horse. Now what did he want? "Do you think it's buried here, or something?"

He closed his eyes for a second, then took her hands in his. Hannah blinked. Was he finally going to tell her he was her father?

"Someone with magic could use the jewel to give magic to all."

Okay, not the father thing then. "That's a lot of power. Who would give all that away?"

He scrunched up his eyes. "I was hoping you would."

Hannah gasped and pulled her hands away. "Me?! I don't even think I want it for myself! And anyway, I don't have the jewel."

"What if I could get it for you?"

It was her turn to narrow her eyes. "I thought you were already trying?"

"Yes, but what if?"

Hannah shrugged. "I suppose…"

But before Hannah could finish her thought, Lucian reached into his shirt and pulled out a thin cord with a small purse at the end. He pulled the little string holding it closed, revealing an ornate black necklace with a large stone in the middle.

23

"Bastard!"

The word came out barely audible, as her lungs refused to work. Even her thoughts didn't seem to go past that one word. *Bastard!* All this time… Eyes wide, Hannah stared at the black, shimmering necklace. He'd had it all along.

When her incredulous gaze finally locked onto his anxious one, little black dots danced across her vision. She forced herself to breathe, her lungs slowly picking up the pace again.

"I could have been home by now." Her blood rose with her voice.

"I wanted you to get to know the people here. I hoped you'd change your mind about leaving."

"The people!" Hannah took a deep breath to prevent her vision from clouding. Through gritted teeth she spat her words in his face. "How noble, thinking about the people. You're nothing but a liar and a thief." She snatched the leather pouch with the jewel from his outstretched hand. "Those people are not my responsibility. My brother is."

Lucian's jaw muscles flexed. "Your brother is a grown man."

"So are your people." Her whole body shook. "My brother deserves my protection. He's my family. Your people are nothing to me."

He'd know that wasn't true. She'd let him see her compassion towards them whenever anyone mentioned magic, or the Baron, or any other wrongdoing. She'd been so relieved to find someone willing to help her. He was already concerned about other people, so she had been eager to assume he'd help her because she needed help. Turns out he was only helping himself.

"You have the power to save them."

"Save *them*. Ha! You just want a pocket witch. Or, what was that again? Magic for all. Magic for you, you mean! Well, you can forget about that! How stupid do you think I…" Her voice broke. How stupid did *she* think she was? She closed her eyes for two shaking breaths.

Why didn't he just leave? He must realise by now that Hannah wasn't going to aid him in his search for power or whatever it was he hoped to achieve. But all he did was stare at her. Not arguing. Not questioning. Simply waiting.

When she spoke again, her voice was calm and cool. "I'm going back to Nottingham to take my brother home. We've lost enough because of this world and the people in it. Goodbye."

He looked her in the eye one last time, a disappointed, almost sad contemplation. Then he sighed, turned around and mounted. "Think about what I said." He turned his horse and rode off inland.

Hannah's shoulders slumped. She bit her quivering lip and gripped the leather pouch tightly as she watched him go. When he had disappeared from sight, she sank down on the cold muddy road, beating her forehead with her fist, fighting back tears. That was twice in one week she'd been played for a fool. Was she really that naive?

Panting, Hannah stared at Allegra, grazing at the side of the road. Lucian had been right about one thing. Sean was a grown man. He could make his own decisions. Hannah could certainly never scold him again for not recognising a dishonest person. If he found out about this, he'd make her apologise. Perhaps she should apologise anyway.

The weight in her hand pulled her attention back to the pouch. Reluctantly, she pushed the leather aside and stared at the jewel. So this was it. Nothing special about it, as far as she could see. A polished black stone, an oval roughly the size of a quail egg, sat in a web of little black-beaded chains like a big, shiny spider. It seemed to emanate an orange glow, yet as Hannah shifted her focus to the encompassing beads, the glow disappeared. She frowned and brushed her finger over the smooth surface. A faint orange shone through her flesh, as if she held her finger on a strong torch, but all around it the jewel was black as ever.

The glow intensified. Sean's face flashed before Hannah's eyes, but it wasn't Sean. This face was distorted, though its features were untouched. It was Sean's character that had changed, as if someone else was inside Sean's body, using his face. Hannah pulled back her hand, gasping. Her whole arm tingled, and she blew on the tip of her throbbing finger, but there was no mark. Was she really going to use this thing? If this is what it did only to memories, using it seemed downright dangerous. But she couldn't rob Sean of his one chance to go home. Nose wrinkled, she drew the string tight and hung the pouch around her neck, where it lay uncomfortably heavy on the top of her corset.

She cast a last glance at the road inland. With the jewel in her possession, any pull towards Lucian was gone. She could kick herself for not realising they were always travelling in the direction Lucian had already taken. Now she was stranded in this dismal place with no means of finding her way back.

Cold seeped into her limbs through her soaked skirt. Hannah closed her eyes, weary from the journey as well as every rotten thing that had happened to her lately. But she couldn't stay here. She'd rest later. Soon, hopefully. As she tried to get up, her wobbly legs gave out and she almost fell. She stretched out her arm to keep her balance, then gasped when a hand clamped around her elbow. She twisted her head, and her heart skipped a beat.

"Ben!" Her breath caught in her throat. "What are *you* doing here? How did you get here?" Amazed, but incredibly relieved to see an actual friend, she threw her arms around his neck. When he didn't react with his usual enthusiasm, her brain switched back on with a vengeance, showing her the most powerful moment from their last conversation. Her passionate 'No' echoed in her ears. Cheeks burning, she released him as if he'd grown quills.

His pulled-up lip was more grimace than smile. "Looks like rain."

Rain. Yes. That too. But mostly… Ben. Here. How? *Why?* Hannah's mind whirled with questions, but a big, cold rain drop right on her nose dragged her back into action.

"The lighthouse." She pointed at the only place that provided cover. Now that she'd sent Lucian packing, she would need to find her own way back. The jewel would probably tell her which way to go to find Sean, but it wouldn't protect her from the Baron when he eventually caught up. She'd be alone. Except now she had Ben. Maybe. Hopefully.

Allegra had wandered off to find some juicier grass. Hannah called to her as she stumbled towards the lighthouse. Her petticoat had soaked up so much water and mud that it hindered her already unstable steps.

Ben, who had started ahead, stopped and turned. "What is it?"

"I just need to undo this." She dropped the heavy wet petticoat unceremoniously at her feet, then hobbled stiff-limbed towards the lighthouse.

The plateau ended abruptly where the lighthouse was built, leading from the side of the building straight into the waves below. The receding shoreline must have been the reason the lighthouse was abandoned, but although no light burned at the top, the sleek round building still stood proudly against the ever darkening sky.

When they reached the door, Hannah prayed it wouldn't be locked, but naturally it was. Ben threw his shoulder against the door, but it wouldn't budge.

"Let me."

He smirked. "You were never very strong, Hannah."

He avoided looking her in the eye, instead trying the door again, only to slip on the pebbles of the path surrounding the lighthouse.

A knot tightened in her stomach. What had she done to this poor man? No matter how he'd managed to show up here, he'd come to her rescue when everyone else had turned against her or abandoned her. Even if she didn't want to marry him, she should have been more considerate. She should have seen that his plans, and his feelings, were different from hers. If she'd taken the time to care instead of playing along. Mum had been right about Hannah being immature. How could she ever make it up to him?

An apology for starters, probably.

"I'm sorry, Ben." Hannah placed her hand on his lower arm, but he withdrew it. "I should have realised, I just... I'm sorry."

He snorted. When he finally looked at her, all familiarity had gone. "It doesn't matter now. In fact..." He took a step back and kicked his boot against the door, breaking the lock. "You did me a favour. You coming?"

She followed him into a dusty, round space full of empty shelves. To one side, a cast-iron spiral staircase led up to the next floor, to the other, a single tiny window was cut into the wall, but the grimy salt caked to the outside prevented most of the light from flowing in.

"What do you mean?"

He sighed, leaving the door ajar to catch what little light came in from outside.

When he didn't answer, Hannah found herself biting her thumb. What was that sigh? Resigned? Frustrated? ... Disappointed? She was about to apologise again, just to break the silence, when he turned to her.

"I wouldn't want you to be unhappy just to make me happy."

Hannah blew out a breath. "I'm so sorry." What else could she say? "What happened since... Aunt Jess... This place... It's made me see how wrong I was not to think about how you'd feel. I think I knew, actually, but… it was too easy to have you around. And fun too. Right?"

Yeah. That sounded bad, even to her. "I'm sorry."

Ben sighed again. After a few uncomfortable moments, he broke the silence.

"So, d'you come here often?"

Her smile was forced, but she reached out to touch his arm, and he put his hand over hers. They stood listening to the rain together, spending another few minutes in silence. He was a good guy. Even after this, he might still forgive her.

And yet… something niggled at the back of her mind. "How *did* you find me?"

His muscles stiffened under her hand. "I followed you."

She withdrew her hand. "How? The portal closed after we came through."

Shaking his head, he made an impatient gesture, but then his hand locked around her wrist. Hannah tried to free herself by twisting against his thumb, but he laughed.

"I told you, you're not very strong. You can't win."

Can't win? Win what? What was this to him, a competition? A fight? Hannah searched for the man who'd asked her to marry him only five days ago, but found nothing but the same exterior. If he was here, then he must have gone through the portal before Sean and Hannah. But if he knew about the portal, then… The realisation made her queasy.

As calmly as she could, she said, "Ben, let me go."

"Hm, no. You see, the last time I thought I could let you go, you ran out my door."

"I said I was sorry. What more do you want? I'm still not going to marry you." Hannah wiped her face with her sleeve. Rain was blowing in through the open door, but her face was wetter than it should have been.

He laughed again, his deep voice gaining a sharp pitch. "I think we've moved past that, yes." He yanked on her arm, making Hannah gasp in pain. "Can't ask for your aunt's permission anymore, can I? Or should I say your mother's?"

"How did you—"

"Strange, right? Why would anyone here tell me that? Me, a stranger, trying to find his beloved, who turned him down." His words poured disgust over her, but then his lip curled back up. "Strange... Unless of course, I already knew. No," he interrupted her again before she could speak. "She didn't tell me. She would never have said anything. If she never told *you*, why would she confide in *me*?"

His mouth twisted into a crooked smile, his eyes colder than Hannah had ever seen. All those little things that Mum liked so much about him, all those old-fashioned courtesies... He knew exactly how to behave, because he had lived here too.

"Did you come to our world... for us? Why? You couldn't have known us. We left when you were just a child."

"Hm." He was silent again, bouncing slightly on the balls of his feet. "Would you believe... I was paid to?"

Could he have been? *Oh please, let me be able to believe him.* 'You can't win.' But this was Ben! Trustworthy Ben! "Who would pay you to find us? And why?"

"To... protect you. Someone wants you dead, you know."

"Of course I know." Familiar bubbles formed in Hannah's blood. This didn't add up. Ben had never been overly protective. Okay, maybe he had, but she'd never been in any real danger. Had she? In any case, where was he when Aunt Jess... when Mum... "Some protection. You failed!"

"As you may imagine, or maybe not, I was somewhat distracted at the time."

"You were already on your way back here." Whether it was her recent stroke of bad luck with trusting people or the way he'd grabbed her wrist, his attitude set off an alarm bell, underlined by a distant roll of thunder. "I don't believe you."

Rubbing one hand over his chest, he turned his gaze from the rain outside to rest on her face. "See, I tried to come up with something you'd swallow. I liked being your hero. I really did. Even though I apparently wasn't, seeing you here again, all alone and unprotected, I still tried to find my way back into your confidence. It's too bad, really."

Looking at his sneer, Hannah felt sick. Even her boyfriend had not been who she thought he was. "If I had married you, I never would have known that Aunt Jess was my mother. You would have kept everything from me."

He shrugged. "If you had married me, Jess would still be alive."

Her sickness disappeared, along with everything else inside her body.

"You…" Hannah whispered. Trembling fingers pressed against her lips, she stared at the face she knew so well and didn't recognise at all. Then her gaze drifted out the open door to the sea, waves building in a rising wind. "The gun was modern." Unlike the one the Baron had used to hit her over the head. She'd never questioned it.

"Hm. You'd have made a terrible policewoman." He hesitated. "I'm just wondering what to do with you now."

Who was this man? How had he masked his character for so long? Was she completely blind? Her insides came back with a vengeance, weighing heavier than ever. She had to get away. She'd wonder at her own stupidity later.

"In case you still had hopes of getting out of here alive, let me kill that hope right now. Like I said, I'm wondering what to do with you. Throwing you off this lighthouse seems like a fitting end. Make you feel something of what you left me with."

He dragged her along by her wrist, but stopped with his foot on the first stair. "Actually, I'm being dramatic."

Hannah's mind was racing. If he would only let go of her arm, she knew she could outrun him. But he knew that too. "Why don't you just shoot me, like you did my mother, and be done with it."

"What fun is there in that? I've wasted years on you, I won't end this as quickly as you did."

Good, that gave her a little longer. "Then at least tell me why!"

"Haven't you figured it out yet? I knew you were naive, but I didn't think you were stupid."

Well, she was. That much was clear. But saying no had obviously been the right decision after all. *Thank you, subconscious. Now can you get us out of here, please?*

"The Baron, of course. He doesn't like other people with magic around, even in the other world. He sorely regretted ever cursing your mother and said he'd make me a rich man if I made sure neither she nor her daughter would ever return, if you know what I mean. Enough explanation for you?"

Wind whistled at the curves of the lighthouse.

"So what stopped you?"

He shrugged. "I liked it there. I had never killed anyone before and I was already wealthier than I had ever been in this world. Something to be said for mod cons."

It sounded surreal, coming from her mother's murderer. Feeling right at home, waiting for the moment he would kill them all.

"And then…" He took her chin in his hand, and she jerked her head back. "I fell in love. No, wait. I *thought* I did. The favour you did me was making me see that. Having been sent to kill you, my obsession turned to keeping you safe. To save you. Ha! You're no more whole, no more pure than I am. You turned me down and I realised I had been dreaming. It's your own fault, really."

"You can't blame that on me, you psycho maniac arsehole!" Hannah burst out.

He chuckled. "There's my Hannah!"

The amusement on his face hurt her more than his grip on her wrist. Her wrist! How could she forget the one weapon she'd found? If she was quick enough, she might take it out and use it before Ben realised what was going on. Holding her arm behind her back, she shook her sleeve and felt the knife drop into her hand. With her pinkie she slid the catch off and slowly flicked Sean's knife open. One moment she hesitated, gripping the weapon tightly. *He killed Mum. He deserves it.* She swallowed, swung her arm forward, and dug the blade into the muscles of his forearm.

He let go, screaming obscenities at her that were lost in the thunder. He growled and reached out as she ran, but all he caught was the button holding up the long side of her riding skirt. The fabric dropped down and trailed after her as she slipped out the door and into the storm outside. She rammed the door closed, catching the train and pinning her to the spot. Leaning against the door, she slashed at the skirt. Curse her slight frame! It wouldn't hold Ben in for long.

Ben thrust open the door, and Hannah fell forward. Her elbow hit the wet pebbles around the lighthouse and she almost dropped the knife. Before she could crawl away, Ben was on top of her, his forearm against the back of her neck, pushing her chin into the gravel. He twisted her arm to her back, forcing her to let go of the knife.

Sleet battered her limbs as Hannah fought the man she once thought she loved. The rain had them drenched in seconds. Hannah could hardly breathe. She tried to move, but the pressure of his knee on her lower spine sent bolts of lightning flashing before her eyes. He twisted her head by grabbing her hair, and whispered in her ear while he traced her hairline with his index finger, blood dripping from the cut on his hand.

"Not serious, am I?" The sound barely made it over the crashing of the waves below, and the wind whipping rain against the building behind them. Hannah winced when he yanked her hair, and the line of his lips hardened.

He took his knee off her back and turned her around, pinning her wrists to the ground above her head with his left hand, while clamping his right around her throat. Warm blood mixed with cold rainwater. "I'm serious now, Hannah. Do you like it better?"

Gasping for air, Hannah fought him with everything she had, not wanting to give in to his superior strength and weight. She kicked up her legs until he simply sat down on them. Writhing and screaming, she tilted her head, but it only increased the pressure on her throat. She bucked and retched, panic taking over her thoughts.

She stilled. Her heart glowed. No, not her heart. And not a glow. Her chest grew warmer until it started to burn. The jewel.

Ben froze. Was he reconsidering, or just curious? He ripped the soaked fabric of her jacket away from her body, exposing her skin to the icy water. But it didn't feel cold. The jewel now radiated so much heat that the leather purse felt like it would melt into her skin.

Ben loosened his grip. "Ah. I'll take that."

He snatched the purse from her neck, letting go of her hands.

Hannah blinked the rain out of her eyes. Had he really... *Dumb move!* Ten fingers clawing in his face, she put all the strength she had left into one shove, and managed to throw him off. She scrambled to her feet. The knife. Where was it? Hannah had moments before Ben would be on his feet, but the rain made it impossible to find anything among the glistening pebbles. Ben stood, bent over and panting, and glowered at her.

No more time. Anywhere else was better than here. She turned, but immediately recoiled. Hooves thumping on wet ground sounded through the rain. Too close. *Lucian?* She didn't dare hope. It must be... *him.*

With the Baron in front of her and Ben behind, the only way out was into the lighthouse. Hannah staggered back over her half-torn skirt. Ben limped toward her, but stopped to stare at the approaching horse. Hannah slipped inside, threw the door closed and rested against it for a moment, taking in large gulps of air.

This was a delay at most. Against the two of them together, Hannah didn't stand a chance. With trembling fingers, she buttoned up her jacket, and ripped off the rest of her side train. Struggling for breath, she tried to move the shelving units. Bolted to the floor. She had nothing to defend herself with but a piece of torn, wet fabric.

What was taking them so long? They should have been in here by now. Winding the cloth around her hands to fashion a makeshift rope, Hannah stood swaying, waiting for the door to open. But nothing happened.

Maybe they'd gone. If they had the jewel, maybe they wouldn't bother with her. *Wishful thinking, Hannah. You're being 'naive' again.* She winced. His words hurt. But in this case, she probably deserved it. No. She would have deserved it if Ben hadn't turned out to be a lying, scheming murderer! He wanted her dead. The Baron wanted her dead. What took them so long?

Hannah opened the door just enough to look out. The streaming rain made it difficult to distinguish the figures until lightning flashed. One of them was on the ground. That made no sense. They were after the jewel and after her. The jewel they already had, and they knew Hannah was in here. Why would they go against each other?

Unless… Could Ben have thought he had the upper hand if he held the jewel? The other man hoisted the limp figure unto the horse, then turned and started for the lighthouse.

<h1 style="text-align:center">24</h1>

An intense heat seared Roderick's chest. *Hannah!* was all he could think. Her image appeared before him, young and attractive, but not nearly as confident as she had been in the castle. Alive, though. When she faded and the room came back into view, Sean was looking straight at him, clutching his chest where he'd doubled up and sank to his knees in front of a chair.

"She's found it. Since she doesn't know how to use it, she can cause these surges if she touches it. But, Sean…" He waited for the boy to look him in the eye to gauge his reaction. "She will know now. She may not have the ability to control her power, but she knows she has it."

The reluctance was unmistakable. Sean's jaw hardened. The hand that rubbed his chest flexed into a fist. This rivalry between him and his sister was one of the most effective—and amusing—ways to spur him into action.

"Brilliant!" Look at that, Sean even managed to produce a smile. "If she's found the thing, I can use it to make a portal and we're out of here."

Still sticking to that one, are you? All right, I'll play along.

"Are you sure she'll want to come? Or even that she'll come back, now that she's found her power?"

He shrugged. "This is Hannah we're talking about. Doing the right thing is more or less her trademark. Along with telling others that their thing is not right. She'll be here."

"If only to show you what's right, you mean?"

"I know what's right," Sean said, teeth clenched.

Roderick didn't doubt it. A little boy not far from there might, though. Roderick gave a small smile that seemed to calm Sean, but wasn't meant for him. The smile came with the memory of learning magic, of becoming familiar with that feeling of power, and of finding new ways to use it. Though Sean wasn't ready for that sort of thing, Roderick remembered the first life he had taken. Oh, it had been nothing special, a delivery boy or some other insignificant person. He'd had to start somewhere, hadn't he? Just to see if he could. And even for that small act, he felt some remorse afterwards.

Sean would feel it too for his own action, as soon as he settled down some more. And so he should, it was only natural. But once he'd rationalised his deed, the next would be much easier. A dog, a boy. Roderick wondered who would be next.

* * *

Staring out the window of the bar room, Sean played with the beads around his neck. He hadn't seen Charlotte yet today. She had been out when he went down for breakfast half an hour ago. He'd read all the papers and made almost no sense of the news. Most of it about affairs in London, and a scandal surrounding the daughter of a man called Lord North. Maybe she'd shown an ankle or something.

With a sigh Sean folded the paper away. His hand found the beads around his neck. What was keeping Charlotte? He was hungry. Should he go find her? She'd want to know that Hannah had found the jewel. But he wouldn't tell her how he felt about it. What he felt that moment his sister appeared to him. He could see her very clearly, stretching her hand towards him, an anxious, worried, even scared look on her face. Yes, she'd found it, that much was clear. But was she in danger?

He wanted to help her, of course. But he also didn't want

217

her to come back just yet. If she returned, the Baron would as well, and Sean wasn't ready. The Baron was at least at level three, and Sean had only once tried level two magic. He still needed to find a body to change, but the village wasn't exactly full of volunteers. If they found out he was playing around with magic, they might not even let him stay at the inn anymore, hero status or not.

No, Hannah would simply have to tough it out a little longer. She never needed him before, so she could do without him now. The fact that she was scared was not a bad sign, actually, because it meant she hadn't yet found a way to beat the Baron. If she had, or if she would, he'd never hear the end of it. He'd stay in this world just to escape her endless boasting.

In the end, even if that happened, he'd still be the old baron's son, so he might still end up in the castle. Maybe he could find a way to free Roderick and rule over the land without the people having to fear him. Couldn't be that difficult, could it? He'd always have Roderick to help him out.

But what if Hannah decided to stay too? Roderick favoured him now, but he hardly knew Hannah. She could turn him around. Or worse, what Roderick thought of them now could very well turn out to be the truth. Roderick helped Sean because he didn't want Sean to be overshadowed by his sister. Kind of nice to finally have someone less than impressed with perfect Hannah, but he seemed to think Sean needed help standing up to her. Which amounted to more or less the same thing: Hannah was stronger.

Sean shuddered. Hannah might have been the stronger one in the past, but that was about to change. In this world, Sean had found his strength. He would be the powerful rescuer Roderick believed him to be. The new baron would guide his people, not scare them. And he certainly wouldn't let anyone take his power from him. If he'd learned anything from Roderick's story, it was to not let personal feelings weaken you.

The door opened and Charlotte blew in, her beautiful, but

rather angry eyes searching his.

"Did you do something to Georgie?"

Ugh, not this again. Sacrifices would have to be made, but he'd rather not be reminded of them. He made a vague gesture that could mean anything.

"He won't stop crying, but he doesn't say why. What did you do?"

He held up both hands in defence. "Nothing! I don't know why he's crying and I don't like the fact that you automatically assume it's my fault. I'm sorry that I left you alone yesterday, but don't pin this on me."

She blushed, biting her luscious lip. Good, she believed him. She placed her fingers on his arm and said, "I am sorry. But he's genuinely upset. I feel so sorry for him. He never said anything about you, but every time we mentioned you, he looked so scared, poor thing. And I know that you're… well… trying to…"

"Yes, and with any luck, that will get rid of the man who's been plaguing your village for years. Do you really think I would use it on a little boy? For a laugh? Ha. Ha."

She swallowed, her eyes fixed on the floor. Why did it feel so good that she believed every word? It wasn't even that hard to lie to her any more. After all, the lie was a small price to pay for all the good he would do her and the villagers. It was unfortunate that she could not enjoy this moment as he did. But if he didn't make her feel ashamed at her accusation, she might take it as an admission of guilt.

Time to be magnanimous and forgive her. He needed to get on with his practice if he was ever to defeat the Baron. And he might be on his way back already. If Sean didn't make it at least to level three soon, he didn't stand a chance. The few times he had tried magic, like last night on a spider in his room, it had worked, but only if he could touch the subject. Where was he going to find a human body to touch? He stared at Charlotte. What woman didn't want something changed on her body?

"It's okay, Charley. Come on, let's have some breakfast."

Over bread and sausages they talked about nothing in particular, avoiding anything that might cause friction. In the back of the room two older gentlemen were having a hushed conversation, but from the looks they gave Sean, it was obvious what they were talking about. At one point Sean looked over, smiled, and gave them a little wave. It excited them more than he had expected and he chuckled.

"You see? You're giving them hope. You don't need magic for that." Charlotte said, her voice encouraging, but her eyes searching for confirmation.

"I feel like a celebrity." Most celebrities didn't really deserve their status either. What hope could he give just being himself? He did need the magic. More than that, he wanted it. He could always stop afterwards. "Wait until I get rid of that Baron. Then I'll have earned their respect."

Charlotte kept silent, watching the two in the back instead.

"I will, you know."

She turned to him and flashed her most radiant smile. "I believe you can."

"But you don't think I will?"

Her smile perished. "I… I'm not sure you're choosing the right path, that's all. Magic is—"

"The only thing no-one else has been able to try. Or have you all really done nothing to stop him?"

"Of course we have, but—"

"Right! So once I'm good enough, I'll kick his butt and I won't use magic anymore, okay?"

She still didn't say anything. There was just no pleasing this girl!

"Because you're going away?"

Ah.

He put his hand to his head to rake through his hair, but stopped at his forehead. "I don't know."

She cast down her eyes. "You don't think there's a reason you were brought here?"

"A reason? Yeh, there's a reason! Me mam was murdered and I'm going to kill the bloody bastard who did it! I would have done it already if people didn't keep telling me it's impossible because of his magic. Well, I've got magic too. I just need to learn how to use it. But I will use it for good. I won't be like him. I will give to people, instead of take from them."

He had her attention, although she wasn't convinced. How could he make her see? "How about you? Isn't there something you want? Or something you want changed? Something you don't like, about your body maybe?"

She recoiled, eyes wide. "You're not using magic on me!"

He took her wrist and she balled her fist, watching his hand with suspicion.

"I only want to help you."

She yanked her arm and he let go. "I don't need help. I'm fine the way I am. I stay as far away from magic as I can."

He jutted out his jaw. "Stay away from me, you mean?"

She frowned and let out a short breath. "No! I want you to stay away from it too."

He gestured widely with two arms. "I can help all these people, and you don't want me to try because you're afraid? Is that fair?"

Again she didn't have an answer, but sat silently scowling at him.

"I do want to help them. But first let me do something for you, just to show you that I can. Don't you want something altered? Your nose, or your hips, or—"

"What's wrong with my nose?" She put her hand to her nose and her scowl melted in insecurity.

"There's nothing wrong with your nose!" This was getting much harder than he thought it would be. Why didn't she just work with him, so he could get on to the next bit? Elements sounded much more fun than human bodies anyway. He never did have the intention of becoming a plastic surgeon. "But don't you think you're a little tall? I could make you a bit smaller."

"Chop off my head, why don't you?" He'd gone too far. She stood up with such force that her chair crashed to the floor, but she made no move to pick it up. "Stop this, Sean. Just don't!"

She stormed off into the kitchen, leaving Sean with the curious glances of the pair in the back. She said no. Of course she said no. Why wouldn't she say no? Every woman in his life seemed to say no eventually. Even his own mother had said no to his way of life, no to his friends, no to his choices. What else was there to say no to?

He got up and left for the factory. Why did nobody ever see things his way? What did he do wrong? Or was he wrong? Had Hannah been right all along? Was he never going to be more than a follower? What if the Baron showed up and didn't even care that Sean had magic too? What if those few days of practising really didn't make him an enemy to be reckoned with, even if he had talent?

Sean, don't. Even with Hannah far away, he could hear her voice clearly in his head. *Just don't.* Charlotte had joined her. Don't try your luck. Don't think you will be stronger. Don't think you can win. *Just don't.*

He felt sick. With the factory already looming through the trees, he stopped in the middle of the path. Were they right? Was he only planning his suicide?

Sean, don't. All the blood seemed to drain from his head, to gather somewhere around his stomach. One more time, Hannah, and I'll—You'll do what, Sean? *Just don't.*

In waves of nausea he got rid of his breakfast. Bent over and panting, his hands on his knees, he stared at his left arm without seeing what was in front of him. Instead, as soon as his stomach settled down, he took off his coat, let it drop to the ground, and rolled up his sleeve. The little tattooed needle pointed at him. Weakling. Look what happens when you try to do things by yourself. You're not strong, you need Hannah to fix things.

He brushed his forehead with his sleeve. Even without the coat he was too hot. Sweat trickled down his back.

Sean, don't!

He grabbed his wrist and concentrated. Nothing happened. His eyes burned. He was not weak! His nails dug into his wrist while he glared at the tattoo, but it kept accusing him. If anything, it got bigger.

Shaking with anger, he wiped at his eyes and nose. His own body didn't even listen to him. Again he stared at the ink in his arm, willing it to disappear. Snot and tears dripped onto his sleeve, darkening the cloth, but nothing else changed. At last he loosened his grip and his arms fell to his sides. He couldn't do it. And if he couldn't even make a tattoo disappear, how could he take on a man?

Just don't.

25

Sucking in a quick breath through her teeth, Hannah slammed the door shut, keeping her hand in place. She pressed the palm of her free hand, still wrapped in the coarse cloth, against her forehead and tried to think, but all her brain came up with were images of Mum, lying on the living room rug.

I wish Sean were here. She never would have thought that's what she'd be thinking right before she died. Hannah pushed away from the door and stumbled up the stairs, using a burst of energy that must consist solely of adrenaline. Whoever it was coming to get her, if he was to win this, at least he wouldn't get her alive. Panting, Hannah tried to focus on Sean. If only she could give him some kind of message, then at least he could make it back.

'Sean,' Hannah breathed, but he didn't answer. Was the jewel too far away for this? Or had something happened? Maybe it didn't work like that at all. She was alone and he'd never know how much she missed him.

She'd reached the second floor, a completely empty round room, when the door downstairs opened. The tones of someone shouting her name mingled with the wailing wind. Not Ben. The Baron had caught up with her after all. Hannah shivered. At least with Ben she knew what she was up against. This man brought magic to the table, and a whole set of rules she knew nothing about.

Heart pounding in her ears, her breathing becoming more laboured with every pace, she scaled the steps to the top floor, finding nothing but empty spaces in between. No hiding places, nothing she could use as a weapon against her attacker. This would be the last one. She wouldn't leave here alive. Her gut told her to fight, but her head was giving up. She'd thought she was tired before, but the idea of even one last fight was too much. What could she do against someone who would use magic to kill her? She stood, panting, listening. Ascending footsteps. Slow but sure. Hannah reached out in the dark. Another flash of lightning showed her a door. Thunder crackled the air almost immediately after. If this door was locked...

Hannah tried the handle and the door opened. Rain lashed her face, and the wind pulled at her hair and what was left of her skirt, inviting her, pushing her towards the obsidian waves below. She inched across the threshold, pressing her body against the rough white stone.

Crashing against the rocks, a huge wave sent salt water spraying her face. A gust of wind yanked the strip of cloth from her fingers. It flew over the railing and vanished into the depths of night. Lightning flashed overhead as thunder hammered her eardrums. In the silence that followed, her name sounded from within the building. Hannah's nails dug into the wall behind her. He would never let her go. He might not even kill her quickly. She whimpered and brought a trembling hand to her lips. No other way. He had won.

As if in a dream, Hannah let go of the wall and moved towards the railing. She looked down into the dark turmoil beneath and balked.

"Hannah!"

Clutching the railing, Hannah jerked her head towards the balcony door, where Victor emerged. Soaked strands of hair clung to his dark skin, partially hiding weary, hollow eyes. His eternal frown deepened when he saw her. He stretched out his hand, his cape dangling from his arm like a drenched Dracula.

Six feet of nothing but icy wind and rain separated him from her. When he took a step towards her, Hannah put one foot on the lower rail and prepared herself to jump.

"Hannah, please!"

She froze. Did he just say please? The wind was howling in her ears, even drowning out the crashing of the waves on the rocks below. In her moment of hesitation he shouted again.

"Please, don't jump!"

Stammering thoughts fought tumbling emotions as Hannah stood motionless in the wind.

Victor lowered his hand, palm up. "I'm sorry I struck you."

Hannah turned around to face him. "You're… sorry?"

"I am! I never meant to hurt you."

Her fingers, seeking support, gripped the wet metal railing behind her. Rage rising inside her like she had never felt before, her palms tingled and her vision turned scarlet. "You had my mother killed, but you're sorry you hit me?"

Rain splashed from his hair as he shook his head. "I did not kill your mother! She was my friend."

Cheeks burning, Hannah hurled her words at him. "That's a lie! She never even mentioned you."

"Naturally. She was trying to protect you."

"From you!"

"No, from the person who did kill her."

Her heart churned. The jolting wind took her breath away, and the rain pummelled her numb skin. *Think!* But her tortured brain came no further than telling itself to work.

"Please, Hannah! I'm not who you think I am. Give me a chance to prove it, please!"

This was the man she had been running from? Tall as he was, he looked pitiful. Her trust was too badly damaged to believe him, but her only other option was to jump to her death. Slowly Hannah let go of the railing and stumbled towards the white wall, still several feet away from him. He breathed out, supporting himself with his elbow against the door frame. His dark gaze pierced her eyes before he turned and went back inside.

Hannah hesitated. But another flash of lightning reminded her that staying out here would not increase her chances of staying alive. One wavering foot in front of the other, Hannah approached the balcony door. Footsteps sounded on the stairs several floors below. Hannah blew out a breath. She hastened out of the rain, slammed the door shut, and leaned against it. Eyes closed, she relished the musty, almost warm air entering her lungs. Only then did she notice her teeth were chattering. Her coat was downstairs in the mud and her blouse was torn. The tweed skirt was so far gone that it hardly provided any decency anymore, let alone warmth. Only the thin suede breeches clung to her skin.

Another deep breath, then a step toward the stairs. Where was he? Downstairs, but what floor? Hannah tried to listen for any sound of him, but the wind and the occasional burst of thunder still made it impossible to discern any other noise. Shivering and on her guard, she descended. When she reached the ground floor, Victor was waiting for her at the foot of the stairs. He took a step back to allow her some space, and exhaled.

"Good."

"Oh yeah?" Hannah couldn't think of a better retort. Whatever evil scheme he was planning, he'd better execute it quickly. But all he did was take off his coat, revealing the thin sword underneath.

"I'm sorry, it's rather wet. But it might be warmer than what you're wearing."

He held it at an arm's length. Hannah took it without thinking, even relishing its leftover warmth for a second before her mind flicked on again.

"I don't have it."

"I don't want it."

That was not what he was supposed to say. The jewel was his heirloom, the thing with the power. Why wouldn't he want it?

Hannah examined his face, but after that slight oversight earlier, it was set in the same scowl as before.

"What are you going to do with me?"

"Take you back to the castle, if you'll let me."

Hannah pushed out her chin, aware that she must look tiny in a coat that was about ten sizes too big. "I don't have much choice, do I?"

"You do. Stay here if you wish, but I suggest you come with me, the sooner to get you and your brother home."

"So you can go back to tyrannising those around you? I won't let you!" Said the mouse to the cat. But he had not killed her yet. Hannah felt brave, like a condemned woman spitting in the face of the hangman.

He looked at her from above, as if she needed to be reminded of the silliness of her words. "If you come with me, I will explain on the way."

Work, brain. The quickest way to get back to Sean with the jewel was probably to go with him, but… Everyone she'd met had told her about the wicked Baron. And here he was, offering her his help. Until she could make sense of it, though, she might as well try and keep her enemies close.

"I'll come."

He nodded, opened the door, and was instantly drenched. He whistled for his horse, and the animal trudged over through the mud, halting just short of the path of slippery pebbles, a weakly protesting Ben tied to its back. The Baron took its reins, then whistled again. Allegra, the traitor, appeared through the grey watery curtains. Hannah had come to think of Allegra as her horse, but she'd lost her allegiance too, if she ever had it.

Wrapping the giant, heavy coat around her, Hannah ventured outside and mounted with considerable difficulty, her mind reeling with what had happened. Victor spurred his horse into a gallop, and Allegra followed her master. It took all Hannah's effort to keep her numb body in the sloshing saddle, so when they reached a village not ten minutes later and dismounted in front of the inn, she was still wondering if she should have steered Allegra away from the Baron and fled.

Victor paid for two rooms, told Hannah to eat something and disappeared, leaving her wondering once more if she should just take the horses and go. But then she caught the look the woman behind the bar gave her. The unbuttoned greatcoat now showed her ragged miniskirt and torn blouse, still soaking wet and mud-stained. Hannah pulled the coat closed, but didn't bother ex-plaining, or even showing an apologetic smile. She asked if she could borrow some clothes, but the barmaid only wrinkled her freckled nose. She told Hannah she'd send something up, and would Hannah like her dinner in her room?

Hannah shivered. Somewhere deep inside a little flame poked at her. Would it kill the woman to be a bit more considerate? What did she think happened to her? But the flame died under the snuffer of exhaustion. No-one in this miserable world had ever cared what happened to her. Except maybe Charlotte. But she was far away. Probably. Actually, Hannah had no idea how far from Nottingham they were. They must not be very close if the Baron decided to stay here for the night.

Hannah shrugged and followed a maid to her room. When the maid had left, she dragged herself to the bed and buried her face in the pillow. Tears that she'd held back far too long came freely, soaking the linen under her head.

"Oh Mum, I miss you so much."

Her mother's smiling face appeared, but it moved away from her, fading into the distance. Sean felt far away too. Eyes closed, Hannah focused on him, but all she heard was that awful laughter.

A knock on the door announced a girl with a tray of steaming vegetables and a big piece of mutton. Hannah slid off the bed, dropping the wet coat on the floor and leaving it where it fell. She shuffled to a chair near the fireplace, where the girl put down the food on a little side table before she left. Hannah didn't think she was very hungry, but when she started eating, the plate was clean in less than five minutes. The girl, returning with dry underclothes, made no effort to hide her surprise, but was too timid to actually say anything. She took the plate and scuffled out, leaving Hannah staring into the fire.

Alone again.

I should get out of these wet clothes.

What pretty flames.

Move, arms.

Look at them dancing.

Why aren't I crying?

Mmm, warm.

She must have sat staring into the fire for quite some time, because when she finally tore away her gaze, parts of her clothes had begun to dry. She made herself take off her shoes, followed by every other bit of sticky wet garment. She longed for a hot shower, but a quick wash from the bowl of cold water in the corner would have to do.

Another knock on the door startled her.

"I'm not dressed!" Hannah yelled, skipping toward the chair with the dry clothes. But as she hoisted herself into the crisp chemise, she heard footsteps leaving. When she finally climbed into bed, all her muscles thanked her, and she passed out until morning.

26

When a maid knocked on the door at seven to wake Hannah
and bring in some breakfast, the rain had thinned to a drizzle.
Hannah groaned as last night's events came flooding back. Ben
killed Mum. She'd still have trouble believing it if he hadn't tried
to finish her off, too. But then she was saved by the man she'd
been hating since Mum died. Her friend. He said he was Mum's
friend. But it didn't make sense. Did it?

Hannah's body rolled out of bed, but her mind did not want
to come along. She'd survived, at least. Not dead! Yay! Now
what?

Facing another day with no allies was something she'd rather
postpone for a few more minutes, so she reached for her clothes
without thinking or feeling too much.

Fortunately, her corset had dried overnight. Now that she
was used to it, it was actually quite comfortable. As long as she
didn't pull the laces as tightly as Nellie had done. Someone had
come in and taken the rags away, though. Probably when they
lit the fire. Hannah had slept through it all. In place of her old
outfit were a new but simple, light blue dress and a pinafore.
Great, all she needed was a hair band and she'd be Alice in Won-
derland.

After a cup of tea and a sandwich that made her wonder
if last night's meal had really been as good as it seemed at the
time, she sat staring at the fire again. She'd soon be back with

Sean. How would she find him? Would he be angry with her? She should never have left him on his own in a strange world, no matter what Roderick had said. Another person she'd been stupid enough to trust.

Was there anything she'd done right? The point of the entire journey had been to find the jewel. Through no merit of her own, she'd finally held it, only to lose it again moments later. Now that she'd had some sleep, not trying to get it back yesterday seemed foolish. This thing that everybody wanted, it should really be hers. She wouldn't use it for herself. If *she* had it, she could kick the Baron out of his castle. The old *and* the young. Free the people. Maybe give the power to Lady Ethel.

Or...

Didn't Lucian say that they would benefit from a leader from the other world? It sounded absurd. And yet... Wouldn't it be great to finally have that calling in life to answer? She wouldn't make the mistake of trusting anyone again. She wouldn't need to. She'd have the jewel.

Both craving and dreading whatever would follow, she went downstairs. She'd look out for opportunities to take back what should be hers. The Baron may have rescued her yesterday, but she'd been taken in by people helping her before. If she could retrieve the jewel, then she would have the upper hand for a change. And then, if he still maintained he was her mother's friend, she might listen to him. *There you go again, trying to trust someone.* The words of one man against those of everyone she'd met, and she still desperately wanted to believe him. Hannah took a deep breath before she opened the door to the bar room.

Fresh and dry in a grey suit, a new coat over his arm and his sword at his side, the Baron stood at the bar, reading a newspaper. The young woman behind the counter sneaked several looks at him before he noticed Hannah.

"Good morning." He folded away the paper and gestured her towards the door. "I've arranged for a carriage. It will be slightly slower, but decidedly less wet."

No bag. He must have the jewel on his person somewhere.

Under the awning outside the Baron halted, donning his hat and coat. A stocky man in a brown bowler hat came towards them. He pointed a thumb over his shoulder across the street.

"That him?"

Only then did Hannah spot a thoroughly drenched and perfectly miserable Ben, chained to a tree, with a saggy bit of cloth around his neck. The man went to fetch him, and when they came closer, Hannah could read the writing on what looked like a tea towel: 'Property of Lord Pryce'.

Property. Ben was a despicable human being, not worthy of her compassion, but that was just it. He was still human. Apparently that meant nothing to the man standing beside her. She glanced at the Baron, but as the two men approached, it was the dark maelstrom around Ben that almost sucked her in. The intense hatred in his eyes robbed her of her breath, yet she could not look away. This was the man who had asked her to marry him. What if she'd said yes?

A horse-drawn closed van appeared around the corner. It stopped in front of them, and the driver went round to open the doors at the back. Keeping an eye on Ben, the man in the bowler hat produced a gun, but held it loosely by his side while the other man prepared the van.

Now or never, take the gun!

Hannah bit her teeth. She couldn't.

He murdered your mother. Shoot him!

Her hands curled into fists. Why didn't she? Ben wasn't worth the cold wet air he breathed. Who would care if he died? She certainly wouldn't. Every muscle in her body on edge, she readied herself.

Hurry!

He was so close. She couldn't miss. He'd die instantly. It would even be too good for him. Her hand came up, just as the man in the bowler hat turned away.

Hannah's cheeks glowed. The idle hand went to her lips instead. Breath shallow, she willed her hands to steady. She never even stepped forward. As much as she wanted Ben gone, she couldn't take his life. That would have been worse than declaring him property. She glanced at the Baron, only to find him staring at her hand. He met her eyes when she let her hand fall. Good thing she couldn't get any redder.

The van departed with Ben inside, leaving Hannah feeling defeated. This was how she avenged her mother, letting someone else do the dirty work. She hugged herself. Though the dress wasn't exactly thin, she could do with an extra layer. Because these shivers were from cold, not from disgust with herself for not being able to take revenge on the man who'd murdered her mother. She swallowed, pressing her eyes closed for a second.

The weight of a blanket being draped around her shoulders surprised her. She gratefully pulled it closer, but did not thank the Baron. It wasn't until they were well and truly on their way that she felt her body relax slightly. With Ben out of the way, however, thoughts of Sean came rushing to the front of her mind. Hannah had promised her brother she'd get them out of here, but the Baron, sitting across from her, but still entirely too close, held the jewel. Why would he let them go now, when he was the one who'd locked her in his castle in the first place?

"Lord Pryce…" After all, when you're British, you can hate someone, but you must use the proper title.

The carriage shook when it hit a pothole. To keep her balance, Hannah grabbed the first thing her hands found. His knee. She jerked her hand back, feeling the blood creep to her cheeks once more. Still he was unmoved, save for a slight deepening of his frown at the mention of his name.

"Miss Taylor?"

"Why are you helping me?"

He blinked slowly. "Your mother was my friend and would have been under my protection had she stayed. That courtesy naturally extends to you."

"Courtesy!" She gave a sharp laugh. The bruise on her head from where he struck her still hurt.

That at least got a reaction. He cast down his eyes. "I have already apologised for that. I was… distraught."

"Because of my mother."

"Yes."

Hannah tried to catch his eye again, but he wouldn't let her. "Ben said he killed her in your name."

His gaze flicked back to her. Something in his countenance changed, almost in… relief? "He admitted to this?"

"Y-yes."

"What did he say, exactly? Did he name me?"

"He said 'the Baron'. It was Roderick, wasn't it." It wasn't even a question anymore. It wasn't him. She'd doubted it before, and though she still didn't trust the man in front of her, his reaction was undoubtedly genuine. "You know, that's very confusing that you're both referred to as 'the Baron'."

Was that a smile? No. No, it definitely wasn't. But the frown disappeared, and for him, that was almost a happy face.

"Call me Victor."

"Hannah."

He only gave a short nod, and continued, rubbing his forehead with his fingers. "I don't… talk… to people… very often. People are either afraid of me, or afraid to be seen with me, so I tend to act, rather than talk. Your mother was my anchor. The fact that there was one person who believed I was a good man trying to do the right thing was what kept me going most days. When I found her there…" He swallowed, eyes closed. "Not only had I lost my one friend, but the only other people who might have believed in me now thought me to be a murderer, too. I had to talk to you both, to explain, but unless I could somehow prove my innocence, you would never believe me. I thought I had already resigned myself to that fact, but when I saw you there, by yourself on the market, I thought… I didn't think. I acted—stupidly.

"I know you have no reason to believe me, but I beg you to at least listen to me. Will you do that?"

Hannah hesitated, his emotional words taking her by surprise. She'd been believing all the wrong people lately. What if what he said sounded convincing? Would she fall for it again? She thought of Ben. She had trusted him. She'd thought she knew him. She'd thought she loved him at one point. No, she would not believe Victor. She wouldn't believe anyone for a long time. But they had a long journey ahead of them, so she might as well listen to his version of the story. Starting with…

"You were there, at Mum's, with the gun."

"I went to see your mother every year. First with my own mother, when you and I were both children. We used to play together then. Don't you remember that?"

She thought of the sad-looking boy in the painting in Nottingham Castle, but nothing else came into her memory. She shrugged.

A muscle in his jaw flexed. "You were very young then. After my mother died, I came by myself, but you were usually in school when I visited. I always made sure no-one followed me, but after all those years I must have become lax. Ben must have followed me through the porthole one day. I never realised your Ben was the same man who disappeared from the village years ago. The man they said I killed. When your mother mentioned a Ben in your life, several years had passed, and I didn't make the connection. I'm so sorry, Hannah. If I had been more attentive, he would never have found you."

It could have happened. He sounded so sincere.

Careful, Hannah.

"So Roderick told Ben to follow you to our house and kill us? Why hadn't he done that himself?"

"My father never knew we visited your mother until I told him one evening during a particularly unpleasant encounter. I wanted to spite him, knowing he could not leave the castle and do anything about it anymore. Unfortunately, I was unaware at the time of his ability to frequent the factory, where Ben worked. But Ben didn't follow me until years later, when I had almost forgotten I'd ever mentioned it. My father never showed himself to me after that night, and I had begun to hope I was finally rid of him.

"Why Ben waited to carry out his command, I do not know. The fact that he did on the day of my visit cannot be other than coincidence, as I never planned these visits. I was yards away from your mother's door when the gun went off. By the time I entered, the murderer had gone, so I didn't know who did it or why. But as I knelt by her body, Sean walked in. Naturally, he assumed I was the culprit, but I never touched the gun."

Hannah put her fingers to her temples. He was making it really hard not to trust him. His story made so much sense. "But they told me all these things about you. The girl in the factory, the shrivelled tongue..."

He was quiet for a breath. "I killed the man who did those things." He narrowed his eyes. "You mentioned Roderick, so you must have met him."

"Roderick did *all* those horrible things? But *he* was always nice to me, and *you*..."

"I put you across my saddle," he said, staring at the floor.

"And you killed him. Your own father! When? When I left?"

"Oh no, I killed him when I was twelve."

She sat blinking at him.

"Didn't they tell you the castle was haunted?"

27

The interior of the carriage blurred. Hannah couldn't breathe. He was mad! Eyes wide, she grabbed the door strap for support. Her boyfriend had killed her mother, whom she thought was her aunt, at the order of a ghost from another world. Why didn't somebody in the mental hospital she must be in wake her up?

"Hannah, please believe that I had nothing to do with killing your mother."

Hannah opened her mouth, then closed it again. Not finding anything to say, she gave up and stared at the grey, wet landscape. This was a different route from the one Hannah had taken with Lucian. The view here was of rolling hills, less moory.

If only her thoughts were as smooth. Something still didn't add up.

"You shot Sean. You shot at me!"

He plucked at a loose thread in the upholstery by his knee. "I did not shoot at you, I shot at the person shooting at you. I did, however, hit your brother and I'm sorry. I'm a horrible marksman. Better with a sword," he added, almost in a mumble.

The thought Hannah'd had on top of the lighthouse hit her again. Was this the man she'd been running from? "Yes, they told me about that. How you use it as your magic wand."

The fingers playing with the thread stilled. "You were misinformed. I do not use magic."

Oh, right! No magic, just ghosts. She snorted.

"And I'm supposed to believe that? If you don't use magic, how come you're still the one in the castle?"

He kept his dark eyes trained on something in the distance. Was he truly sad, or just coming up with an explanation?

"My father still has the people thoroughly frightened, though he's been dead for seventeen years. I have tried to help the villagers, to make them see that I am not like him. But after he caused all the accidents and eventually a death in the factory, people made up their minds. The new baron is just as bad as the old."

Strange as it was, Hannah was starting to believe him. Crap. But she still couldn't quite forgive him for hitting her. Rubbing the back of her head, Hannah frowned at him.

He sighed. "Again, I am deeply sorry. You had made up your mind about me before you even knew who I was. I thought I might talk to you more rationally in the castle, but then you wore my mother's dress and… I wasn't ready. When you took my keys, I realised my father must have spoken to you. I'd ruined my one chance to change your mind. But the fact that he was still around did confirm that Minnie's death was somehow his doing. All I could do at that point was try to find you, and hope the killer would not get to you first.

"What my father had always wanted most, was to recover the jewel, but although he never found it, he believed it was in Highlow. I counted on him having sent you there first. Of course, once I got to Highlow, I learned you had not been there, and must have lost your way. You could be anywhere. I was afraid I had but one undesirable option left, until I remembered one of the paths had gone out of use since my father died, so if he'd given you instructions along that route, the most logical place you would have ended up was Ravenshead. When I reached there, however, you'd already left for Highlow. Unfortunately, people in Ravenshead were not very cooperative, and it took some time before I found this out.

"Back in Highlow, I visited lady Ethel, whom I had not seen

since before my mother died, hoping Lucian would have taken you to her. She was reluctant at first, but listened to me for my mother's sake. Though she did not seem too eager, I must have convinced her, because she told me you had been there, but were already on your way again. It was at that moment I saw the man I supposedly killed five years ago stalk around the garden. Whatever his intent, I reasoned it must have something to do with you, so at last I had to… do the one thing I had spent years setting myself against. I had to open my mind and let magic in, to use the jewel to guide me to you, or at least to it, your destination.

"I would have reached you sooner, had I not encountered a party from a neighbouring noble."

Hannah raised her eyebrows. He couldn't mean those beat-up bowler-hatted men that had passed her when she was travelling with Lucian?

"I'm sorry for what you have had to endure, partly on my account. But I am pleased I was able to reach you in time."

So was she. Hannah shifted in her seat. Forgetting her costume for a minute, she had leaned forward, and now, with the corset's pressure on her bladder, she had to pee. Funny how a triviality like that could settle the nerves.

"Last night, after I secured Ben, I went to talk to you, but you were—" Something outside caught his attention, and his frown returned.

Hannah followed his gaze to the edge of the wood bordering the field they were crossing. A group of men, holding horses by their reins, were watching the carriage pass. Another appeared on horseback from the trees, pointy beard leading the way.

"Lucian!"

Was he going to rob them? To think that less than twenty-four hours ago, her allegiances, such as they were, had been reversed. The carriage shook and then accelerated. The driver must have spotted the group as well.

"Yes." Victor kept a sharp eye on Lucian. "Ben used to have

connections with Lucian's band. If he managed to contact those friends, that is probably how he found you. Whether Lucian is explicitly aware of this, I'm not certain. However, I don't think he will try anything now. Like all the others, he's too afraid. Although he's still not sure."

"Not sure about what?"

Some of the men mounted. Lucian said something that didn't reach the carriage. Instead of answering Hannah's question, Victor put his hand on the pommel of his sword. After another word from Lucian, one of the men broke away from the group and galloped towards them. A second followed. Then a third.

Hannah's heart rate shot up. Wouldn't try anything, huh? She clutched her apron, wishing it held something she could defend herself with.

Lucian now followed the three, while the rest of the men stayed behind. Halfway across the field he overtook his friends, but instead of leading them, he changed direction and barricaded them with his horse. As the carriage barrelled past, they quickly disappeared from view.

Hannah's hand rose to her throat, as Victor's grip on his sword loosened. A familiar prickle at the back of her neck calmed her as much as it riled her.

"That's the second bloody time," she burst out, "He needs to take control of those hooligans. First they take my horse, and now they're attacking me!"

Victor pinned her with one of his stares.

"All right, *your* horse. You did get it back." *Now stop looking at me.* She wound a curl around her finger. "You said he wasn't sure? About what?"

Victor stared at her a second longer, but then leaned back and continued as if nothing had happened. "No doubt he has told you that he robs nobles to feed those around him?"

Hannah nodded.

"What he has no doubt failed to mention is that not all nobles are like my father. Many of them have the good of their people at heart and will only use their magic to defend themselves against the hunger for wealth and power magic has caused in others. Naturally, it's only those peace-loving nobles that Lucian robs. He's a pest, but he has people convinced that all nobles are the same and that one day he will save them."

"And how will he do that? By giving everyone magic?"

He narrowed his eyes. "Is that what he told you?"

"He wanted me to use the jewel for it."

Victor flexed his cheek, but it still wasn't a smile. "Would you know how?"

Hannah shrugged.

"It's manipulation. Using sheer willpower to change the world around you. But giving magic to all and sundry would be a terrible idea. Not to mention the impact on the one wielding magic in the first place."

When Hannah raised her eyebrows, he continued, "I understand why he thinks it would be the answer. This world is a bed of glowing embers, it only needs a little fuel to turn into a blaze. But simply presenting people with that kind of power would create chaos. A very dangerous chaos."

"You'd rather keep it to yourself." Hannah folded her arms across her chest.

"Yes." He looked at her frankly, not impressed with her provocation. "I would keep it to myself and anyone else who has proved to use it wisely, that is, not at all. There is so much fear when it comes to magic. Those without magic fear those who do possess it, but even among nobles fear is widespread. Once word gets out that a person doesn't use magic, they become an easy prey for other nobles looking to extend their territory. Which is why I have to let the people fear me in order to help them."

"While you continue to hold the power."

When he spoke again, his tone was flat. "If only I can find enough nobles who want what's best for the country and its people, then maybe we can create unity and acceptance in society. Lucian knows this sentiment exists among certain nobles, but he is unsure whether I subscribe to it, and I prefer it that way. It means he stays out of my territory."

What an incredibly lonely life.

What, you believe him now?

Oh, shut up.

For a while she sat staring out the other window, mulling over everything he'd said. She did believe him. Or at least his intentions. But was that enough to trust him? She'd believed Lucian too, but he'd been lying from the start.

Hannah groaned. "Great. My father is a coward."

Victor narrowed his eyes. "He has told you he is your father?"

Hannah shrugged. "No, but from all the other things he said, I kind of gathered…"

Victor kept quiet, scrutinising her once more before turning to the window. Why didn't he say something? Did he know more about this?

"You don't think he is?"

"I don't know." He kept his eyes on the window, but flexed his hand.

"But if he isn't, then who—"

"I don't know. I was only seven when your mother took you all away, and twelve when my own mother passed. I never found an opportunity, or the courage, to confront your mother on the subject. Perhaps I should have. But she'd found her way out. She was happy. And she was my friend. The only person in two worlds who wasn't afraid of me. I couldn't…" He took a deep breath. "I only know what my father has hinted, but he is the least trustworthy person."

"You mean…"

"I. Don't. Know."

Hannah considered the implications of his words for about two seconds before she felt the urge to spit. Remembering the way Roderick had acted when they first met, she shuddered. He wouldn't have done that if he was her father. Right? She pulled the blanket tight around her and wished she could ball up and have a good cry. Maybe she could go back to believing the lie about Uncle Tom and her parents dying in a fire. With this new bit of information it was easy to see why Mum would have lied.

"Will you let us go?"

Again she was fooled by a huff that could have been a laugh, but definitely wasn't. His look was one of surprise. "Of course. I will help you to go home in any way I can."

"Will you give me the jewel?"

He hesitated. "If you need it. And then I will destroy it."

Hannah cocked her head. "How do you know I won't use it against you?"

"You wouldn't."

Aren't we sure of ourselves. "You don't know me."

"You and Sean were practically the only topics of conversation during my visits with your mother."

"You're basing your decisions on what my mum told you about me?"

"She was your mother."

Who believes a person's mother when they're talking about their child? "Gullibility is not the best quality in a leader. If you're so sure of my good intentions, give me the jewel now."

He remained calm enough to irk her. "No." All he did was rub his chest, the way she'd seen Lucian do before.

Well, she knew where the jewel was, but she'd never get it off him by force. Did she even want it anymore? Funnily enough, she did, but the want didn't feel like her own. *She* didn't want it, but then, she did. Or maybe… it wanted her. She shivered. Okay, that was creepy. Unless… it wanted to be with her because she wanted to use it for other people. Maybe everyone said it was bad because they couldn't stop using it for themselves, and it didn't want that.

She became aware of his eyes on her, and suddenly realised she'd been staring at his chest for the last few minutes. Blood shot to her cheeks as she searched for an explanation that made more sense than 'the jewel wants me'. Her first reaction was to fight for possession of the stone, but that anger melted away when she caught him staring at her lips. She sucked them in and averted her gaze to the window. If he wanted to look at her that way, he should not have told her they might share a father. Yuck.

But… she had been looking at the jewel. What if he'd only wanted to distract her? He'd admitted to wanting to keep the power, and thus the jewel, to himself. Easy to say he would give it to her if she needed it. Would he really? She'd keep looking out for opportunities to take it back. It was the only way to be sure.

The landscape changed again. From the carriage she had a wide view over fields with sheep, because the hills were lower. They must almost be back in Nottingham. A sense of unease slid its cold fingers around Hannah's shoulders. Whether it was the proximity to Sean, or a general dread of what was coming, it had Hannah rub her sweaty hands together under the blanket to regain some warmth.

Victor grunted and furiously pulled the leather pouch from under his shirt. Panting, he held it up in the air. His evident concern matched Hannah's own. She felt it too. Over the last few days she'd ascribed sudden uncomfortable changes in body temperature to her own state of mind, but that last blast of heat had hit her with a new realisation. Sean was using magic.

28

Sean stumbled in, ignoring Roderick's questioning looks. He'd failed. Over a lousy tattoo. In his own world, he could simply have it removed. Here, he'd be stuck with the reminder of Hannah's superiority for eternity. He dragged himself over to Roderick, snatched the bottle off the table and put it to his lips.

Why didn't he just make the portal already? He could do that at least. Leave this whole stinking place for what it was. Hannah could always come through when she got back. If she got back. Why should he care? Sean stared at the back wall, then took another swig. On the next he choked and when he slumped on the bench coughing, Roderick said, "Tell me. You'll feel better."

The coughing stopped after two more swigs, but it took three more for Sean to start talking. He wasn't too eager to tell his father about his failure. Roderick had been the only one remotely positive about his efforts lately.

"Charlotte asked if I didn't think there was a reason for me being here. To be honest, I can't come up with any." He stared over Roderick's shoulder, his hands limp on either side of the bottle. "Hannah's still doing all the important stuff, and I can't even get magic to work on myself."

Roderick put a hand on Sean's shoulder. "Your power is beyond any I have seen. Greater than my own, greater even than the Baron's. The only thing you need to practice is confidence."

A half smile played around Sean's lips. "That's what Mum

used to say. Long ago. Maybe you're right. I guess I'm not ready for level three, though." He showed Roderick the tattoo. "I tried to get rid of that, but it didn't work."

Roderick took his hand off Sean's shoulder and leaned back. Sean hadn't told him what the tattoo meant, but Roderick clearly understood this was more than a simple practice run.

"My dear boy, you have much to learn. Do you not think that if we were able to change our own bodies at will, we would stop ageing and live forever?"

Sean frowned. "So I tried to do something that's not possible?"

Roderick shrugged. "The ink in your body is not alive. As I have told you, the manipulation of elements is something only the most powerful minds can accomplish. Attempting magic on your own body requires not only magical skill, but also the power to invade your own mind. A body with magic naturally acquires a greater resistance to it. To change the body, one must first change that part of the mind that tells the body to resist. You have attempted a highly complicated procedure. I am not at all surprised that it did not work." He sighed. "I'm sorry I can't be of more help to you. Even with the use of my powers, I would have had difficulty showing you. As things are now…" He raked his hand through his hair and stared into the fire.

Guilt tickled Sean's stomach. He'd been so involved with learning about this newfound power, that he hadn't given one thought to what it must be like to lose it. But maybe there was a way this could work out well for both of them. "Hey. Couldn't I practise on you?"

Narrowing his eyes, Roderick studied Sean's face. "Why?"

"To help you out, of course!"

Roderick waved a dismissive hand. "I couldn't possibly ask that of you. Even if you found a way, it would take too much of you."

"It's not just for you, you know. I need the practice."

Roderick sent him a small smile. "I know. I wouldn't mind

you practising on me, but this is too much for you. You have so little experience managing that kind of energy, it could break you."

Sean frowned. "But—"

"Sean, listen to me. I am honoured that you would help me. I know you have the power to do this. But learn to control it, or you will hurt yourself. Trust me."

Rejection again. Sean pressed his lips together to keep from swearing. He moved from the table to one of the armchairs, grabbing the bottle of wine as he went. But his earlier dejection had made way for angry resolution. All he had to do was allow himself to change his body. That portal could wait. If he could do this, the Baron didn't stand a chance. Sean would move into the castle tonight, and wait for him there, to tell him he was finished.

He put the bottle on a little table, and settled back into the armchair, rolling up his sleeve. With the support of the armrest, he held the tattoo upward.

Just don't.

Sean clenched his teeth. He could do this. He would show them he was stronger—better—than any of them. He tried to clear his mind, rid it of all the negative voices. All female voices. His own male voice found a way to silence them, which was a satisfying realisation. He *could* do this. He would not allow his sister to literally invade him with her condescension any more. His body *would* open up and drive her influence out.

Sean's movement was slow and deliberate. He placed his wrist in his right hand, carefully aligning his fingers. Taking in a deep breath, he stared at his arm. Focusing on every little detail of his act drove out the last anxiousness, until he was left with an odd, almost expectant tranquillity.

This was his body. He knew it through and through. He concentrated on the ink, the intrusion, the part of his body that was not part of him. He would no longer allow it to stay. His body was subordinate to his mind. It always had been. But in this world, it would carry out a command it would not have received back home. Open up.

A sharp pain burned through Sean's gut, splintering into tiny fragments all over his body. He gasped, eyes wide but vision blurred, as he clutched his own wrist. Electric jolts seared his skin, twirling and shattering into needle-points, piercing him from the inside out. At last the pain dissolved into a tingle, leaving him panting, trying to focus on the thin dark line in front of him.

His pale skin turned slightly pink around the tattoo. Sean blinked, not wanting to give in to the elation over this visible effect. This was nothing. With Hannah on her way back, time was running out for him to show his power. He would show her. Ink, out.

The pink disappeared.

Concentrate on your body, not the ink.

His skin was his. His skin would obey. Sean gritted his teeth against the stinging pain that kept rolling over him in waves. A frustratingly long time passed before the pink glow returned, but then it rapidly turned to red, to the point where individual blood vessels appeared as tiny purplish and red ribbons, snaking towards the black ink. A small drop of blood formed at the tip of the needle. It grew and trickled down Sean's arm, but he hardly noticed. The ink was still there. He would have to concentrate harder. No more needle. No more weakness. Instead of that needle opening his skin, *he* would open up his skin to drive it out. Forever. Other droplets of blood appeared around the tattoo, drowning it until the needle was no longer visible.

Sean's vision blurred as his energy leached away. He held on several seconds longer, wondering where that eerie laughter came from. Then darkness took over.

* * *

Roderick was thoroughly in awe of the display he had witnessed. Admittedly, Sean had been unconscious for over an hour, so clearly he needed to replenish his strength. But after Roderick had cleared away the blood, the tattoo had no longer shown, and the skin was as smooth as that around it. The bandage from the earlier bullet wound on Sean's upper arm, however, was in need of redressing.

Whatever reason Sean had for removing the connection to his sister, he might have been wiser to heal his wound than to create another. Whether or not that embellishment graced Sean's skin was of no importance to his role in Roderick's future. Removing it had only left him physically drained. Roderick could only hope he would recover in time for the imminent confrontation with his sister and the part Roderick needed him to play in that.

A faint smile darted across Roderick's lips. He had once tried to make his own appearance more impressive. The experience, the knowledge of his own body and of his own competence, had nurtured every further magical endeavour. But the girl he attempted this for had been anything but impressed, as he had failed, and it took him three days to recover, both physically and emotionally.

Disillusionment was only part of the process. How differently things could have turned out if someone, anyone, had ever told Roderick he had done well. Especially when it came to magic. Sean's disappointment with the reactions of those around him was natural. In time it would be followed by disgust for those less powerful. That's when they would have some real fun, Sean and he.

If only Victor had been more ambitious, he could have used his looks and powers of persuasion to great advantage. They could have had the country at their feet. What a waste to throw it all away.

But to have encountered this new potential was more than a relief. It was the rebirth of hopes that had been reduced to ashes. Roderick suppressed a triumphant smile. He'd held off

Sean's offer to undo some of this curse, but knowing the lure of magic, Sean would be back with a reformulation. And who was he to say no to that? Roderick's patience would finally be rewarded.

Expecting Sean to wake up soon, Roderick set to peeling some of the hardboiled eggs from his new, well-stocked personal pantry. Food would help replenish the boy's energy levels. Sweet foods worked best, but someone had eaten all the apples. Not someone Roderick would give another thought, though. He'd served his purpose.

* * *

The first thing Sean checked when he woke up, was his elbow.

"It's gone!" He jumped up from the chair, the blanket Roderick must have draped over him falling to the ground. He beamed at Roderick. "And you said I couldn't do it."

"I never said that." Roderick smiled. "I said you should wait and learn more control. Had you had more control, you would not have bled. Nor slept so long. Welcome back. And well done."

"Thanks." Sean couldn't take his eyes off his arm, now rid of blood and pale as ever, but without the inky reminder of reproach. He showed Roderick again. "Completely gone." With that, he stuck an entire egg in his mouth, and tried to chew without spitting bits. His mouth full of mumbles, he stroked the inside of his elbow. Wow. It had actually worked. He'd been determined, but not exactly convinced he'd be able to pull it off. Now that it was gone, all its history seemed less important too. It had been his idea to get matching tattoos all those years ago, but Hannah's choice of image had always bothered him. She'd said this was a needle for keeping things together, but to him it had always just been a needle, plain and simple. It had become a symbol of everything about her that bugged him. Now that it was gone, all those strong feelings about her simply vanished. Compared to what he was about to do, she was... insignificant.

Halfway through peeling another egg, Roderick tapped his finger on the table. "Have you thought about what you will do with Victor?"

"Well, no. I've been distracted. And asleep. But if I can do this, I really don't think Victor will be a problem."

"Don't be too sure. If you let him come too close, he will simply run you through with that sword of his. No magic required."

"So I need to keep him at a distance." Sean took the egg and bit off a chunk. "Again, can't I practise that on you? You've seen what I can do. I feel fine now. Just attack me, and I'll block you, or something. I won't hurt you."

Roderick pulled on Sean's sleeve to make him sit down on the bench next to him. "Sean, listen. Victor is on his way. Whether or not he has found Hannah, he knows she has recovered the jewel and will probably come back to Nottingham as quickly as possible. Though he cannot know what you are now capable of, he will see you and your sister as a threat, and he will do anything to secure his position. Victor doesn't care about you. He will put himself first. The only way to deal with that is to *be* like that. Put yourself first. You have tremendous power. You *should* be first. Or life will not be worth the living. Believe me, I know."

With those last words, he looked Sean in the eye, only to avert his gaze a moment later. "There is something I have neglected to mention to you until now. It is the reason why I'm unable to leave this place. It is how Victor took my power from me."

Sean perked his ears. This should be interesting. "I was wondering about that. If I could do that to him, then we'd all be in the clear, right?"

"Unfortunately, yes." Patting Sean's arm, Roderick produced a weak smile. "As much as it pains me to say so—he is my son after all—"

Sean snorted.

"—I think it might be best if you repaid him equally for what he did to me."

Again with the pauses. "Which is…?"

"He killed me." Roderick swallowed. "Ran me through with the sword he still carries. The body I had before is buried on the grounds somewhere."

Silence. In the room as well as in Sean's head. He blinked a few times, frowned, opened his mouth and closed it again. "I don't—"

Roderick disappeared. Sean's eyes bulged. *No way.* He checked around the room for smoke and mirrors, or… something. But Roderick was gone. Sean rose, moving towards the spot where Roderick had been not a second ago. Roderick reappeared and stepped back to avoid a collision. Sean screamed and jumped behind a chair.

"Holy— Oh, just… no. That shit is too weird, man. That is too… no. Nope, no. Nuh-uh." He spun around, one hand to his forehead. With fingers gripping his hair, he ventured another look at Roderick. "Are you serious? You're not… real?"

"I am very real, Sean. That is why Victor wants rid of me so desperately. I was the only one who stood up to him."

Eyes wide, Sean stared at Roderick, heavy breaths his only movement, while he tried to wrap his thoughts around the latest bit of insanity this world had thrown at him. "Is that… normal… here? I mean, if I kill Victor, is he even going to die?"

"As you might have guessed from the lack of other spirits, my condition is very rare indeed. I can only assume it was my intense love for your mother that kept me here. Or perhaps the injustice of Victor's action. But I see no reason why the same should happen to him. The only real advantage he has over you, is that he has already killed." He spread out his arms. "Obviously. But you already knew that. It's what brought you here."

That focused Sean's thoughts. So Victor had murdered both Sean's mother *and* his father. A father Sean had thought to be alive after all those years, who now turned out to be dead after all. But the grief, or the rage he had expected did not manifest. Roderick never felt like a father to him. Even friend might be a stretch after the few days they'd spent together. True, Roderick had taught him a lot, and Sean was grateful for the confidence he'd shown in his abilities. But what little affection he felt could dwindle very quickly if Roderick wanted to exert too much influence on him. Once Sean had paid the debt he felt he owed, would he need, or even want, the older man to play a part in his future here?

But that was a question for later. Right now, he needed to concentrate on Victor. After they came to this world, Sean had always assumed he would simply kill Victor in vengeance. But now that the moment was nearing, his plans had changed. He wouldn't return home afterwards, but take over Victor's place in this world.

Poetic justice. If Victor had never come to the other world, he could have kept his wealth and position. Of course, there was the little matter of the actual deed of killing a man. That was bound to have some kind of impact. But it was a justified act. The man was a murderer. Sean was simply the executioner. There was only one more thing to consider.

"Do you think Hannah will be with him?"

Roderick hesitated. "Will it matter?"

"She may object to killing a man without a trial. Even one who's murdered her mother."

"Well…" Roderick raked a hand through his hair. "I don't think she's the one we need to worry about. I'm more concerned about what will happen afterwards. The people need someone to guide them."

Sean studied the older man's face. Was he really suggesting…?

"You can't do that. You're stuck here."

Roderick looked him in the eye. "But you could."

He *was* suggesting Sean take over. That at least simplified matters. With the backing of the old baron and Sean's status as a hero in the village, the castle was practically his, with all the wealth and power that was always supposed to be his, though his mother had tried to keep it away from him. He would be a good leader. Give back enough to keep the people happy. No fear and no revolts in his territory. See, Mrs MacGregor, he *had* paid attention in history class.

"I'm sorry, Sean. I know you ache to return home, and now I'm asking you to take on this responsibility. Now that I have come to know you better, a new hope has settled in my heart. There will be a chance. Frankly, I would prefer you take it, rather than Hannah."

Sean didn't answer straight away. She'd love that. Hannah would move into that castle and start bossing people around in the blink of an eye, given the chance. But then, he would not give her the chance. He wasn't dominated. Not anymore.

"You're right."

Roderick's face brightened.

"It would be irresponsible for me to leave these people without someone to have their backs." Sean made an effort to look like he was making a sacrifice. "But I don't want to stay forever. Once we find a good replacement, I'm out of here." He could always change his mind later, or never find the perfect replacement.

"Sean, I… I did not suppose ever to be released from this life of involuntary solitude. Having you here has changed my entire existence. I will do anything in my power, limited though it is under the circumstances, to help you."

"I wish there was something I could do to help *you*. But how could I make you live when you're already dead?"

How to create a zombie in seven simple steps. That ought to be fun. Less than a week ago, Sean would have laughed at the idea. Now he was actually considering it. He wouldn't do this with just anyone, only to be able to shout 'It's alive! Alive!', but this was his father. The father part may not have been all that warm to begin with, but now it was pretty deadly cold. Still, if he wanted Roderick's help, he would have to stay on his good side.

Roderick sighed. "Alas, living a true life is out of the question for me. Even if you did possess elemental power, asking you to form a body would be ludicrous.”

“There must be something I can do, though.”

“Well… The one thing I miss most dearly is the ability to touch people.”

Sean pulled up an eyebrow. “But… you’ve touched me.”

“I’ve touched your clothes. I cannot touch your skin. All these years, it never would have done me any good, but now that I’ve met you…” He spread his arms in a helpless gesture.

Sean nodded, biting his lip. How does one give touch to a ghost? He rubbed the inside of his elbow, then raked a hand through his hair. Shrugging at last, he grabbed Roderick’s shoulders and looked into his eyes. If he could make his own body obey, Roderick’s would have to concede as well. Though he didn’t know what it was that made Roderick’s clothes solid enough to touch, that would simply have to extend to his skin. Sean wanted it to, so it would.

Roderick doubled up with a gasp. That would be the pain, then. Magic was not a great thing to be on the receiving end of, even if it’s your own. As he watched Roderick writhe, he marvelled again at how little it affected him. Stronger magic must mean stronger mind.

The sizzle in Sean’s veins grew weaker, a by now familiar sign that his feat was accomplished. He released his hold on the older man, who slowly unclenched his teeth. Then he reached for Roderick’s hand, and helped him up. His father managed a weak smile. It wasn’t undying gratitude, but it was better than nothing.

“So, if I want to stay here, are there any more differences between my world and yours that I should be aware of? Or are magic and ghosts the only things?”

<h1 style="text-align:center">29</h1>

High on his victories, but a little low on energy because of them, Sean was on his way to the village. He'd informed Roderick it was to get something to eat, so as not to deplete Roderick's stock. In reality, he wanted to start preparing the villagers for the change in government they were about to experience. Roderick probably realised what Sean was up to. He was a ghost. He didn't need any of that food. But so what if Roderick knew? They had the same ideas for the future now, or at least similar ones. The excuse had served mostly so that Roderick couldn't tell him he wasn't ready. He tended to play it safe, whereas Sean had proved to himself that he was more than ready. The Baron was history, and it was time the villagers knew.

Where to go first? The pub was probably the most practical place this time of day. He'd be seen before he even arrived. They'd have a drink ready for him as soon as he dismounted. They'd…

They weren't in the pub. They were in the streets. Huddling together, like a few days ago when those thieves had come calling. Except this time they didn't seem afraid. Excited chatter carried from one group of people to the next. When he rode past, they looked up and smiled. Grateful, big smiles, yes, but not surprised.

Sean dismounted in front of the pub, but hesitated before going in. Charlotte would probably be there too. She'd always believed in him, even when he doubted himself. But she didn't approve of his methods. And what was he without these 'methods'? In fact, disapproving of his methods was disapproving of him. But maybe, now that he was about to take care of the Baron, she'd change her mind. Maybe, if she grovelled a bit, he'd forgive her.

Ignoring people who wanted to shake his hand, he went inside. Charlotte was balancing plates piled high with scrambled eggs on her arm, while sliding another one onto someone's table. She only looked up to see who had entered when the entire room went quiet.

"Sean," she breathed.

He took her by the elbow and led her to the back room where he first met her.

"What's going on?" He closed the door with his foot, still holding her elbow.

Her big eyes opened wider still. "Don't you know? Hannah's back. She came in here just a few minutes ago, asking for you."

"I did not know." He'd taken a little detour to have a look at his new abode. Well, as of tonight, probably. "Did you send her to the factory?"

Charlotte nodded.

"Did she say anything else?"

She shook her head.

"So why is everyone so excited about Hannah returning? They hardly know her."

Charlotte glanced at the door, then at his hand on her arm, and gave him an uncertain half smile. "Well… She was seen… together… with the Baron. In a carriage. So… we all assumed… Well, she must have him under control, mustn't she? If he would have caught her, she'd be dead!"

Sean's breath grew deeper as his eyebrows sank. "*That's* their conclusion? She comes to the village in the presence of its tyrant of so many years and everyone thinks Hannah saved them from him?"

Unbelievable! Without doing anything at all, she still managed to trump him! *He* was the one who was supposed to defeat Victor. *He* should be the object of their adoration, not her!

Charlotte whimpered under his tightening grip. "Sean? You're hurting me. What's wrong?"

Sean's vision reddened. He had been right here all this time. They'd got to know him. They'd called him a hero! Yet the minute Hannah returns, they forget about him and carry her on their shoulders. Hurrah for Hannah.

"She doesn't know what she's doing. She's under his spell."

Her eyebrows shot up. "Hannah?"

"Yes, Hannah!" he barked. "She's fallible, you know. You have all lived with this Baron for years. None of you ever managed to stand up to him. And you really think that Hannah, who is no better than any of you, could withstand his magic, and capture him. You don't think he has her under a spell? This is just the latest way in which he's manipulating you. You people are so gullible. It's no wonder he exploits you."

Narrowing her eyes, Charlotte paled. "Sean… Did you use magic?"

Slowly, a wide grin spread over his face. She was such an open book. She wanted him to say no, but she knew he wouldn't. Of course not! How could he not be proud of the fact that he had mastered this power in a matter of days?

She drew in a sharp breath. "Oh, Sean, no. *No!*"

"You will still choose her judgement over mine, won't you. It doesn't even matter what I say. *I* say *she* was wrong. *I* say he killed my mother and I'm going to kill him for it."

There. It was out. With the words his anger bled away to make room for a cold tranquillity, like a windless day on a snowy plain. Now she knew he would do it. For his mother, who never thought him worthy. For the people in this village, who didn't believe he could do it, but did believe his sister could. He would kill Victor even for Hannah, to free her of his magic and send her home.

Charlotte cringed, casting quick glances at the door. Then she squared her shoulders. "I saw Hannah. She was fine. You won't need to…"

This girl. She didn't grovel. She didn't change her mind. She'd even stopped believing in him. Loosening his grip on her elbow, he let her go.

"I have to tell the others." She started for the door, but froze mid-motion.

No need for physical violence. Not even a touch was necessary anymore. Holding her in place hardly cost him any energy at all. "No, you don't," he said calmly. This had lasted long enough. The people would have to be told about his decision, but he would do it himself. They were his people now, after all. And they would not doubt his leadership because some silly girl refused to accept his superiority. Forcing her back against the bricks by willpower alone, Sean marvelled at the ease with which magic came now.

Such a pretty face, even with that cornered bunny look. He reached out and stroked her brown curls. Such curves… He stepped closer. Her big brown eyes bulging, she stood crippled against the wall. Tears streaming down her face, she stared at Sean, whose hand was on her throat, thumb on her chin. He looked down on her with a thin smile.

"You should have said yes. I've no time for no anymore." His thumb brushed her lips. "Pity."

Out of the wall trickled tiny streams of water that combined and flowed into larger currents, meandering up and down the bricks towards her quivering body. She shook when the first drops touched her skin, but couldn't tear her eyes away from Sean. *That's right, I'm the one doing that. Elemental power. It'll be the last thing you'll feel.* More and more water engulfed her body, reaching her cheeks, then her lips, her nose. Sean chuckled softly and pressed his lips against hers one last time. Then he stepped back as she struggled for air that could no longer reach her lungs.

He flinched. Maybe he didn't care whether she lived or died

anymore, but this wasn't pretty. He turned away, feeling a little cowardly. He'd had no problem seeing Roderick in pain, but watching someone die at his hand still made him uncomfortable. He'd better make sure to take strength from the magic before he faced Victor.

His blood stopped sizzling. Without looking back, he evaporated the water, opened the door and entered the bar room. A soft tinkle reached his ears, followed by a crunching sound. The necklace Charlotte had given him had broken, the amber beads falling to the ground. He'd crushed one of them under his heel, the other he now kicked to a corner. 'Magic takes away things you're not prepared to lose', Roderick had said. If this was all it took, good. Who needs a necklace made of hair? He took a breath, and strode out into the street to meet his people.

Convince Nellie, and you'll convince the village. Sean had only needed about a day to figure that out. Since the town didn't have any local government apart from the Baron, the most influential person was the one who always knew everything that went on and never had nothing to say about it.

Sean found her surrounded by curious villagers, but she put him in the spotlight as soon as she saw him. "Sean! Have you heard?"

"Yes," he said solemnly, "But I'm afraid it's not good news."

The faces around him fell.

"Hannah has fallen under the influence of the Baron. He intends to use her to win you all over to his side." To his own ears his words sounded fake and melodramatic, making him wish he'd prepared some kind of speech, but all eyes were on him. He'd have to make the best of it. "While Hannah was gone, I have stayed here with you. I have listened to your stories about the Baron's atrocities. I have… felt them deeply myself." *Let's have a dramatic pause here.* It seemed to be working. A murmur rose from the growing crowd. "The Baron should not be the one up in that castle. He doesn't deserve it."

Someone in the back cheered. Nellie's eyes narrowed. "We know all that. What do you propose we do about it?"

"I don't have time to explain, but I believe I have found a way to rescue Hannah and end the tyrant's reign."

More cheers.

"I've already shown you that I want to help you. I want that Baron gone too. Are you prepared to help me?"

A thin man in wire-frame glasses clapped him on the shoulder. "What do you want us to do?"

"Absolutely nothing. I want you to stay here and carry on as you would on any other day. Trust me to take care of you. If I fail, you won't be implicated, but if I succeed, I will lead you to freedom."

Most of the bystanders now wore big smiles, but Nellie pursed her lips. She tugged on her mob cap, then told Sean to wait there, and went inside. The others took turns shaking his hand, but Sean threw several anxious glances at the pub door. If Nellie went into the back room, it was game over. She returned holding the gun Hannah and Sean had brought with them from the other world, and Sean released a breath.

"Take it. The Baron doesn't allow us weapons. I took it off Hannah, because it could only make things worse. But if you are going to confront… him…" She thrust the gun into his hands.

Sean welled up. He hoped Nellie would take it the right way, because it was all he could do not to burst out laughing. She meant well, but seriously! He hugged her, and got out of there. Time to confront Hannah and answer that nagging question at the back of his mind: had she really succumbed to the Baron, or had she abandoned her brother in favour of a murderer?

* * *

Hannah entered the factory with Victor on her heels. "Sean?"

No-one answered. Where else could he be? She'd thought he'd be at the inn, but when she talked to Charlotte, it seemed that budding relationship had fizzled out. Charlotte wouldn't say too much, but she'd directed them here.

She stomped upstairs to take a look, but the office up there was empty too. "He isn't here," she said, returning to the dining hall, "Is there another room he might have gone too?"

Sitting down in the chair closest to the fire, Victor shook his head. "We will wait for him. The castle is the only other place he'd be able to communicate with my father, but I suspect Roderick has yet to extend that invitation."

The fact that Sean had preferred Roderick's company over Charlotte's was alarming. The fact that her brother wasn't here even more so. Maybe Victor was wrong. Maybe they should go to the castle. Hannah paced in front of the fireplace. "I should have talked to him before I left."

"If you had, I could have prevented you from leaving."

Oh, here we go again with the smugness. "Maybe it's a good thing I didn't, then."

He examined her from under a pulled-up eyebrow. "Really?"

"Yes. Because now we have the jewel."

"*I* have the jewel."

He reached into his pocket and pulled out the necklace, its chains draped over his fingers.

Mine!

Where did that come from? She didn't really want it. But it might come in handy. Victor said he wouldn't use it anyway. He'd been under magic's influence so long, though. The jewel would probably have a stronger hold on him. If *she* had it, she could use it to do some good, without it affecting her too much. Hannah jutted her chin out ever so slightly.

"Good girl, don't let him intimidate you," a voice broke through the silence.

Hannah drew in a sharp breath.

Victor only frowned, not looking too surprised. "Show yourself."

"Insolent pup," the voice snapped.

When Roderick appeared right next to her, Hannah yelped. She jumped away from him, her eyes flicking back and forth between the two men. "He listens to you?"

"He has to." Victor kept his gaze on Roderick. "Since I killed him, I have a degree of control over him. Unfortunately, not enough. He calls me his master, but the sarcasm hits him harder than it does me. As long as I endure, he will have to listen to me. He has expired into his worst nightmare."

Roderick smirked, looking down on his son. "And he can't get rid of me unless he uses magic. Which he refuses to do. Pitiful." Turning to Hannah, he shrugged. "But practical, for me. My dear, may I say it is lovely to see you again. I confess I had my doubts sending a girl after my most precious possession, but it has turned out delightfully."

"Where's my brother? I have to talk to him. Now."

Roderick cackled. "Look at you. So pure. So righteous. So very naive." But then his face transformed back into the charming man she'd met at the castle. "Don't worry, dear child, Sean is quite well. But perhaps less eager to see you than you are to see him. He has taken it upon himself to free the people of their current oppressor. It shouldn't be difficult, but he wants to show you his worth. That's important to him. And the people, of course, will be free. Isn't that what you want? Why don't you join your brother? This is what you were meant to do. Free the people."

"Don't listen to him!" Victor interrupted, clutching the delicate chains of the necklace in his fist.

It took Hannah half a second to let his words register. She was still in awe of how quickly Roderick could switch from insults to convincing, soothing tones. She heard the words. She knew they were false. And still she felt compelled to listen.

Victor's words put the venom back into Roderick's voice. "No, don't listen to *him*. I will be damned if I grant *that* slug of a son any kind of victory." And then the honey was back. It was truly enchanting to see Roderick's whole being smooth with his voice. "Of course, I'm damned already. Squashed by a slug. Still, that won't last much longer, thanks to your talented brother.

"Hannah, dear, you and Sean have been the brightest lights in the dark hole of my existence. Your selflessness towards the people in a land you never knew was your own, and your courage to stand up to established tyranny, have given hope to a desperate community. Surely you and your brother should be the ones to hold the power?"

As he mimicked the hand with which Victor was still holding the necklace, his words danced around in Hannah's brain.

Hold the power.

She wanted to.

She was entitled.

In one smooth move, she jumped forward and grabbed the jewel from Victor's hand, cringing as her fingers brushed the glistening gem. The wave of energy it emitted not only heated her core, but brought Sean to the forefront of her mind. No longer with a sad smile, he stood grinning widely, before opening his mouth and uttering that same nasty laugh Hannah had heard from the moment she'd opened herself up to the jewel.

Taking a few steps backwards, Hannah held Roderick's gaze.

Roderick concentrated on her with a twinkle in his eye. "Feel that power, girl. Let it fill you. Let it become you."

Oh, there was power there, all right. Other than before, the jewel practically vibrated in her hand. In the presence of three people cursed with the same magic, it was ready to release its energy. Hannah swallowed. There must be a way to use it for good. It wanted to be used. It wanted to *be*.

Could it be good? Hannah glanced at Victor, who had his intense glare fixated on her. He didn't want it used. Not even with good intentions. Could she trust him to be right? Her gaze flicked to Roderick, and his confident smile. She knew she couldn't trust him. But out of the two of them, he was the most relaxed, the most reassuring.

"Feel it. The power to take. No, not even that. The power to make others give."

She wanted to give him the jewel. He would know what to do. What *would* he do? Wait, no. She didn't want to give him the jewel. Did she? No!

Her frown made way for a smile. A decision! She'd finally made one that was absolutely the right one. She lifted her head, the necklace lightly between her fingers now, and winked at Victor, who shifted in his seat. Roderick chuckled at the sight.

Hannah raised her hand, gathering all her determination. Willing it to destroy itself, she threw the jewel on the factory floor.

The sound of the gemstone shattering drew Roderick's attention back to her. He jumped forward, but had to hold on to the back of one of the chairs when he saw the scattered fragments of his future. He wheezed. "Witch!"

He stretched out a hand towards Hannah, but before his feet could follow, Victor had taken him by the arm. He jerked around to face his son. Victor now exuded the calm his father had displayed moments before. The serenity in his face might even hold a sense of triumph.

"You knew," Roderick growled, "How could you have known?"

The door swung open and Sean sauntered in.

* * *

Sean froze as he took in the scene. Roderick, Hannah, and the Baron. And a shimmering mass of black shards on the floor. He'd felt the pull of the jewel when Hannah had touched it. But now, as anger rose from his stomach to his head, he wondered why she'd destroyed it. The jewel had been their ticket out of here. Wasn't that what Hannah wanted most?

"Sean! You're safe." Arms outstretched, Hannah ran towards him.

How could she be so calm after she'd effectively thrown away the one thing that set them apart? "What did you do?"

She slowed, dropping her arms. "It would have brought us nothing but trouble."

"So you leave me alone to fetch this thing, and now you've destroyed it. Without ever thinking to ask me." She had the good sense to blush, but Sean was only getting started. "Now that you're here—finally—perhaps you'd like to tell me your next plan? Seeing as you so graciously destroyed our chance of going back home?"

She held up her hands. "Sean, don't be like that."

Sean, don't.

"You're all I thought about. You're my brother! Now that Mum's gone, we only—"

"Ah, yes, it's 'Mum' now, of course." He let out a short, sneering laugh. "You must be so pleased. But you were never important enough to be called a daughter before."

Hannah gasped. "Mum did that to protect me. To mislead anyone who would come looking for us."

"Oh, I see." His voice was bitter. Not even that held up. "She didn't think *I* was important enough to protect that way."

Narrowing her eyes, Hannah frowned. "How could she? You were born there. Besides, he"—she pointed at Roderick, who pulled his arm free from where Victor was still holding him—"didn't know you existed, so there was no need."

Fists balled, Sean now raised his voice. "She should have told us 'he' existed. He's our father!" He wrinkled his nose and pointed at Victor. "*That* is who she was running from."

Victor's chin lifted slightly, but other than that he stood idly by, hand on his sword, dividing his attention unequally between Roderick and Sean. Apparently he still thought his father was a bigger threat than his brother. He'd soon be corrected.

Hannah bridged the gap between them, laying a hand on Sean's arm, which he immediately withdrew. "You're wrong, Sean. Don't believe…"

"DON'T!" Sean's cheeks flushed. "That's all you ever say to

me! Don't hang with them, don't listen to him, don't talk to her! Did you consider the fact that *he* may have used magic to make you believe he's the good guy here?"

Hannah glanced at Victor. She wasn't even sure herself. At last, Sean had cracked the great and mighty Hannah's confidence. Maybe, if she had shown a little more trust in him when she saw him just now, he wouldn't have been wondering what else he could crack. Years of biting his cheek, of stoically undergoing the constant ribbing, were agitating the bubbling volcano in Sean's gut.

But he needed to be calm in order to use magic. As much as he was starting to hate Hannah, he wasn't going to waste his magic on her. That, apparently, was needed for the passive bloke in the back.

Look at him. *This* was the evil Baron he'd been preparing to kill? All he did was hang around watching everyone. Pathetic. Killing helpless women and suppressing non-magical people must make him feel so tough. In the presence of equals and superiors, however, he shrunk away.

This was why Sean was here. It was so obvious, that he wondered why he hadn't seen it when Charlotte questioned the value of his presence. He'd thought it was all about Hannah, but Hannah was insignificant. Whether or not she was under the Baron's spell didn't matter. Sean would be the one living in Nottingham Castle. Jewel or no jewel, at last he would be the one with the power, and everyone would be grateful for it.

30

"I do not use magic." Victor said it both to Sean and to Hannah. Hannah frowned. Though she mostly believed him, Sean's words had hit a sore spot. What if she only believed Victor because he made her?

Sean snorted. "No, not in the other world. That's why you killed my mother with a gun."

"Sean, I did not kill your mother."

Hannah chimed in, "That's right. Ben did that. He told me so himself." Of that, at least, she was absolutely certain.

Sean wore his most incredulous face. "Ben. Killed Mum. I'd like to hear that from him, then."

"We sent him to London, but—"

"'We'? Conveniently getting rid of the so-called witness together now, are you? You don't think he made Ben confess? I didn't see Ben there, when we found Mum, did you? Saw *him*, though."

This was not going the way it was supposed to. Why didn't Sean believe her? Hannah had expected to have to convince Sean of Roderick's guilt, but not of her own innocence. "Victor and Mum were friends. He knows things only Mum could have told him."

Sean paused. This was her way in! Hannah opened her mouth to elaborate, but Sean turned and pointed at the wall near the door. A second door appeared. A familiar, weathered wooden door. The way home.

"Take it, Hannah. Open it. Go back."

He'd done it. He didn't even need the jewel. All she'd accomplished by going away was leaving Sean alone with the worst influence imaginable. And now he thought she was against him. How could he think that? Just because she'd teased him a little when he'd done something wrong? It wasn't her fault he did so many things wrong.

She was never a bad sister. Nor a bad cousin. Her first instinct was to tell him how wrong he was, but that was exactly what had driven him to this point. He *was* wrong, though. It couldn't all be her fault. Could it?

Shaking her head, Hannah stared at the door. All she'd wanted since she came here was to go back. Now she could. Her mother's killer was behind bars. There was nothing left for her here. Except her brother. "I'm not going without you."

Sean laughed without humour. Roderick joined in, sneaking Hannah a victorious sneer as he made his way towards the counter to obtain a bottle of wine.

"Why would *I* go back? I was a loser there. I'm a leader now. Don't stand in my way, Hannah. I'm warning you. Go home."

Hannah wet her lips. Stand in his way? He'd never talked like that before. Had he really felt like a loser? And whose leader did he think he was here? His bitter attitude had her hesitating between contradicting and appeasing him. Roderick had made her out to be Sean's enemy, and for some reason he'd believed it. Now what could she say?

Victor spoke up. "Sean, this man will cast you aside as soon as he can take no more from you. Expect no benefit from him that will not serve him first."

Taking a glass of wine from Roderick and gulping some down, Sean held up his index finger. When he'd swallowed, he wiped his mouth on his sleeve. "Unlike some other people in this room, he hasn't taken anything from me. I haven't even given him all that much. Especially when you compare it to what he's given me."

Roderick gave a smirk that Sean didn't seem to notice.

"A whole town full of people. If he hadn't helped me, they wouldn't have given me a second's thought. But you know what they did? They believed me. They think I'm…" He made a big gesture, wine spilling over the sides of his glass. "Magnificent."

"And you think I don't?" That niggling unease in her stomach was growing into panic. This wasn't the Sean she knew. He completely ignored her.

Downing what was left of the wine, he strode up to the fireplace, pushing Victor aside. "They cheered me, is what they did. Welcomed me into *his* castle. They. Love. Me. Ooh!" He reached into his coat, producing Ben's gun. "Look what Nellie gave me. She says the *Baron*"—he side-eyed Victor then turned back to Hannah—"doesn't want them owning guns, so she thought I should have it. Not you. Me."

That wasn't so strange, was it? He seemed to think she wanted to be better than him. All she'd ever done was take care of him. And maybe make a few jokes at his expense. He'd never been so sensitive about those before, but perhaps it would help if she apologised? "Sean, I… I want to say I'm sorry."

"Oh!" His eyes widened in mock astonishment. Then he smirked, the flickering light from the fireplace distorting his features. "Little late for that, innit?"

That was what he wanted? Hannah didn't even know what she was apologising for. Then again, if she'd shown a little bit more support during the rest of his life, maybe he wouldn't have had any reason to think badly of her now. Even if it was the influence of magic that made Sean turn against her, there was some truth to what he said. "Really, Sean, I—"

"Don't bother, Hannah." His smile had vanished. Roderick came over and put his hand on Sean's shoulder. "I've found someone who does want me. Who wants me to be me. Who encourages me to do, because I can." His words must indicate Roderick, but instead of looking at the older man, he moved away from him to fill his glass. He laid the gun on the counter, leaning against it while Roderick ambled back towards Hannah, wine in hand.

"Sean has the support of the people. He will be a great leader."

Victor now moved to Hannah's side, clutching the hilt of his sword. He seemed to think Roderick was the bigger treat here, the way he tracked his father's every move. But to Hannah, Roderick was of secondary importance. He was dead anyway. As creepy as that was, what could he do? She would stand her ground, though she couldn't help balling her fists.

Roderick laughed. A pleasant, confident laugh. The same laugh he'd used to charm her earlier, and probably countless others before her. Poisonous words in silky tones. And yet, that debonair attitude was still attractive, even in a man planning your downfall. He was entirely too close, but Hannah was making a point, here. She shivered when he spoke.

"Sean doesn't need me. He doesn't need any of us. But he seems hesitant to rid himself of you completely, which, I have to say, I do see the merit of."

Uttering a low growl, Victor went for Roderick, but Sean tutted and flicked his wrist. Victor halted mid movement, sword half drawn. He didn't even move when Hannah reached out and touched his arm.

Roderick, who hadn't flinched, held up his glass and examined it. He continued as if discussing the weather. "That sword won't stop me now, boy. You've tried it before. You didn't succeed then and you won't now. In fact, you never will. Sad, but true." He shrugged. "All things considered, you did me a favour. I can't die twice. So in effect, you granted me eternal life." His gaze wandered around the factory. "Of course, it hasn't been much of a life so far. But Sean will see an end to that." He toasted Hannah's brother, who inclined his head.

Hannah pushed between Roderick and Victor. "Sean, you can't mean to help him. He's the one who told Ben to kill Mum."

Sean only shrugged. Hannah's shoulders sagged. Her brother had turned into her enemy while she was away on a useless errand. She should never have left. It really was her fault after all. She stared at her brother, not knowing whether to cry, or scream, or plead with him. Instead, she remained frozen to the spot, feeling the gaping distance between them.

Roderick faced Victor again, leaning back slightly, so he wouldn't have to look up. "Did you think you would have a chance now that you've found a little friend?"

Jaw clenched, Victor stared over his father's shoulder. "This is not about her."

A twinkle sparked in Roderick's eye. "What, you feel for this girl?"

Dropping his volume, he leaned closer to his son. "Did she talk to you? And you said something back?" He laughed. "How thrilling!"

Hannah tore her gaze away from Sean, who looked on with mild amusement. Why didn't Victor stand up to his father? If she said something, what would Sean do?

Roderick leered at Hannah from the corner of his eye. "Did you get close enough to smell that sweet scent of hers?"

Hannah narrowed her eyes. "Roderick…" It was the tamest warning in the world, but Roderick was on Sean's good side and she didn't want to do anything to widen the gap between her and her brother. Not before she'd found a way to bridge it. Sean cocked his head, but said nothing.

Now leaning towards Hannah, Roderick continued, "Did you look at her? Really… look."

The wine on his breath made her recoil despite her resolution to stay where she was.

"Oh, don't be shy. Remember, I've seen it all before. That sweet little birthmark, just there."

He stretched out the middle finger of the hand that held the wine glass and pointed between her breasts.

Hannah's heartbeat quickened. How did he—the bathroom.

"You creep!" She clenched her fists, glancing at Sean. She didn't expect him to stand up for her, but how would he react if she stood up against Roderick?

Roderick inclined his head towards Victor. "Did you know? You didn't, did you. Of course not."

Victor's breath grew heavy, straining against Sean's hold.

"Oh, but don't worry," Roderick continued. "I took good care of her. Didn't I, hmm?"

Hannah rolled her head back to get rid of the tingling in her neck.

Victor's eyes shot fire, but he still couldn't move. "You couldn't have touched her."

Roderick emptied his glass and shoved it against Victor's chest. "Ah, you're right, I couldn't have. But..." Holding her gaze, he reached out and slowly traced her jawline. "Things have changed." He moistened his lips, his voice no more than a whisper now. "Even your mother gave in to me in the end."

Without thinking, Hannah raised her fist and punched him on the jaw. The jolt of pain in her fingers was extremely satisfying.

Roderick first looked perplexed, then turned to Sean, who was grinning widely and now shrugged, palms up.

"You wanted to touch skin."

Roderick's eyes narrowed. He did not join Sean, but slunk to the fireplace. Her brother couldn't have heard his last remark, but Hannah was happy to get a glimpse of the old Sean. She had to say something to get through to him. Sean was her brother. He wouldn't hurt her. Then why was she this scared to face him?

With Roderick out of the way, Sean released Victor, who turned to him. "Sean, there is no need for you to kill me if you truly have the good of the people in mind. I would be more than willing to share my plans with you."

Sean grinned, folding his arms over his chest. "And what if I don't believe you?"

"I have papers at the castle proving my intentions."

"It's true." Hannah took courage from Victor's presence. "He's told me all about his plans. They sound good, Sean. He'll really help the people."

Sean paused. He took a few steps to the side, but then moved resolutely forward to get in Victor's face.

"I will not be caught up in your manipulation. I'm not worthless anymore!"

His words shredded Hannah's heart. She had to force the words out so they'd be more than a whisper. "You never were. I'm so sorry I made you feel that way."

He stood very still, looking down on her. Never before had Hannah felt small in his presence, but years of her belittling *him* now diminished *her* to almost nothing. It took all her strength not to hide behind Victor. She crossed her arms over her stomach, driving her nails into her elbows when he spoke again, his voice icy.

"Whatever I did, there was always something wrong with it. I was never good enough. Not for you and not for Mum. She should have told me my father was an important man. But she never even told him I existed. This life, this power is my right. I shouldn't have had to put up with years of being nobody."

Hannah blinked away her tears. All those little ribs she made in good humour. All those years she'd teased and mocked him, hoping to annoy him out of that circle of bad influence. She never thought how he'd feel about them. All he had done was laugh and wave it away. It had seemed so innocent at the time. But while she thought she was protecting him, he had resented her for it.

"You don't need to be a leader to be somebody. And you were always strong, Sean, I never doubted that."

Pushing her nails deeper into her flesh to drown out the memories, she continued, "You got clean. That was *you* doing that and it took so much strength! I'm only sorry I never told you how proud I was. But I am! And so was Mum."

She undid the button on her sleeve and pushed it up to show

him the spool of thread on her wrist.

"Remember what she said? It takes a needle *and* a thread to sew. You need both. I need you!"

With a crooked smile, he pulled up his shirt sleeve inch by inch. When the fabric reached his elbow, Hannah's vision blurred with tears. No needle. It once mattered so much to them that they had it embedded in their skin, and now he had erased it.

"It's been a constant reminder of how *I* did it wrong and *you* had to save me. Even though you would never let me forget it." He stroked the empty patch of skin. "So it's gone. I'm already forgetting it was ever there."

31

"Sean… You're my brother." The sound of her strangled voice seemed strange and as small as she felt. "I love you. Please remember who you've always been."

"Who I was was never as good as precious, perfect Hannah. Even here, where nobody knows us. People have never followed me. They follow you. How could I go against you? I'd be standing alone."

Was that really what he thought of her? "I'm not against you." He'd never believe her. *Don't give up, Hannah.* "Don't be against me. You've proved that you can do it. Now prove that you can stop it. Don't let him take you from me as well."

Sean scoffed, "Doing it wrong again, huh, Nana? I'm still not good enough. You've found another brother and you instantly prefer him to me."

Sean faced Victor. They were of equal height, but Sean's frame was slighter and Victor was armed.

"You've been here long enough. Time for you to go."

When Victor didn't move, Sean swung at him. Hannah threw herself between them, but stumbled and fell backwards when her brother shoved her aside.

Victor caught Sean's wrist easily before the fist could connect, but then Sean smiled.

Victor's surprise was followed by a frown. He looked at their hands as his breath grew ragged.

"Look at that," Sean sneered, "From a distance, this looks as though you're in control, doesn't it? Just like your life. Funny."

"Stop!" Hannah screamed. She pulled herself up on her brother's shirt, hoping to loosen his hold, but Sean held on.

Victor's body convulsed, his knees buckling, the hand clutched around Sean's fist dragging Sean down.

Roderick, looking on from his spot by the fireplace, gave a snigger that turned into a very familiar nasty laughter. Sean took his eyes off Victor long enough to wink at Roderick with a smirk.

Hannah took the opportunity to wrench Sean's arm free. How did she end up fighting her own brother? They had shared so many good things. Now all she wanted to do was run away from this… thing that had taken him over. If only she could take him with her. Leaning against him in an attempt to separate him from Victor, her eyes darted to the wall where Sean had created a portal. Magic couldn't go through. Would he return to normal if she could get him to the other side of that weathered old gate?

Despite her efforts, Sean flung her aside. He lifted his hand above his head, and sliced the air in Victor's direction.

Victor gasped. His waistcoat darkened, the white shirt above it turning red. Clutching his chest with both hands, he sank to his knees. Drops of blood mixed with the dust on the factory tiles.

Hannah screamed. She dropped down to Victor's side. *So much blood. What do I do?* Hands floating uselessly in mid air, Hannah racked her brain for anything on where to press or how to stop the bleeding, when Victor touched her knee. When she looked up, he held her gaze with dark, sad eyes. *No, don't give up. Don't give up!* Tearing yet another dress to pieces, she pressed the fabric onto Victor's chest. Why was he so calm?

"Hannah."

This was not going well at all. What was she going to do against Roderick if Victor couldn't help her? And Sean was…

She'd never—

"Hannah, the gun," Victor whispered.

What? Shaking and panting, she looked up. Victor put his hand over hers, but before he could say any more, Sean's voice cut in.

"And now you're on the floor. That's really quite pathetic. Roderick was right, wasn't he? You're—"

"Sean!" Hannah burst out, tears streaming down her face, "Look what you're doing! This isn't you, Sean, it's—"

Sean gave a short, frustrated sigh, and bent down, grabbing both their hands to pull them apart. "Hannah! Will you stop blaring! How can I enjoy this with you yapping in my ear? I'm trying to use his body to—"

A sharp flash of light blinded Hannah as a massive explosion rang out. She ducked, covering her head with her arms, expecting to be covered by a collapsing building. Apart from the whistle blowing in her ears, however, nothing happened. Slowly, she lifted her head, holding her arms over it. Sean was still standing right beside her. He looked around him, then chortled. Hannah couldn't hear him over the ringing in her ears and the sound of her own panting, but Sean doubled up laughing. Hannah watched him in bewilderment, other sensations creeping up on her, then hitting her sharply. A light breeze played in her hair, cooling her face. The stinging scent of burnt wood reached her as she realised her back was warm. Looking up at Sean, she now made out a huge black cloud behind him, visible even against the darkening sky. Sky?

Hannah whipped her head around. The entire factory was blown wide open. The roof was gone, as well as the better part of the walls. None of the debris had fallen into the dining area, but the trees around the building all had bits of bark ripped off and branches broken. Stones and chunks of mortar littered the ground outside. Inside, frayed edges of walls still glowed a fiery orange. Other sections shone like polished metal, the stone having melted into an almost mirror-like surface.

Behind Hannah, a gaping hole had swallowed up most of the floor, the long tables and benches burning and smoldering at the bottom. Several yawning black cracks branched outwards from the crater, breaking up the few yards of tiles left around the edges. One of the fissures separated Hannah, Sean and Victor from the part of the floor that held the fireplace where Roderick stood, uttering an amazed chuckle, while he held up nothing but the stem of his wine glass.

The ringing in Hannah's ears softened, making way for Sean's whinnying. He caught his breath long enough to shout out to Roderick, "Whew! That felt good! Did you see… Do you know what I—" He hiccoughed and laughed at his own silly noise. "That ought to do it, don't you think?"

Roderick shook his head in disbelief, but his smile widened when he saw Victor, who had lost consciousness. At least, Hannah hoped it was only that.

"Well done, son. You have liberated me."

Heat rose to Hannah's cheeks. She got up and stood in front of Victor's body, trembling with fury. "*That* is your son!"

Roderick barked out a laugh. "*He* killed me. Thought it such a merit that he carried the weapon proudly, everywhere he went." He stepped closer, his hand already outstretched towards the sword at Victor's side.

Hannah jumped back, and pulled it out of its sheath. It wouldn't do her any good, but it sure felt right to point the weapon at Roderick. It was heavier than she'd expected, but she managed to keep the tip from shaking too much. "Don't come any closer."

"That sword can't kill me twice. Do you not realise the futility of your actions?"

"Oh, she realises all right." The coldness in Sean's eyes punched her in the gut. The disgust in his entire attitude hurt her more than his words ever could. The sword clattered to the ground.

Hannah's voice quivered. "Sean, please come home with me."

"What home? My new home is up on that rock. I earned it." He chuckled again. "Look at all this! I did this."

Her stomach contracted. "'This' is chaos. Is that who you want to be?"

He glared at her. "No, this is who I *am*."

"Then maybe it's a good thing Mum hasn't lived to see you turn into... this." Hannah swallowed back her tears. At that moment, in a factory still sizzling with the force of its destruction, she felt more alone than she'd ever been. "The old Sean might well have been a good leader, but this one will do the people no good at all."

Sean snarled. "They'll follow me now, whether they want to or not. I can do anything. I won't hear no anymore." Closing his eyes, he inhaled. The air tingled, then grew heavy and light at the same time. Stifling. Choking.

Roderick let out a ragged scream that sounded even when his body disappeared. From all around the room microscopic elements sped in his direction, leaving tiny trails of light, like spider silk glinting in the sunlight.

Slowly, Roderick reappeared. A translucent, huddled shape, almost a shadow against the dusty stones in the background. His fingers took shape first, denser parts of his body following.

Tortured screams echoed off the walls, where more and more mirror-like spots developed, growing and flowing into each other, reflecting the deep orange of the remnants in the crater.

Sean's hands shook. Drops of sweat formed on his brow when Roderick solidified. Something was wrong. The hideous display was taking too much of Sean. This was a look of determination rather than the confidence he'd displayed earlier.

Alarmed, Hannah turned back to Roderick. Panting through his teeth, he straightened slightly, hands on his sheer thighs. More and more of the minuscule parts hit his body, and as Sean renewed his efforts, Roderick's fingers began to glow. The nails took on a liquid shine, tiny bubbles forming in several of them.

Roderick doubled up and fell to the floor.

Over Roderick's cries, Hannah shouted, "Sean! He will kill you! Your power…" This wasn't helping. She launched herself on her brother, hurtling him to the ground. He cursed, pushing her aside with such force that her back hit the counter, and renewed his efforts.

With that lapse in Sean's concentration, Roderick let out another roar. As he cried out, he threw his head back. His skin turned almost white. It stretched and smoothed, first waxy, then glass-like. The effect was that of a life-size porcelain doll. But instead of the fine features usually painted on figurines, Roderick's were exaggerated and deformed. His skin stretched over his face, as if it had been pulled backwards. His hair clumped together in places, dripping off his head like candle wax. Crouching naked on the floor, parts of his torso still vague, he grunted.

Captured in horrified fascination, Hannah gasped. Sean staggered back when he saw the distortion. The elements stopped flying. Sean stumbled, a look of exhausted shock on his face, and fainted.

Roderick didn't even seem to notice. Still breathing heavily, he stood, rubbing his arms and chest, frowning at the luster. Then his thin, taut lips pulled away, flashing long shiny teeth in a gummy, triumphant grin.

Hannah's stomach turned. *Sean, what have you done?* Her brother was just a few yards away, barely breathing. If only she could get him out of here. The portal was right there behind him. If they were lucky, Roderick might still be confined to the factory, even with his new body.

Hannah darted to Sean's side, but before she could reach him, the Baron was done admiring his pale porcelain skin.

"Now then," he whispered, his voice gradually gaining stability and volume. "Let's see what this new body can do for me."

Seemingly unaware of his nudity, he strutted towards Victor and tutted.

"Oh no, this won't do at all. I'll want that pleasure for myself."

He bent down, grabbed Victor by his hair and pulled his head up. Victor groaned and coughed.

"Wake up, you ninny. See if you can kill me now." Roderick threw his son's head back and straightened.

Hannah reached for the gun Sean had left on the counter. She wet her lips.

Roderick smirked at Victor, condescending brow already in place. "Come on, ask me to leave. Ask me nicely. Didn't work, did it? Ignoring me, trying to kill me again. None of it worked. Commanding me to destroy myself. That was a good one, though. Even I didn't know if it would work. But I won't be your problem much longer. Mainly because you will cease to be my problem."

With rattling breaths, Victor managed to pull himself up on his elbow and reach for the sword lying next to him. He hewed at Roderick's leg, but the blade deflected with a soft clink. Roderick laughed heartily.

She had a clear shot. He was close enough. She couldn't miss. *Breathe, Hannah.*

"Happy now?" Roderick chuckled. "Give it here."

Teeth gritted, Victor held on a few more seconds, then tossed his sword to Roderick.

"Thank you," Roderick sneered. "That's all, really."

He pointed the blade down at his son, playing for a moment, then hardening his glassy features.

Hannah released the safety and aimed. *Please let this work.*

Roderick stiffened. As he turned, Hannah pulled the trigger.

Roderick's last look at Hannah and the gun in her hand was one of amused arrogance. Then the porcelain skin over his heart cracked open.

Hannah ducked, crouching against the counter. A shockwave surged through Roderick's body, breaking it, shattering it. All the power Sean had invested in this creation now shot the needle-like fragments apart. Victor was hit by the full blast, blood-red darts sinking into his flesh and slashing his skin where they grazed it.

Hannah squeezed her eyes shut. It had worked. Though Roderick had proved once again he could hurt people even after he was gone, this time he was actually gone.

When the rain of lustrous splinters stopped, Hannah hurried to her brother's side. Sean's body shook, and he opened his eyes. Hannah touched her hand to her lips. Even when she'd dropped him off at rehab all those years ago, before the tattoos, he had not looked this hollow. He seemed even thinner. Drained. Depleted. As Hannah knelt beside him, palms stinging with ineptitude, a ghost of a smile played around the corner of his mouth.

"Old magic."

Then realisation and fear flooded his eyes. He grabbed her wrist with a strength she hadn't expected.

"Hann—" A cough prevented him from going on. His breath came in ragged bursts. "Charlotte… I… Hannah… I'm so sorry."

"Sean?" She called his name again, but he didn't answer.

Everything stopped. Nothing else mattered. She sank down, her face buried in his shirt, and cried.

32

Sunlight can be so deceptive in its cheerfulness. For the first time since she entered this world, there was no mist, no rain, no thunder, just happy little beams of sunlight, playing in the trees.

Hannah sat staring at them from the floor of the factory, Sean's head in her lap. When he'd gasped for breath after a few seconds, Hannah had been ecstatic. But it turned out that only his body returned to life. He'd opened his eyes, but there was nothing in them. No recognition, no emotion. All that had been Sean was gone.

Stroking her brother's hair, Hannah took a deep, faltering breath. Her hand still shook from pointing a gun at a man and pulling the trigger.

Not a man. A monster. And he was already dead.

What she'd done was right. She truly believed that. But it didn't stop her hand from shaking.

The fire in the crater was dying. All that was left of the long tables and benches were some charred spikes in a heap of ash. Victor had collapsed dangerously close to the edge of the crater. She should move him before he rolled in, but she couldn't get herself to abandon her brother.

Shouting outside the walls drew her attention to the edge of the trees. Bart, the giant innkeeper, appeared, taking in the destruction before him with his mouth open. A small man wearing a cap stepped out as well. He stalked past Bart and entered through the remains of the door. As soon as he spotted Victor, he scurried over, put his boot to Victor's side and pushed.

"No!" yelled Hannah, clawing at Sean's shirt.

William hesitated long enough for Nellie to push past her husband and shove William aside.

"Think, William. Look." She turned to Hannah. "What happened?"

"Rod… rick… Baron…" Somehow talking turned on the tears, and she had to stop, sobbing violently.

Nellie knelt down, rubbing Hannah's back. "Go get the doctor," she instructed the men.

"But he's with Charlotte," replied William.

"He said he couldn't do any more for her. Go get him."

Nellie sat with Hannah, making soothing noises, until Hannah had calmed enough to form comprehensible sentences.

"Victor," Hannah rasped. She coughed. "Please, can you check on him?"

Nellie hesitated. She stopped rubbing circles on Hannah's back, but then got up and advanced towards the heap of man on the crater's edge. When she crouched down and rolled him over, she gasped. The look of horror she cast over her shoulder spoke volumes.

"Is he dead?"

"No, but…"

Hannah closed her eyes in relief.

Nellie picked up one of the red splinters scattered around the room, and held it up for Hannah to see. "What are these?"

Hannah swallowed. "Later. Can you help me bring Sean to that door? It's a portal. I have to get him home."

"No." Nellie's eyes were full of understanding, but her voice was resolute. "You need to rest before you take anyone anywhere. If the doctor approves, we will take you to the inn, and—"

"Castle." Victor's deep voice startled Nellie. She scooted away from him, her eyes wide. "Take us to the castle."

"It's all right, Nellie, he's not the enemy." But he was alive. And talking, which was more than Sean did. Hannah clamped her brother to her chest. She'd get him home. He would get better.

The men returned with the doctor, who was a kind man, and seemed genuinely concerned, but she needed modern medicine for Sean. If she'd felt strong enough, she would have dragged him through the portal as soon as she was sure the villagers weren't going to lynch Victor. But although Victor was sitting up by the time the doctor was done examining him, Hannah felt what little energy she had left ebb away.

She was vaguely aware of being taken to the castle, Nellie's comforting presence always close. A familiar scarlet canopy was the last thing she saw.

Hannah woke late the next morning with a start. *Sean!*

She jumped from the bed, ignoring her weary, aching muscles. In her shift, she darted to the corridor, where she knocked into Nellie.

"Where's Sean? I have to see him. Where is he?"

Shushing, Nellie took her by the shoulders. "Calm down, ducky. He is asleep. He woke during the night, rather… in a state, but the doctor gave him something to calm him, and he has been sleeping peacefully since. Now, let's get you dressed, and you can go see him."

Hannah hugged the buxom woman. Nellie stiffened then relaxed and held Hannah in her arms. "Come," she finally said, and led Hannah back into the bedroom.

Sean did look peaceful. Apart from a few scratches and a slight darkening around his eyes, nothing seemed out of the ordinary. She almost wanted to wake him, to tell him Roderick was gone, and that she would never make fun of him again. He would tease her, say she wouldn't last a day. They'd go home, and everything would be back to normal.

But without Mum.

Hannah stroked the blanket at the foot of the bed, wanting to touch him without waking him. He *would* be fine. She'd take him home as soon as he was able.

Sean's eyes opened.

"Hi," she tried.

No reaction.

Nellie fluffed up his pillows and took a bowl of porridge from the nightstand, of which she held a spoonful to Sean's lips.

No reaction.

"Roderick's gone."

Still nothing.

"We're going home soon."

That time, Hannah didn't even expect a reaction. "Don't worry," she whispered.

Nellie placed an arm around Hannah's shoulders, guiding her away from the bed, and down towards the kitchen.

Victor was busying himself lighting a fire in the stove. He didn't look up, only asked, "Any change?"

"Well… not with Charlotte."

Victor kept his head down, blowing gently on the baby flames. "Oh?"

Nellie patted Hannah's shoulder. "I'll leave you here. I only came down to see what the noise was."

That made Victor look up. "Hannah! How are you?"

She shrugged, sitting down on one of the kitchen chairs.

Victor took one of the gleaming copper pans, filled it with milk, and put it on the stove.

"How are you?" It seemed an odd question, but what else was she going to say?

"Not dead."

It would have been funny if it weren't so true.

Hannah gave a half smile. "I'm glad you're better."

She sought his gaze to show her sincerity. He met her eyes as he placed a steaming mug in front of her and sat down opposite. His face was covered in tiny scabs, and he sat slightly hunched, the bandage visible under his shirt. But some of his earlier solemnity had lifted.

"How is Sean?"

Biting her lip, Hannah hugged herself. "He's… bad."

"I'm sorry."

"Hot chocolate?" Hannah sniffed the cup.

"It is the best remedy for magical blows."

Makes perfect sense.

"Is that why you're up already, when yesterday you were lying in a pool of blood? Did you give some to Sean?" Though she tried, she couldn't keep her voice from betraying some of the resentment she felt.

Victor took a deep breath, but winced half way, making Hannah regret her pointed words.

"We share the same curse. It bonds us, lets us know when one of us is using magic. That's how you found the jewel. The magic in these curses, it wants to be used, it wants to grow. It's strongest when its members unite and work together, but turned against itself it isn't nearly as powerful, and will try to undo its own damage to help it survive. For it to be strong, I have to be strong, and so does Sean."

Hope sparked. "You mean… the magic will make Sean better?" Something good might come from this power after all.

A muscle in Victor's jaw flexed. "If he remains under its influence, yes."

"Oh. Right. That's bad. But at this point he can't do anything. Couldn't we stay until he's better, but leave before he starts wanting to use it again?"

"Did you know Sean attacked Charlotte?"

Hannah's mouth fell open. "But he liked her."

"Nellie found her in the back room of the pub, barely alive. It appeared she'd coughed up water, but no-one understood where it had come from. Sean was the last person seen coming out of that room. Though he'd gained their trust, enough suspicion remained that they picked up the courage to visit him at the factory. The explosion hampered that courage, but concern for Charlotte drove them on eventually. I had her brought to the castle, where she regained consciousness this morning, and confirmed the suspicions. "

Hannah pressed her eyes closed. Why? None of Sean's actions here made sense. But it did explain his last words.

"He said he was sorry," she whispered.

That was that. Sean couldn't stay here. If magic would make him better only to make him worse, she would take her chances with the doctors back home.

"We should go. Will you help us?"

Victor nodded. "Of course. And thanks to your intervention, I have now found an ally in Nellie. Should I be unable to accompany you, I'm certain someone from the village will offer their assistance."

"Thank you. I think it's probably best if I go alone first, to make sure we can get back unseen." Hannah wasn't so sure they'd be able to count on the courage of the villagers. Nor would they be likely to offer help to a man who'd attacked an innocent young woman.

"I'm glad you came, Hannah."

His soft tone surprised her.

"I have something for you." He reached into his trouser pocket and pulled out her mother's locket.

Hannah's eyes widened. "Lucian gave that to you? When?"

Victor placed the little portrait on the table, staring at it pensively. "This morning, before you woke. He and I had a long conversation. He... I think he might be willing to help me."

"That's great!"

They were quiet for a while, both drinking their hot chocolate.

"Stay." Pleading eyes locked onto hers. "I know I have no right to ask, but..."

No. Her life wasn't just hers anymore. What happened to

Sean was partly her fault. Even though leaving Victor broke more pieces off her heart than she wanted to admit, she had to go. For Sean. "My mother is dead. My brother is…" She swallowed. Pretty soon she wouldn't have a heart left to care. "I may have been born here, but I have a life there. Sean has to go there. He needs me. And I… have nothing to lose."

"I do."

She didn't answer, but pushed the little portrait towards him. "Keep it. She was your friend."

Tears flowing down her cheeks, Hannah found her way through the streets, familiar even in the dark of early morning, but no longer home. With her hand on the door handle of her mother's house, Hannah hesitated. She had been so sure coming back to this world was the right thing to do. But was it?

EPILOGUE

Daylight filtered in through a dirt-covered window. For years, dust had been settling on the bookcases lining the walls. What once had been the study of the castle's owner—his pride, his home, his sanctuary—was now no more than a storeroom for the relics of his life.

A parchment on the antique desk fluttered. It encouraged Roderick no longer than an instant. A draught. Bloody old castle. The breeze blew up layers and layers of dust, gathering it around the piles of books that were scattered on the floor across the circular room. The shelves lining the walls had long been insufficient to hold their sheer quantity.

Again Roderick concentrated. He could almost imagine his own hand again, flipping the pages of the book in front of him. *Turn, page. Turn!* He slapped at the book, kicked it with all his might. Willed it to move.

The book remained. The dust remained. And Roderick remained. He screamed. But no matter how frustrating the howl, it never sounded.

Thank you so much for reading this novel. If you liked it, your review could help the author reach more readers. A few stars, a line or two on Amazon, Goodreads or any other website of your choice is all it takes. Thank you again!

I am very grateful to everyone who has read this novel during its creation and told me about all the horrible mistakes I made. They've made the novel so much better.
Thank you, I couldn't have done it without you!

Of Dutch origins, formerly in France and presently based in southern Britain, C.M. Bakker spends her days gazing at romantic countryside, wondering how to describe it to do it justice. She loves good food, good puzzles and good villains.

With her debut fantasy novel out of the way, she now devotes her time to writing cosy mysteries. Find her efforts at: https://cmbakkerwrites.wordpress.com